ROMANCING THE CROWN

With the help of their powerful allies,
the royal family of Montebello is determined to find
their missing heir. But the search for the beloved
prince is not without danger—or passion!

Meet the major players in this royal mystery:

Duke Lorenzo Sebastiani: With the crown prince still
missing, the world awaits word that Lorenzo will one
day ascend the throne in his stead. But now that new
clues to Prince Lucas's whereabouts have been found,
what will Lorenzo's future hold?

Eliza Windmere: Because she holds the key to the
mystery of the missing prince, this royal-watching
reporter is about to get up close and personal with the
bachelor duke himself. But will the royal search bring
her happiness—or heartache?

King Marcus Sebastiani: His Highness of Montebello
never gave up hope that his firstborn son still lived.
And now that the search is on, the king hopes to secure
the crown prince's legacy.

Ursula Chambers: Ursula never did care much for
babies, but now that her sister has a royal bun in the
oven, ever-ambitious Ursula is about to cash in on the
tiny tot's royal legacy. But her first order of business is
making sure the Prince of Montebello is never found....

Dear Reader,

Happy New Year! And happy reading, too—starting with the wonderful Ruth Langan and *Return of the Prodigal Son,* the latest in her newest miniseries, THE LASSITER LAW. When this burned-out ex-agent comes home looking for some R and R, what he finds instead is a beautiful widow with irresistible children and a heart ready for love. *His* love.

This is also the month when we set out on a twelve-book adventure called ROMANCING THE CROWN. Linda Turner starts things off with *The Man Who Would Be King.* Return with her to the island kingdom of Montebello, where lives—and hearts—are about to be changed forever.

The rest of the month is terrific, too. Kylie Brant's CHARMED AND DANGEROUS concludes with *Hard To Tame,* Carla Cassidy continues THE DELANEY HEIRS with *To Wed and Protect,* Debra Cowan offers a hero who knows the heroine is *Still the One,* and Monica McLean tells us *The Nanny's Secret.* And, of course, we'll be back next month with six more of the best and most exciting romances around.

Enjoy!

Leslie J. Wainger
Executive Senior Editor

Please address questions and book requests to:
Silhouette Reader Service
U.S.: 3010 Walden Ave., P.O. Box 1325, Buffalo, NY 14269
Canadian: P.O. Box 609, Fort Erie, Ont. L2A 5X3

The Man Who Would Be King
LINDA TURNER

Silhouette®

INTIMATE MOMENTS™

Published by Silhouette Books

America's Publisher of Contemporary Romance

Special thanks and acknowledgment are given to Linda Turner for her contribution to the ROMANCING THE CROWN series.

 SILHOUETTE BOOKS

ISBN 0-373-27194-8

THE MAN WHO WOULD BE KING

THE SEBASTIANI FAMILY

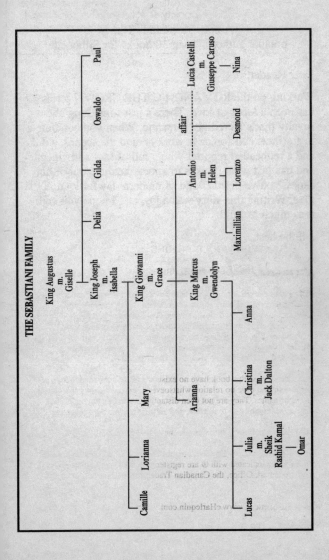

King Augustus
m.
Giselle

King Joseph
m.
Isabella

Delia · Gilda · Oswaldo · Paul

Lucia Castelli
m.
Giuseppe Caruso

Nina

King Giovanni
m.
Grace

affair

Antonio
m.
Helen

Desmond

King Marcus
m.
Gwendolyn

Maximillian · Lorenzo

Camille · Lorianna · Mary

Lucas · Julia
m.
Sheik
Rashid Kamal

Omar

Arianna · Christina
m.
Jack Dalton

Anna

A note from Linda Turner,
popular author of over 30 books for Silhouette:

Dear Reader,

Working on the ROMANCING THE CROWN series
has been a labor of love. There's just something about
royalty that's incredibly romantic. When you combine a
lost prince, evil forces at work behind the scenes, a duke
and a redheaded reporter who's full of sass and vinegar
and has just what it takes to knock the duke out of his
shoes, you've got the kind of modern-day fairy tale I
love. Writing this story was a joy, and I hope you enjoy
it as much as I did.

All the best,

Linda Turner

Chapter 1

"Eliza? Willy called three times while you were out. He wants you to call him back. He said it was important." All decked out in designer labels and looking every bit the socialite she was, Deborah Jones couldn't wait to relay the message to Eliza the second she returned from lunch.

Witch, Eliza fumed, hating her smirk. If snooty little Debbie had been anyone else but the daughter of the owner of the *Denver Sentinel,* the newspaper Eliza sweated blood, sweat and tears for, she'd have told her to eat woolly worms and die. But that would have been playing right into her hands, and Eliza wasn't that stupid. She'd spent nine years working her way up from copygirl to reporter to columnist, and she was protecting what was hers. From the moment Deborah had walked into the office a month ago as a new reporter for the society page, she'd made it clear to Eliza that she was not only after her job, but just looking for a reason to run crying to her daddy so she could get Eliza fired. Eliza didn't intend to give her that reason.

But, damn, it wasn't easy. Eliza wasn't one of those meek, mild-mannered women who let people walk all over her. She stood up for herself, and was proud of it. So biting her tongue and forcing a smile took some effort. "Thanks," she said as she took the pink message slip Deborah held out to her. "I'll call him later."

"Better you than me," the younger girl retorted, her smirk more pronounced than ever. "That man still thinks Elvis is alive. Why do you waste your time on him? He's a fruitloop."

Eliza couldn't argue with that. There was no doubt about it—Willy Cranshaw was a few cards shy of a deck. He was a hermit who lived in the mountains north of Boulder, and he was constantly calling the police with one outlandish tale after another. He had no credibility whatsoever with the authorities, and for the life of her, Eliza didn't know why she continued to accept his calls. Over the years, he had given her a few good tips, but those times were rare and not always worth the effort of dealing with Willy. He was, to say the least, high maintenance. Still, she felt sorry for him. He seemed so lonely, and she knew what that was like. She and Robert had broken up two months ago, and she'd never been lonelier in her life.

"He just needs someone to talk to sometimes," she replied, and wasn't surprised when Deborah sniffed in disdain. Her daddy's money and position guaranteed her a place in the world and someone to talk to, even if it was only a therapist. She'd never understand what life was like for a man like Willy.

"If that's how you want to spend your time working, go ahead," the younger girl said with a toss of her head. "I'd rather talk to someone who can give me a real story."

When she turned and walked away with a superior smile and her pert, plastic surgery-perfect nose in the air, Eliza was half-tempted to throw her Rolodex watch at her. Her phone rang then, however, thankfully distracting her. Giving Deborah's retreating back one last glare, she snatched up the phone. "Eliza Windmere."

"Eliza! Thank God! I've been trying to reach you all morning. Didn't you get my messages?"

"Hi, Willy," she said with a wry grimace. Speak of the devil. "I just got your message. Deborah said you had something important for me."

"I don't like that girl," he retorted, immediately distracted. "She treats me like I'm some kind of moron."

Eliza had to laugh at that. "Yeah, I know the feeling. She does the same to me. But that's not why you called, Willy," she reminded him, bringing the conversation back to the matter at hand. "What's going on? You didn't call three times because you don't like Deborah."

Just that easily, he was back on track. "It's the prince!" he said excitedly. "He's alive!"

Eliza didn't have to ask him which prince he meant. There was only one that was missing, and that was Prince Lucas Sebastiani, the firstborn of King Marcus and Queen Gwendolyn of Montebello and heir to the throne of the small island country in the eastern Mediterranean.

Athletic and handsome, he had a wild streak in him that had, no doubt, given his father more than a few gray hairs over the years, but Prince Lucas had always been great fodder for the nationally syndicated column Eliza wrote that chronicled the lives and loves of the royals. And she'd loved him for that. He had a great personality and was well loved throughout the world. When his plane crashed in the Colorado Rockies last winter and he was declared missing, Eliza had grieved just like everyone else…and followed up on every lead. But there had been no new information for well over six months, and she, like everyone else, had no choice but to believe he was dead.

"It's been a year, Willy," she said gently. "There's no way he could be alive after all this time."

"But he has to be," he insisted. "I have proof."

"Really? And what might that be?"

"Just something I found in the woods," he said craftily. "If you want the rest of the story, you have to come here and talk to me."

Eliza told herself he was blackmailing her and she'd be a fool to fall for it. She'd dealt with Willy too many times in the past to believe every wild story he told. This was the same man who'd claimed he'd seen Elvis, the Pope and an alien or two in the remote mountains where he lived. Before she jumped in her car and went racing up to Boulder, she had to make sure he wasn't pulling a fast one on her.

Deliberately sitting back in her chair, she said, "Let me get this straight. You found something in the woods that proves the prince is alive, and you called me instead of the police. That looks more than a little suspicious, Willy, and you know it."

He didn't deny it. "I couldn't call the cops," he said simply. "They said if I called them again, they'd put me in jail for harassment."

Eliza didn't doubt that. She knew from personal experience that he was like a dog with a bone when he came up with one of his stories. He'd been known to call her as many as eight or nine times in a day. In spite of that, though, he really was a harmless old coot. He just wanted some attention, some acknowledgment that he mattered, just like everyone else.

Knowing that, she should have just pacified him and hung up, but she couldn't, not if there was even the remotest chance that he was telling the truth. "You'd better not be lying to me about this, Willy," she warned. "If I drive all the way to Boulder and this turns out to be just another Elvis sighting, I swear I'll never take one of your calls again."

"I wouldn't do that to you. I know how you feel about the royals. I wouldn't make this up."

Deborah would have told her she was a fool to even consider believing him, but there was something in the old man's tone that she couldn't ignore. If he was telling the truth and the prince really was alive, this would be the biggest story of her career.

"I'll be there as soon as I can," she promised. "Okay?"

Across the phone line, he sighed in relief. "I'll be waiting for you."

Even though Eliza had been to Willy's cabin several times before, she was amazed every time she managed to find the place. Located high up in a deserted canyon that was far off the beaten path, the cabin was all but lost in the thick stand of snow-covered trees that surrounded it on all sides. Anyone who hadn't known where it was could have driven right past it without even seeing it.

Pulling up before it in her red Jeep, she knew better than to knock at the front door. She didn't know what had happened to him in Vietnam—he shut down at the very mention of war—but he'd been living in seclusion for the past thirty years. He only allowed a select few people into his life, and even then, it was on his terms. He never talked to anyone who knocked on his front door.

She could feel his eyes on her, and wasn't surprised that he was watching for her. He might have withdrawn from the world, but that didn't mean he didn't know everything that was going on around him. If anyone invaded his space, he knew it.

Striding through the snow around the side of the house to the back door, she knocked twice, waited a beat, then knocked again. She knew from past experience that even though he was expecting her and was well aware of the fact that she had arrived, he wouldn't answer the door if she didn't knock correctly…because she might be an imposter sent by the government to arrest him.

And this was the man she trusted to give her the story of a lifetime.

Amused at the thought, she watched the door slowly open and wasn't surprised when he glanced past her to the forest of trees behind her to make sure no one had followed her. "It's all clear," she assured him. "There's no one here but you, me and the squirrels."

Not taking her word for it, he checked behind her and was apparently satisfied. Opening the door further, he motioned her inside. "I thought you'd never get here. Look at this." And before she could thank him for inviting her in out of the cold, he shoved something soft into her hands.

Surprised, she frowned down at what appeared to be a dirty rag. Then her eyes focused on the embroidered patch that was sewn onto it. A lily with crossed swords. The Sebastiani family crest. It was grimy and weathered, but she still would have recognized it anywhere.

Her heart slamming against her ribs, she glanced up sharply at Willy. "Where did you get this?"

"In the woods about five miles from the crash site. It's the prince's, isn't it?"

Without a word, Eliza spread out the cloth and saw it was a scarf. A light blue cashmere scarf that she had seen around the prince's neck in a picture of him taken just days before his plane crashed last year. According to published reports, his mother, Queen Gwendolyn, had had it specially made for him and there wasn't another one like it in the world.

It was then that it hit her. Willy hadn't lied. There was no way a scarf belonging to the prince would have ended up five miles from the crash site unless it had been around his neck. Dear God, he really was alive!

Light-headed with excitement, she didn't know whether to laugh or cry. Prince Lucas was alive. And thanks to Willy, she had the story, she thought, stunned. Who would have thought it?

Given the chance, she would have given him a bear hug, but she had a feeling that probably would have sent him into apoplexy. So she smiled at him instead and said, "It certainly appears to be. Let's sit down, Willy, and you can start from the beginning. When did you find this? Did you find anything else that belonged to the prince? Who else have you told?"

"Stop the presses! Prince Lucas is alive."

Striding into Simon Maxwell's office, Eliza wasn't surprised when her boss responded to her announcement with a snort of disbelief. Gruff and cynical, with a personality that was as caustic as sandpaper, Simon didn't believe anything until the facts were laid out before him in black and white. "Yeah, right. And I'm the queen of England. I thought you were working on a real story, Red. You don't get paid to write fairy tales."

At any other time, Eliza would have snapped at the hated nickname he invariably used to tease her, but not today. Not when she was walking on air and feeling so darn good about herself and her job. Thanks to Willy, her position at the paper had never been so secure. She had a story to kill for and Ms. Nepotism was nowhere in sight. Life didn't get any better than that.

Beaming with triumph, she reached into her oversize purse, pulled out the scarf, and dropped it on his desk. "The way I see it, LaGree, there's nothing better than a happy ending. Take a gander at that if you don't believe me."

Simon hated his nickname as much as she did hers, but he hardly noticed. His eyes on the scarf and its golden crest, which he was as familiar with as she was. Motioning to the lone chair in front of his very messy desk, he growled, "Sit down. It looks like you've got something to tell me."

That was all the encouragement she needed. Plopping down into the chair, she immediately launched into the story, leaving nothing out. Unfortunately, she didn't have the happy ending—yet. "I know he's alive, Simon. He's got to be! This is proof he walked away from the crash site."

"Not necessarily," he argued, playing devil's advocate. "An animal could have dragged it away."

"And built a campfire?" she tossed back. "Willy said he found the scarf near the remains of a campfire five miles from the crash."

Put that way, Simon couldn't argue with her. "Who else knows about this?"

Not surprised that he'd asked the same question she had, she grinned broadly. "Just you and me and Willy. The king and queen don't even know yet. Willy was afraid to tell the authorities."

She didn't have to tell him why. Willy's reputation with the cops was well known by every reporter in Denver. A slow smile sliding across his chipmunk cheeks, Simon leaned forward just to be sure he'd heard her correctly. "Are you telling me that the king and queen don't know there's new evidence that their son is alive?"

Her blue eyes sparkling, she nodded. "You got it in one, LaGree."

"Then you've got to go to Montebello and tell them!"

Whatever Eliza was expecting, it wasn't that. "What?! But don't you think we should tell the police?"

"And let them leak the story to every Tom, Dick and Harry who writes a gossip rag? Hell, no! Go home and pack your bags. I'll make the airline reservations and get you some spending money. You've got to move fast. I want a play-by-play of everything that happens. Everything!" he stressed. "The king and queen are going to wig out when they find out the Prince is alive—"

Throwing instructions at her like darts, he never noticed that Deborah Jones had stepped into the open doorway until she demanded, "What prince? Who are you talking about? My God, is this about Prince Lucas? Are you saying you've found him?!"

Caught off guard, they both looked up and swore. From the look on Deborah's face, it was obvious that she'd heard more than either one of them wanted her to.

Shooting her a hard look, Simon growled, "You're barging in on a private conversation, Missy. Your daddy may own this place, but that doesn't give you the right to just waltz in here without so much as a by-your-leave."

He might as well have saved his breath. Ignoring his lecture on etiquette, she retorted, "If you have proof that Prince Lucas is alive, then I should be the one who goes to Montebello. I've traveled all over the world with my father. *I* have connections that will not only get me in the front door of the palace, but an audience with the king and queen. She doesn't."

Furious with the younger girl for trying to steal her thunder, Eliza felt her heart sink. She couldn't summon a single word in her own defense. Deborah was right—she'd never been to Europe and didn't have a clue how she would get in to see the king and queen. All she had were her wits and the Prince's scarf. That might or might not get her anywhere, and what was important here was that Prince Lucas's grieving parents be told that there was a very good possibility that he was alive. If Deborah could do that and get the story, Eliza couldn't blame Simon if he sent her. He was caught between a rock and a hard place. Not only did he have to do everything he could to put out a good paper, he had to keep the owner happy. That meant keeping Deborah happy.

But this was her story, dammit! Hers! And she didn't want to give it up...especially to a little blond-headed twit who used her father's money and influence to get whatever she wanted. Glancing at Simon, she braced for disappointment. "It's your call. Who gets to go?"

He didn't even blink. "You do. It's your story."

For a moment, Eliza couldn't believe she'd heard him correctly. But then Deborah started to sputter in protest, and she knew she'd won. Thrilled, she jumped to her feet and impulsively launched herself at Simon. "Thank you, thank you, thank you!" she sang, giving him a bear hug. "You won't regret this. Wait'll you see the finished story. It's going to be great!"

Patting her shoulder, he tried and failed to hide a crooked grin. "Don't get sappy on me," he said gruffly. "Go on and get out of here. You've got a plane to catch."

"But I want to go!" Deborah cried. "This isn't fair!"

"I've got a more important assignment for you," Simon said as Eliza hurried out the door. "I need someone to go to Hollywood and interview Brad Pitt. You're just the girl for the job."

The throne room at the royal palace of Montebello was seldom used for official business anymore. Years ago, the coronation ceremonies for King Marcus and Queen Gwendolyn had been held there, but most palace guests who visited the room were usually interested in viewing the mosaics on the walls that depicted the country's history. Not today. King Marcus had called his family together, as well as Kyle and Tyler Ramsey, two American allies assigned to protect his interests, and the ruling family of Montebello's neighboring country, Tamir. Both royal families had long-awaited King Marcus's decision, especially now that the two long-feuding countries had been united by the marriage of King Marcus's eldest daughter, Princess Julia, to Sheik Ahmed Kamal's son, Rashid, the crown prince of Tamir. Recently, Julia and Rashid had given King Marcus and Sheik Ahmed their first grandchild and as a result, the ruling family of Tamir was concerned about who would take over the Montebellan throne and how this might affect future relations between the two countries.

Now as the guests mingled about and talked among themselves in hushed voices, their eyes lifted time and time again to the clock on the wall. And with good reason. King Marcus was late to his own meeting. Speculation rippled around the room like heat lightning on a summer day. Where was the king? Had he decided not to make a decision today, after all? What was going on?

"Maybe you should go see if something is wrong," Prince Rashid told his wife, Julia. "This can't be an easy decision for your father. He doesn't want to admit Lucas is dead."

Julia could well understand that. Her brother had always been so full of life. She couldn't imagine him dead at thirty-six. But it had been a year since his plane had crashed, and even though his body had never been found, what choice did she and the rest of the family have but to accept the fact that he must have died during the winter storms that blanketed the Colorado Rockies after the crash? If he had survived both the crash and the storms, surely he would have found a way to return to them by now.

It was the not knowing that was killing her parents. She'd watched them struggle with hope and despair and, finally, resignation, and her heart ached for them. Now that she and Rashid had their own baby boy, Omar, she didn't even want to think about what it would be like to lose him. How did a parent handle the death of a child?

"Father just needs some time," she said huskily, blinking back tears. "He'll be here in a moment."

Standing nearby, Rashid's father, Sheik Ahmed, and Rashid's brother, Hassan, surveyed the crowd with the sheik's advisor, Butrus Dabir. There had been a time in the not too distant past when the Kamals wouldn't have been caught dead anywhere near the Sebastianis or Montebello. A broken betrothal between the two families in the late 1800s had caused a century-long feud that might have gone on indefinitely if Princess Julia and Prince Rashid had not fallen in love. With their wedding and the birth of their baby, everything had, thankfully, changed, but no one had forgotten the past.

"I was hoping the king would name Princess Julia and Rashid as heirs to the throne, but the word on the street is that he's leaning toward Duke Lorenzo Sebastiani," Butrus said quietly.

"That's understandable," Sheik Ahmed replied. "The Sebastianis have ruled Montebello since the 1880s. King Marcus will protect that heritage by guaranteeing that the monarchy remains in Sebastiani hands. Julia is now a Kamal…as is her son," he added proudly. It went without saying that Omar was the apple of his eye. "I have no issue with his choice of Lorenzo, if that is, in fact, Marcus's choice."

"Lorenzo is King Marcus's nephew and top aide," Hassan added. "He's a military hero and well respected by Montebellans. He's the natural choice to succeed the king since he has no other sons now that Prince Lucas is dead. And Lorenzo is a good man, one who will follow in Marcus's footsteps and maintain our newly formed ties with Montebello."

"True," Butrus said. "But as the king's heir, Lorenzo will eventually have to forfeit his position as head of Royal Intelligence. That won't be easy for him to do."

Across the room, Lorenzo's thoughts ran along the same lines. He loved his uncle, and for the sake of the country, he would do what was asked of him. But privately, deep in his heart, he hoped Marcus would not choose him. He had little desire to be king.

His illegitimate half brother, Desmond, however, had a very different take on the whole situation. Waiting for Marcus to put in an appearance, Desmond almost rubbed his hands together in anticipation. "This is the day you will be named king," Desmond told Lorenzo proudly. "No one deserves it more."

Lorenzo had to laugh at that. "Aren't you rushing things a bit? The king has kept his own counsel about this. We don't know who he's going to pick."

"Of course we do," his brother replied confidently. "You're perfect for the job, and the king knows it. Trust me. Today's going to turn out to be the most important day of your life."

Lorenzo wasn't surprised that he had Desmond's total support. He always had. From the time Desmond had come into his life when Lorenzo was thirteen, he'd been there for him in a way Lorenzo's older brother Max never had. Oh,

Lorenzo knew Max loved him, too, but Max had joined the Montebellan army at eighteen, then eventually moved to the United States. Since then, he only came home occasionally for visits. Desmond, on the other hand, was the one Lorenzo could count on in spite of the fact that they'd had different mothers and had not been raised together from birth.

"I don't know about that," Lorenzo replied wryly, "but if the king does choose me, I hope you'll be one of my advisors. I'm not much of a diplomat. I'm going to need all the help I can get."

"Of course I'll help you," Desmond replied smoothly, delighted with his brother's words. He kept his glee, however, carefully hidden behind an easy smile. "Haven't I helped King Marcus all these months since poor Lucas was lost? I'll do the same for you. More, in fact. You're my brother. I can't imagine being anywhere else but at your side."

He spoke with a sincerity that was well practiced, and he wasn't surprised when Lorenzo swallowed it whole. His brother was nobody's fool, but Desmond had come into his life when Lorenzo was young and vulnerable and feeling lost, and it hadn't taken much effort on Desmond's part to win his trust. At the time, Desmond had to use his brother to get close to the king. That, it turned out, had been a stroke of genius on his part. Because now it was his brother who would be king. As his trusted advisor and closest family member, Desmond intended to take full advantage of his new position. After all, Desmond was the son of a duke, just like Lorenzo—a bastard son, but a son nonetheless. It was about time he came into his royal due.

What a shame that Prince Lucas had foolishly crashed his plane into the side of a mountain, Desmond thought snidely. Maybe one day, he'd summon up the strength to shed a tear for him…after he celebrated his own good fortune.

First, however, the king had to name Lorenzo his successor, something he should have done ten minutes ago. Troubled by the delay, Desmond frowned at the closed door where the king was expected to make his entrance. "I don't understand the king's tardiness. Maybe you should see if there's some kind of problem," he suggested. "Something isn't right."

Knowing how his uncle grieved for his son, Lorenzo wasn't surprised that Marcus wasn't his usual punctual self. With the announcement of a new heir to the throne, he was publicly admitting that he was accepting the fact that his son was dead. That would be difficult for any parent.

Wondering how he would find the strength to deal with such a situation himself, Lorenzo said quietly, "He probably just needs a little more time to come to terms with everything. I'll go check on him."

Whatever Eliza was expecting when she caught a cab at the Montebellan airport and went directly to the royal palace, it wasn't the mob of reporters that crammed the front gates, trying to gain admittance. Surprised, she asked the cab driver, "What's going on? Nothing's happened to the king, has it?"

"Oh, no, miss," he assured her as he took the fare and tip she held out to him. "He's fine. Or at least he's as fine as any father can be when he announces his son is dead."

"What?!"

"It's true," he said sadly. "It's been a year since Prince Lucas's plane crashed and he went missing. No one wants to believe he's dead, but there hasn't been much hope for a long time now. I guess that's why the king decided to name a successor. Like it or not, the living have to keep on living.''

Horrified, she hurriedly collected her Notebook computer and pushed open her door. ''Oh, my God! I have to stop him. He can't do this!''

Puzzled by her reaction, the cabby laughed. ''Sure he can, lady. He can do anything he likes. He's the king!''

Struggling with her things as she rushed toward the crowd at the gate, Eliza didn't hear him. This couldn't be happening! She should have tried to contact the palace the second Willy showed her the scarf. But she'd known she wouldn't be allowed to speak to the king and queen, and the news she had wasn't the kind that should be relayed over the phone. Besides, would anyone believe her without seeing the evidence?

She should have called anyway, she thought as she fought her way through the mass of reporters. She could have convinced someone to listen to her, and the king would have been spared the agony of picking someone to succeed his only son. Now, she had to convince the guard at the gate that she needed an immediate audience with the king and what she had to say to him was more important than the hundreds of other reporters who wanted the same thing.

''Hey, watch it!''

''What do you think you're doing, lady? Get at the back of the line. We were here first.''

''Too bad,'' she snapped. ''I'm in a hurry and you guys are in my way. Move it, will you? I've got to talk to the king.''

The minute the words were out of her mouth, she knew it was the wrong thing to say, but it was too late. All around her, her fellow reporters mimicked, ''Move it, I've got to talk to the king.''

"You can wait, just like the rest of us, mademoiselle," a skinny Frenchman told her, looking down his nose at her. "And you can forget about talking to the king. His press secretary will tell us whatever he wants us to know."

Eliza knew he was right, but his attitude irked her, and she didn't even bother to respond. Quickly stepping around him, she told the guard at the gate, "It's very important that I see the king. I have some information he needs…"

Surrounded by competing reporters, she didn't dare tell him what that information was, but he wasn't interested, anyway. "Nice try," he drawled, "but I've got my orders. No reporters allowed inside the palace. You'll have to wait, just like everyone else."

Frustrated, she swore softly. So much for trying to go through channels. She liked to play by the rules, but sometimes it just didn't pay. Now it was time to follow her gut and do what she should have done when she'd first seen the crowd of reporters fighting to get inside—find another way in.

"Fine," she retorted, pretending to pout as she let herself be pushed to the back of the crowd. "You can't blame a girl for trying."

The front door of the palace opened then, distracting the crowd at the gate, and that was just the opportunity Eliza was looking for to slip away. As the press secretary informed the crowd that the king's announcement would be released momentarily, she quietly hurried along the palace wall hoping to find some place to scramble over now that the guard was distracted. As luck would have it, she saw a delivery truck enter the service gate at the far end and before it could close automatically behind the vehicle, she slipped inside.

After getting over her initial shock at suddenly finding herself within mere yards of the royal palace, she quickly made her way around the corner of the stone and marble building, looking for a way in. But every door she came to was locked!

"I can't believe this!" she muttered, continuing around the building. An entire staff of people took care of the daily operation of the palace. Surely someone had mistakenly left a door open somewhere!

Frustrated, she was about to give up hope when she rushed around another corner and suddenly found herself at the rear of the palace, facing the sea. And there, right in front of her, were the royal gardens...and a veranda with a set of French doors that looked like they'd been placed there just for her.

"Yes!" she whispered triumphantly. Now, if they were just unlocked.

Her heart thundering wildly, she dashed up onto the veranda and turned the doorknob, half expecting an alarm to blare at any second. But the door opened effortlessly, silently, and just that easily, she found herself standing inside what appeared to be the ballroom of the royal palace of Montebello.

Take notes! a voice in her head ordered sharply. But there was no time. The room was deserted, and she took advantage of that to quickly stow her computer and overnight bag behind the drapes at the window. Hopefully, they would still be there when she got back. *If* she got back, she silently amended. She'd just broken into a king's palace. In some countries, they threw you into the dungeon for that if you got caught.

"So don't get caught," she told herself. "Act like you have a right to be here and no one will even spare you a second glance."

It was a simple plan, one that had worked well for her in the past. Over the years, her job—and curiosity—had led

her into any number of places where she had no business
being, and she'd discovered that she could go practically
anywhere if she acted like she knew what she was doing.
So she smoothed her hair, slung her purse over her shoulder, and strode out of the ballroom like she owned the
place.

Just as she'd hoped, it worked. Stepping into a wide,
impressive corridor lined with a collection of paintings the
likes of which she'd only seen in a museum, she passed
several members of the staff, and they didn't even blink at
the sight of her. Relieved, she would have laughed, but she
didn't dare. The less attention she drew to herself, the better.

Unfortunately, she didn't have a clue where she was going. She knew nothing about the layout of the palace or
where the king planned to meet with the guests he'd invited
to witness the naming of his new successor. Logic told her
that the announcement would be made in one of the palace's public rooms, but that was strictly a guess on her part.
For all she knew, they could be meeting in the family quarters, which could be anywhere.

Frowning, she reached an intersection of hallways and
hesitated, not sure which way to turn. And just that easily,
she made her first mistake. Suddenly, a door on her left
opened, and before she could summon the look of confi-
dence that had gotten her that far, she was caught.

"Who the devil are you?"

Swearing softly under her breath, she silently told herself
to bluff her way out of this. But then she turned to face her
captor and whatever she was going to say next flew right
out of her head as she gasped in recognition. His Grace,
Duke Lorenzo Sebastiani, the man everyone had been spec-
ulating for months might one day be named king!

They'd never met, of course, but she would have known

him anywhere. Over the years, she'd lost track of the number of stories she'd written about him—first as a military hero who was rewarded with the title of duke by the king, then as head of the Montebello Royal Intelligence—and she'd enjoyed writing every one of them. There was just something about the man that had always struck her fancy. He was tough and smart and loyal, and his pictures hadn't begun to do him justice. Lean and well-muscled, his sandy-brown hair streaked with golden highlights, and his green eyes dark with a mixture of emotions she couldn't begin to understand, it was easy to see why he, like the rest of the Sebastiani men, was one of the heartthrobs of Europe.

"Your Grace! Thank God! I need you to get a message to the king—"

"You're an American," he cut in, frowning in puzzlement. "How did you get in? There are no tours today."

"No, sir, I'm sure there aren't. I'm not a tourist. My name is Eliza Windmere. I'm with the *Denver Sentinel*—"

That was as far as she got. "A reporter," he said with a grimace of distaste. "I should have known. The palace is crawling with them. C'mon. You're out of here." And before she could begin to guess his intentions, he grabbed her arm and started tugging her toward the nearest exit.

"Wait! You don't understand. I have information about Prince Lucas."

His jaw set, he didn't so much as spare her a glance. "Yeah, right. Let me see if I can guess. You found him waiting tables in L.A., and for the right price, you'll tell King Marcus where he is. Save your breath, sweetheart. I've heard it all before. The king gets a hundred letters a week from people just like you. I don't know how you all live with yourself. Don't you have any conscience?"

"Of course I do," she retorted, stung. But heat burned her cheeks and deep inside, she had to wonder if he was right. The king and queen had lost a son, and though she had come to give them news they longed to hear, she also wanted an exclusive when they learned he was alive. So how was she any different from the con men trying to cash in on the Sebastianis' grief?

Uncomfortable with the question, she reminded herself that she wasn't trying to extort money from the king or keep his son's whereabouts from him. Of course she wanted the story, but she had that already. At this point, she was just doing the right thing and bringing the king news of his son. "Look, I know how this must look, but I'm serious. I have vital information—"

"And I'm the tooth fairy," he retorted. "Put that in your paper and smoke it. It's probably one of those scandal rags, anyway."

That was the wrong thing to say. Stopping abruptly, she jerked free of his grasp and drew herself up to her full five foot seven inches and gave him a narrow-eyed look that should have reduced him to the size of an ant. "For your information, I wouldn't be caught dead writing that kind of trash, so I'd appreciate it if you'd keep a civil tongue in your mouth."

She'd caught him off guard, and for a moment, he had the grace to look embarrassed. But then he obviously realized that he'd just been brought to task by a reporter, of all things. "That was good," he told her dryly. "For a moment there, I actually forgot that you broke in here."

"I didn't break in. The door was unlocked—"

"So you thought you'd just walk right in," he finished for her. "I wonder how you'd feel if I did the same at your house."

"Dammit, I just need to talk to the king!"

"Not a chance," he growled, and grabbed her arm again. Indignant, she tried to jerk free, but this time, the duke had a firmer grip, and there was no escaping him. Still, she had to try. Struggling, uncaring that she'd probably have bruises on her arms tomorrow, she cried, "You're the most irritating man. I don't know why I ever thought you were charming."

Before she could say another word, they were interrupted by a servant, who hurried forward with a worried frown. "Is there a problem, Your Grace?"

"As a matter of fact, there is," he said flatly. "Show this lady to the door, will you, Rudolpho? She's a reporter. And make sure she doesn't get back in."

"Of course," the older man replied, and took Eliza's arm in a grip that was surprisingly firm.

"No! Wait! At least talk to the king for me," she called after the duke, but it was too late. Without sparing her a glance, he turned and walked away.

Chapter 2

"Please don't give me any trouble, Miss," the servant said quietly. "I don't want to call a guard."

Trapped, Eliza considered her options. Old enough to be her grandfather, Rudolpho seemed a gentle soul, but she knew better than to mistake him for a soft touch. The duke wouldn't have turned her over to him if he hadn't felt he could trust the old man to throw her out. And that could only mean one thing. She had to talk fast.

"I know you're only doing your job, Mr. Rudolpho—"

"Sabina," he interjected with a half smile as she fell into step beside him. "The name is Rudolpho Sabina. I'm the king's personal servant."

"And not easily snowed, I'll bet," she replied solemnly.

His lips twitched, but he only said, "No, Miss, I'm not."

That made it more difficult. Falling back on the truth and praying it didn't let her down, she said earnestly, "Then I hope you'll believe me when I tell you I didn't fly all the way from America just to get a scoop on the king's announcement. I didn't even know he planned to name a new heir today. If I had, I would have tried to call to convince him he doesn't need to do this. You have to believe me, Mr. Sabina. That's why I'm here. I have news of the prince.''

For a minute, she thought he was going to listen to her. He hesitated, but just when she began to hope that he would help her, he continued his pace steadily toward the nearest exit. ''You seem like an intelligent woman,'' he said quietly. ''I'm sure you must realize that over the course of the past year, the king has been hounded by dozens of fortune hunters who claimed they'd found the prince. None of them could produce him. Can you?''

Just that easily, he had her neatly cornered. ''No,'' she sighed in defeat. ''No, not yet. But I'm sure I'll be able to with time.''

''The world is full of people who might be able to do that, Ms. Windmere. That's not a good enough reason to see the king.''

His decision made, they reached an exit then, but before he could show her out, they were joined by a woman who hurried toward them with a frown, scolding Rudolpho all the while. ''Rudy, thank God! I've been looking for you everywhere. Where have you been? The king is about to greet his guests—''

''Oh, please, you must stop him!'' Eliza said quickly, interrupting. ''There is no need for him to announce a new heir. Prince Lucas is still alive! I have proof!''

''She's a reporter, Josie,'' Rudy said when his wife gasped. ''She broke in—''

''Because the guard at the gate wouldn't let me in. I was desperate.''

Josie Sabina, to her credit, didn't dismiss her out of hand. ''Well, I suppose I might do the same thing if I was des-

perate,'' she said with a slight smile. Studying her specu-
latively, she suddenly held out her hand and introduced
herself. ''I'm Rudy's wife, Josie. And you're...?''

''Eliza Windmere.'' Sensing a kindred spirit, she took
her hand with a sigh of relief. ''It's very important that I
talk to the king, Mrs. Sabina. His son wasn't killed in the
plane crash. I live in Colorado. I wouldn't have flown halfway around the world for a hoax. I'm not that kind of
person. I really do have proof.''

When Josie glanced at her husband for guidance, Eliza
felt her heart sink. This was her last chance. If Josie didn't
help her, she was going to be tossed out on her ear, and
she could forget getting a message to the king. Duke Lorenzo would spread the word that she was a crazy American
reporter and nothing she said would be taken seriously.

''Duke Lorenzo said to show her out,'' Rudy told his
wife. ''I'm just following orders.''

That was her clue to do the same, but just when Eliza
felt sure Josie was going to tell her she couldn't help her,
the older woman hesitated. ''If there's the slightest chance
the prince is alive, you know I have to tell the queen,
Rudy,'' she told her husband finally. ''She would want to
know.''

''But what if this is nothing but a scam?'' he argued.
''The king won't be happy that you upset the queen for
nothing.''

''That's a risk I'll have to take,'' she said simply. ''If
the prince was my son and there was the slightest chance
he was alive, I would want to know.''

Put that way, Rudy knew when he was beaten. ''All
right,'' he sighed. ''We'll wait here for you.''

Thrilled, Eliza wanted to hug them both. Finally, someone was listening to her! Now, if only the queen would!
Sending up a silent prayer as Josie rushed off to talk to her,

she waited with Rudy and tried not to be concerned when one minute turned into two, then three, then ten. It wasn't easy. She didn't like letting other people speak for her, and her too-active imagination was jumping to all sorts of conclusions, none of them good. What was taking so long?

Impatient, worry eating at her stomach, she would have gone looking for Josie and the queen if Rudy hadn't been watching her like a hawk. And he obviously knew that. Standing nearby, he had the patient look of a man who had no intention of letting her out of his sight, even if that meant watching her for the rest of the day.

Trapped and hating it, she was looking around for a way to distract him so she could slip away when she spied Josie quickly approaching from the far end of the hall. Her heart in her throat, she stepped toward her. "Well? Will she see me?"

"You have ten minutes," she replied solemnly, only to laugh when Eliza pulled her into a hug. Patting her, she smiled. "Come. You don't have any time to waste."

With Josie now as her escort, they made their way through a maze of corridors before they finally reached a small solarium at the back of the house. Stopping outside the elegantly panelled double doors, Josie gave her a quick lesson in royal etiquette.

"You wait for the queen to speak first, and you curtsy when you are introduced. And don't worry. The queen isn't a stickler for such things, but it is the polite thing to do, and she will appreciate it." Amusement glinting in her dark eyes, she added, "Smooth your hair, dear. That's it. Ready?"

No! Eliza almost cried. She was about to meet the queen of Montebello. Of course, she wasn't ready! Too late, she realized she should have taken time to freshen her makeup and clothes at the airport before rushing to the palace, but there was no time for that now. The queen was waiting and the clock was ticking.

Drawing in a calming breath, she nodded. "Let's do it."

Without a word, Josie knocked lightly on the door and pulled it open. A heartbeat later, she found herself ushered into a beautiful room with pale green walls, mosaic floors and the most gorgeous plants and flowers Eliza had ever seen. And there waiting for her was not only Queen Gwendolyn, but King Marcus, as well.

Her heart pounding crazily in her breast, Eliza told herself there was no reason to be nervous. They weren't ogres. In fact, according to all accounts, they were amazingly friendly and down to earth, considering they lived in a palace. And even though Eliza had never met them, she'd written about them and their children and extended family so much over the years that she almost felt like she knew them.

But even as she went over all the reasons why she should be perfectly at ease in the presence of royalty, she curtsied awkwardly before Josie had a chance to announce her. "Oh, I'm sorry," she said, blushing as red as her hair. "I was supposed to wait until I was introduced—and you spoke first."

Queen Gwendolyn smiled with understanding, and it was easy to see why she was still considered one of the most beautiful women in Europe. In her early sixties, her porcelain skin was clear and virtually unlined, her eyes sparkled, and her figure was as trim and slender as a girl's in a blue silk suit that exactly matched the color of her eyes.

Extending her hand, Queen Gwendolyn said, "For the most part, we don't stand on ceremony in our home, Ms. Windmere. Please…may I call you Eliza?"

"Oh, yes, of course, Your Highness."

Liking her immediately, Eliza shook her hand and could have easily sat down and chatted with her like they were old friends. The king, however, stood protectively at his wife's side and looked every inch the royal. The past year had not been easy for him. Regal and aristocratic, his once dark hair was now nearly completely white and there were lines at the corners of his dark eyes that had not been there last year before his son's plane crashed in Colorado.

Quietly greeting her, he got right to the point. "Josie tells us you have news of our son."

"Yes, sir, I do. I believe he is alive."

"According to Josie, you have proof," Queen Gwendolyn said, her eyes dark with entreaty. "You don't look like a cruel woman, Eliza. If this was all just a trick on your part so you could gain an audience with us, please admit it now, and there'll be no hard feelings."

When she took her husband's hand and they stood side by side, their pain was visible. Eliza could have cried for them both. She'd never been married, never had children, so she couldn't begin to imagine the extent of their hurt. Royalty or not, they were parents and they obviously loved their son, and if she could help them in any way, she would.

"I know this past year had to be extremely difficult for you, and I know that you've had people coming out of the woodwork claiming they had found the prince," she said huskily. "I'll be honest with you. I haven't found him, either, and right now, I don't have a clue where he is. But I truly believe he's alive. Because of this." Reaching into her purse, she pulled out the scarf Willy had found and held it out to the queen. "I believe this belongs to Prince Lucas, doesn't it?"

Her gaze locked on the dirty, tattered scarf, Queen Gwendolyn gasped softly. Tears flooded her eyes, and when she reached out for the scarf with trembling fingers, it was almost as if she was afraid to touch it. "Oh, Marcus, look!"

The king didn't say a word. His expression as hard as granite, he shot Eliza a look that would have had a lesser woman shaking in her shoes. "We gave this to our son for Christmas last year. Where did you get it?"

"From a man named Willy Cranshaw," she replied. "He found it in the woods in Colorado...near an abandoned campsite about five miles from the crash site."

"You think Lucas dropped it there?" the queen asked, brushing away the tears that spilled from her eyes. "That he somehow survived the crash? All this time when we thought he was dead, you think he's been wandering around the mountains? Is that what you're saying?"

Eliza would have bet everything she owned that that was exactly what happened, but she couldn't prove it. And until she could, she wouldn't give the queen false hope. "I don't know, Your Highness. I just know that the scarf didn't walk away from the crash site on its own."

She was trying to be cautious, but she might as well have saved her breath. The king and queen exchanged a long look, and suddenly they were in each other's arms, laughing and crying and dancing with joy.

"He must be alive, Gwen!" the king laughed joyfully. "Can you believe it? After all this time, he's really alive!"

Ecstatic, he whirled her around, then kissed her soundly, not caring who saw. "I have to tell Lorenzo," he exclaimed, "so he can reopen the investigation. And the girls! They're going to be thrilled. Rudy?" he yelled, all dignity gone as he glanced around for his personal servant. "I need you, man. Where are you?"

"Here, Your Highness," the older man said quietly as he stepped into the room.

Surprising the older man, the king embraced him like a brother. "Lucas is alive, Rudy!"

To his credit, Rudy admitted that he'd already heard the news. "Ms. Windmere said that he was, Your Highness, but I thought she was another fortune hunter. Forgive me, Miss," he told her solemnly. "But I couldn't take any chances."

"It's okay," she replied with an easy smile. "I know you were only doing your job."

Pleased by both his old friend's honesty and Eliza's response, the king patted him on the shoulder. "Go get Lorenzo for me. He needs to know about this so we can reopen the investigation."

At the mention of the duke's name, Eliza stiffened. *No!* she wanted to cry. *Don't bring him in on this!* But even as she bit back the words, she knew she was going to have to deal with the duke whether she liked it or not. He was, after all, the head of Royal Intelligence and had been in charge of the search for the prince from the moment his plane had gone down. Of course the king would want him to know about the scarf.

"Please sit down, Eliza and tell us everything," the queen said, motioning her over to the pretty cream-colored couch and wing chairs that flanked the marble fireplace, which was the focal point of the room. "I know you said Mr. Cranshaw found Lucas's scarf near a campsite in the mountains, but can you give us all the details you know?"

"Did he find anything else?" the king asked as he joined his wife on the couch and Eliza sank into one of the comfortable chairs. "Was there any way to tell if Lucas was hurt? Where has he been all this time? Why hasn't he called? Doesn't he know we're worried about him?"

Hesitating, Eliza didn't quite know how to answer that. As far as she was concerned, the very fact that Prince Lucas hadn't notified his family that he was alive said a lot about his mental state, but that was strictly her opinion. She wasn't a doctor and wasn't about to comment on the prince's mental or physical condition to his worried parents. So she avoided the issue and turned the conversation back to what she did know.

"Willy found the scarf at an abandoned campsite in a remote area up in the mountains. He couldn't tell how long the prince stayed there—if it was just overnight or possibly longer, but someone had stayed long enough to build a campfire. As for the scarf, we don't know if the prince dropped it or just forgot it, but it was on a log near the campfire."

"Do you trust this Cranshaw fellow?" the king asked with a frown. "What do you know about him? Could he have found the scarf at the crash site and just made this all up so we would think Lucas is still alive? There are sick people out there who get their kicks doing that kind of thing, you know," he told her grimly. "Gwendolyn and I found that out after Lucas turned up missing. Unfortunately, we live in a twisted world."

"Willy has his moments," she said honestly, "but I trust him. He's not lying about where he found the scarf. He wouldn't do that."

She would have said more, but Duke Lorenzo arrived then, and the second he saw her sitting with the king and queen, he stiffened, his sharp green eyes dark with irritation as they locked with hers. Ignoring his aunt and uncle, he growled, "I don't know what the devil you think you're doing, but you're not getting away with it." Striding over to the chair where she sat, he grabbed her arm. "C'mon, you're leaving. And this time, I'll make sure you don't sneak back in."

Shocked, Queen Gwendolyn cried, "Lorenzo! What in

heaven's name has gotten into you? Eliza has brought us news of Lucas. Stop that!'' she cried when he hauled Eliza to her feet. ''Have you lost your mind? You know better than to treat a guest that way!''

''She's just a reporter looking for headlines,'' he retorted with a scowl. ''Don't believe anything she says. I caught her wandering the halls earlier and had Rudy escort her out of the building, but I guess she found a way to break back in.''

''She didn't break in,'' his uncle said, frowning. ''We invited her in. She has news of Lucas. He's alive. Look.'' Holding out the scarf to him, he made no attempt to blink back the tears that pooled in his eyes. ''This was found five miles from the crash site, Lorenzo. At an abandoned campsite,'' he added huskily. ''Can you believe it? He must be alive!''

Seeing the hope in his uncle's and aunt's eyes, Lorenzo wanted more than anything to believe that his cousin had somehow survived the plane crash. But how could he? It had been a year. If Lucas had walked away from the crash, where had he been for the past year? Where was he now? And even though he knew in a glance that the scarf Marcus held was Lucas's, how much stock could he put in the word of an American reporter who no doubt lived and died by the outrageous headlines she wrote?

''I think it's a little too early to jump to that conclusion,'' he told Marcus stiffly. ''This woman is a reporter. She's just looking for a sensational story.''

''I am not!''

''She writes a gossip column about royalty,'' he continued, ignoring her indignant cry. ''I thought her name sounded familiar when I ran into her in the hall, so I did a little investigating. She writes for the *Denver Sentinel*, and he prides herself on beating the competition to a story. She'll go to any lengths to get material for her column.''

"I don't lie!"

"No? So you're going to stand there and say Count Baldwin really had a child with his governess?" he taunted, referring to a twenty-five-year-old English count who had a reputation for being as pious as a monk. "That's the most ridiculous thing I ever heard. The woman's fifteen years his senior!"

"And a paternity test proved the child was his," she retorted. "If you don't believe me, I have a copy of the test results back in my office in Denver. I'll send it to you when I get back home."

Her blue eyes sparking fire at him, she dared him to top that, and with nothing more than that little act of defiance, she set his teeth on edge. And for the life of him, Lorenzo didn't know why. He liked women and enjoyed their company. He didn't usually get short with them, let alone hostile, especially with someone he didn't even know, but there was something about this little redhead that rubbed him the wrong way.

"The point is," he said through his teeth, "that that was a private situation that you had no business exposing. You have no boundaries, and neither does the paper you write for."

"Oh, really?" she snapped. "Then if I'm the monster you think I am, why did I even bother to come all this way in the first place? I certainly didn't need anyone's permission to write this story. I had the scarf and knew where it came from. I could have splashed pictures of it all over the front page and let the wire services pick it up. Wouldn't that have been a nice way for the king and queen to find out their son was alive? They could have read all about it in the papers."

Far from impressed, he laughed shortly. "Yeah, right! That sounds good, but I'm not buying it. You saw a bigger story and you came after it."

Expecting her to deny it, she caught him off guard when she admitted the truth without batting an eye. "Of course I want the bigger story! Unlike you, Your Grace, I don't have a trust fund or a king for an uncle. I work for a living and I make no apologies for that. That doesn't make me a bad person...or unprincipled. If I had lost a son, I wouldn't want to learn that he was alive by reading it in the paper. That's why I'm here."

With that, a heavy silence fell, and her sincerity seemed to echo throughout the room. Suddenly realizing what he'd said to her in the heat of his anger, Lorenzo felt like a heel. "If I misjudged you, I'm sorry," he said stiffly. "But I still don't trust you."

"Don't shoot her, Lorenzo," his aunt said with a smile. "She's just the messenger, and she's brought amazing news. Why should we begrudge her a story? What's important here is that Lucas is alive. We've waited a year for this day. Now we have to figure out a way to find him."

"That's right," King Marcus said. "I'm reopening the investigation."

Relieved, Eliza considered childishly sticking her tongue out at the duke—it was no more than he deserved. If she'd known just how arrogant he was, she wouldn't have been nearly as complimentary of him as she had been in her columns all these years. Irritating man. It would serve him right if the king gave him a royal dressing-down.

But instead of chastising him, the king said, "Eliza got the scarf from a man named Willy Cranshaw, who found it in the mountains in Colorado. I want you to return to America with her and talk to this man. He may be able to tell you something else that will lead us to Lucas."

Stunned, Eliza couldn't believe she'd heard him correctly. After all the awful things Lorenzo had said to her, the king actually expected her to travel all the way back to Colorado with him? "What? Oh, no! He can't."

"He has to, dear," the queen replied. "He can't very well carry on the investigation from here. And you did say you wanted to help us find Lucas," she reminded her. "Here's your chance."

"But you don't understand," she protested. "Willy won't talk to him."

"He's in charge of the investigation," the king said with a frown. "He has to talk to him."

If she'd been dealing with anyone but royalty, Eliza would have laughed. How did she explain Willy to people who only had to snap their fingers to have anything in the world they wanted? They lived in a palace, for heaven's sake! How could they possibly comprehend a man who avoided other people like the plague and lived in a shack that looked like it was going to fall down about his ears any moment?

"Willy's different," she said. "He fought in Vietnam, and it must have done something to his mind. He's a little squirrelly."

Queen Gwendolyn lifted a delicately arched brow. "Are you saying he's crazy?"

"No, actually, I think he's quite sane," she replied. "I guess the best way to describe him is eccentric. He doesn't trust many people. He sees intruders in the shadows, and he's called the police so many times that they put him on hold whenever they recognize his voice. That's why he called me when he found Prince Lucas's scarf. I'm the only one who'll listen to him."

"Lorenzo will listen to him."

"I'm sure he will. The problem is Willy won't talk to him. He won't talk to anyone but me."

"I knew it!" Lorenzo snorted in disdain. "This is nothing but a scam." Turning to his aunt and uncle, he said, "Can't you see she's just stringing you along? How do we know this Willy character even exists? She could have made this all up, bought the scarf over the Internet and trampled it in the dirt to make it look like it had been in the weather."

Indignant, Eliza snapped, "And why would I do such a thing? For a story? According to you, there is no story. And that would come out soon enough if I tried to slip something so outrageous past my readers. I'd lose my job, and I'm not going to risk that for a story that doesn't exist."

"Then tell us more about Mr. Cranshaw," the queen said. "If he truly does exist, Lorenzo really needs to meet with him. There might be something he didn't think to tell you about the scarf that could lead us to Lucas."

She had a point, one Eliza couldn't disagree with. But they were talking about Willy, for God's sake! How in the world was she going to get him to cooperate? If he got it in his head that the duke was suspicious of him, he might take off up into the mountains because he was afraid he was going to be arrested or something, and there was no telling how long he'd be gone.

"Willy is a hermit, Your Highness. I can't predict how he will react to Duke Lorenzo—or me, for that matter, if I introduce them. But I'll try," she promised. "I came here because I truly believe Prince Lucas is alive. I'll do anything I can to help find him."

"For a price," Duke Lorenzo said dryly. "You want the story."

"I already have the story," she reminded him. "I'll admit that I would love an exclusive, but whether the king grants me that or not, I'll do whatever I can to help find Prince Lucas. That's the real story here.''

"I agree," King Marcus said in a tone that warned them that he had had enough of their bickering. "The only thing of importance is finding Lucas. You can't do that from here, Lorenzo. Not when he may be wandering around the mountains of Colorado, lost and confused and no doubt suffering from some serious injuries. So I'm reopening the investigation and sending you home with Eliza."

"What?!"

"Your Highness, Duke Lorenzo doesn't need me to show him the way to Colorado."

"That's true," he replied, his lips twitching. "But he needs you to take him to Willy. And you did say you would help in any way you could. You meant that, didn't you?"

Trapped, Eliza could hardly add that her help didn't include doing any favors for the duke. She'd just have to bite her tongue and learn to tolerate him, like it or not. After all, it wasn't as if she was going to have to spend weeks at a time with the man. The minute they reached Denver, she'd arrange a meeting with Willy, and drive him out to his place. Willy, of course, wouldn't have anything to do with him, and that would be that. The Duke would admit defeat and fly back home, end of story.

So what was she worried about? She might have to spend another twenty-four hours in the duke's company? If she couldn't handle that in order to get a story, she had no right being in the newspaper business.

"Of course I meant it," she said quietly. "I'll call Willy as soon as we get back to Denver and set up a meeting."

Pleased, he smiled. "Then it's settled. You and Lorenzo will work together. Between the two of you, with your investigative skills and his years in intelligence, you're bound to find Lucas."

Lorenzo wasn't too sure of that—the prince had been missing for a year and could be anywhere!—but at the moment, the king had another pressing problem to handle. Down the hall, family and new allies were waiting for him to announce his successor. Now that there was a strong possibility that Lucas was alive, that announcement would, of course, be put on hold.

"For the moment, I think it would be wise if you didn't say anything specific about this new evidence, Your Highness," Lorenzo said quietly. "Just as a precaution."

"I agree," he replied solemnly. "Lucas obviously isn't himself or he would have been in touch with us by now, so we must do what we can to protect him." Turning his attention back to Eliza, he gave her a hard look. "I need your word that you won't reveal my son's whereabouts until he is safe, Eliza. If you can't do that and still write your story, then I need to know now."

Eliza didn't pretend to misunderstand what he was saying. If she couldn't promise to write the story the way the king wanted, there would be no exclusive. "I like to think I'm a responsible reporter, Your Highness. I believe in freedom of the press, but I also realize that what I write can have repercussions. I don't like withholding information from my readers, but in this case, I agree that there is a need to protect the prince as much as possible. What I'd like to do is write a feature story on him—his life, and hopefully, his rescue. The search for him will have to be included in that, of course, but the story won't be printed until after Prince Lucas is back home, safe and sound."

"And your editor will agree to this?"

Simon would have a stroke, but that was something she had no intention of telling the royals. "He won't like it," she said honestly. "He would much rather cover the search as it's happening, but he'll accept whatever terms I agree to.'' He had to. She was writing the story. He couldn't force her to divulge anything she didn't want to. ''I give you my word that I won't write anything that will place the Prince in danger.''

Considering that, the king glanced at the queen. ''What do you think, sweetheart? Should we even consider giving anyone an exclusive at this point? We have to do what's right for Lucas.''

Before she could respond, Lorenzo said, ''Then the real question here is whether you can trust a woman you don't know from Adam. She's a reporter. She has her own agenda.''

Her eyes flashing with irritation, Eliza didn't say a word in her own defense. How could she? He was right. She was a reporter and she did have her own agenda—she wanted a story that would rock the world back on its heels. That didn't mean, however, that she was a liar.

''We all have our own agenda,'' Queen Gwendolyn replied. ''I want my son back, and just this morning, I didn't think that was possible. Thanks to Eliza, now I do.''

Turning to Lorenzo, she said, ''So the answer to your question is yes, I think we can trust her. By granting her an exclusive, it's in her best interest to keep Lucas's whereabouts a secret. Not only will she have more to write about, but she'll protect her source so someone else won't find him before we do and steal the story right out from under her.''

''I agree,'' the king said. ''Eliza will do the right thing. The exclusive is hers. Lorenzo, find my son for me.''

''I'll do my best, Your Highness.''

''I know you will,'' he said gruffly. ''Now that that's settled, I have an announcement to make. I've kept my guests waiting long enough.''

Only he and the queen knew for sure who he had chosen

to succeed him, and that was information they chose to keep to themselves. Watching them stride out, Eliza couldn't help but envy Lorenzo as he joined them. Given the chance, she would have found a way to follow them, but before she could even think about moving, Rudy stepped into the doorway, blocking her path.

"Duke Lorenzo will meet you at the airport for your return flight to the United States. You do not need to make flight arrangements, as you'll be traveling on one of the king's private jets," he informed her. "The king has ordered a car to drive you there now."

When he motioned for her to proceed him out another door across the room, she could hardly take offense. What did she care if she missed out on the king's announcement? She had the real story. The prince was alive, and she had an exclusive! Life didn't get any better than that.

With every tick of the clock, the volume of the conversation in the throne room seemed to escalate as more and more guests speculated about the growing lateness of the hour and the king's tardiness. Standing off to the side of the podium that had been set up earlier for the king's announcement, Kyle Ramsey could well understand the concerned whispers being bandied about by the other guests. The king, as a rule, was generally a punctual man. Unlike some men of power, he respected other people's time as much as he did his own. He wouldn't be this late unless something was seriously wrong.

"What do you think's going on?" his brother, Tyler, asked as he propped a shoulder against a pillar and studied the crowd with watchful eyes. "Something's happened."

"I don't know," he murmured, "but I don't like it."

He had just cause to be concerned. Last year, as a top gun pilot and newly recruited member of the Noble Men, a covert team of peacekeepers that traveled the world protecting women and children, he had, along with the rest of the team, helped restore relations between Montebello and its neighbor, Tamir, after a century-long feud. Peace in the region was of utmost importance, and for the past few weeks, he'd been training his brother to help with the monitoring of the skies over the eastern Mediterranean. When they'd received an invitation to the palace to witness the king's announcement of his new heir, Kyle had assumed the invitation was just a matter of courtesy. Now he wasn't so sure.

Before he could start to worry about what was going on, there was a stir at the door and the king and queen entered, followed by their nephew, Duke Lorenzo. Considering the fact that with the naming of a successor, the king was virtually acknowledging the death of his son, Kyle was surprised to see him smiling. He'd expected the meeting to be tense and tearful. Instead, King Marcus was almost beaming as he moved to the podium.

Silence fell over the elegant confines of the throne room. "I apologize for the delay," the king said, greeting his elite group of guests with an easy smile. "First, I would like to thank you all for coming. As you must all know by now, I invited you here to name my successor to the throne."

The guests exchanged speaking glances, and suddenly, there was a tension in the air that hadn't been there before. *Who would be king?* The question seemed to float around the room, but if the king noticed, he gave no sign of it. Still smiling, he held out his hand to the queen, and with a love that lit up her entire face, she moved to his side.

Together, they faced their family, friends and allies. "As you all know, the past year has not been easy for us," King Marcus continued. "Queen Gwendolyn and I both believed with all our hearts that Prince Lucas was alive, but with each passing day, it was harder to hang on to hope. Eventually, we reached a point where we had to face the fact that life had to go on. I had to have an heir. Choosing someone to succeed me other than my son was not something I was looking forward to. Now, thankfully, it turns out that I don't have to.''

When a collective gasp rose from his guests, he had to smile. ''No, it's not quite what you think. We haven't found Prince Lucas...yet. But there are some new developments in the case, and although I'm not at liberty to tell you what they are at this time, the queen and I wanted you to know that we have high hopes that he will be back with us soon. Thank you all for coming. You'll never know what your prayers and support have meant to us.''

Chapter 3

With the king and queen's exit, silence fell like a shroud, and for what seemed like an eternity, the guests just stood there, unable to believe the sudden turn of events. Then, an invisible switch seemed to be flicked, and in the next breath, everyone was talking at once.

"Can you believe that?" Hassan Kamal exclaimed. "Talk about timing!"

"I personally find it a little too convenient," Butrus Dabir replied, his hawklike features hard with suspicion. "Think about it. The prince has been missing for a full year, then the very day the king is prepared to announce a successor, suddenly there's some mysterious news that he may be alive, after all. Obviously, he doesn't want to name Princess Julia and Sheik Rashid as his successors."

"You always were suspicious of the Sebastianis, Butrus," Sheik Ahmed said dryly. "It must be that legal mind of yours. You see a conspiracy around every corner."

Not the least offended, he didn't deny it. "They are too

closely aligned with the West, sire. They do not think like us.''

"That, unfortunately, is too true," he agreed. "In this particular instance, however, I don't think King Marcus is deliberately conspiring to deny his daughter the throne. He's just a grieving father who isn't ready to acknowledge his son's death. I can't say I blame him. I would find that equally difficult.''

Standing nearby, overhearing the entire conversation, Princess Julia could have hugged her father-in-law for that. There was no question that her family did think differently from her husband's family, but much of that had to do with the feud that had existed between their two countries for the past century. Trust was not something that came automatically just because peace had been declared.

When it came to family, however, there was very little difference between the Sebastianis and the Kamals. They believed, as she and her parents did, that nothing was more important in life than the love of family.

Reading her thoughts, her father-in-law looked right at her at that moment, his black eyes alight with sympathy and understanding, and it was all she could do not to cry. She missed her brother terribly and couldn't blame her parents for wanting to believe Lucas was still alive. She did, too.

At her side, Rashid took her hand and twined his fingers with hers, his dark eyes smiling into hers when she looked up. He didn't say a word—he didn't have to. After everything they'd been through, they had a knowledge of each other that went soul deep.

"The king may be grieving, but he understands that it's his duty to protect the monarchy at all costs," Rashid told Butrus and his father. "He wouldn't postpone naming a successor unless he truly believed Lucas was alive.''

"I agree," Hassan said. "Whatever's going on, it has nothing to do with some kind of secret plot to deny Julia and Rashid the throne. They never had much of a chance at it anyway. No offense," he told his brother and sister-in-law with a quick grin. "It's just a matter of common sense. If the Sebastiani monarchy is to continue, it has to be handed down through the male line."

Julia agreed. "That doesn't mean there won't be a strong alliance between our two countries," she said. "Now we are not only linked by marriage, but by blood, thanks to baby Omar. The friendship between Montebello and Tamir can only grow stronger."

"I hope so," Butrus said coolly. "I just don't like this new development."

He wasn't the only one. Moving to join his brother, Desmond couldn't imagine what new evidence the king was talking about, but he was absolutely livid. Lorenzo would be king, dammit! It was his right. Marcus had raised him like a son, and it was time he let go of this pipe dream that Lucas was still alive and give Lorenzo the position he deserved in the family. Then, when his dearly loved brother ascended to the throne, he, Desmond, would have the position he, too, deserved. He would be the next best thing to king! That was only just. After all, as the oldest son of the king's deceased brother, Antonio, he was also the king's nephew. It wasn't his fault his mother had been a household maid, he thought bitterly. If he had been legitimate instead of his father's bastard child, *he* would the one the king was now considering as his heir to the throne.

His resentment of that was, however, something he had kept well hidden over the years. So when his brother joined him again, he greeted him with a pretended look of pleased surprise. "This is wonderful news, Lorenzo! So what is this new evidence the king was talking about? Does he really have proof that Lucas is alive?''

''You know I'm not at liberty to say anything about the investigation,'' he said. ''All I can say is that there's some new evidence.''

''Oh, come on,'' Desmond chided him. ''I'm your brother. You can trust me. I won't say anything to anyone.''

''I didn't say that you would,'' he replied smoothly. ''But the case has been reopened, and I don't talk about active cases. Especially when the palace is virtually surrounded by reporters. The very walls have ears.''

Left with no choice, Desmond graciously accepted the fact that he would have to wait just like everyone else to find out what this new evidence was. But he didn't like it. He didn't like it all. Forcing a smile, he said, ''You know best, little brother. I'm sure you'll tell me when you can.''

From across the room, the Ramsey brothers silently gauged the guests' reaction, and neither liked what they saw. ''That one bothers me,'' Kyle said quietly, flicking a look toward Desmond. ''His eyes are cold as hell.''

''He's close to the king,'' Tyler reminded him.

Unimpressed, Kyle shrugged. ''That's only one more reason to watch him…along with everyone else. In case you haven't noticed, he's not the only one who's less than happy with the king's announcement.''

Tyler had noticed, all right, and he didn't mind admitting he was worried. Some of the Kamals had been openly speculative, and where there was speculation, there was still distrust. ''Peace with Tamir is still fragile. Anyone who wanted to shatter the Kamals' relationship with Montebello could find a way to use this to their advantage.''

His expression grim, Kyle had already thought of that. ''It's our job to make sure that doesn't happen.'' It went without saying that they had their work cut out for them.

* * *

Cooling her heels at the airport, Eliza could just imagine the scene at the palace when the king announced that his son was alive. The place was probably in an uproar. Simon was going to hate that she missed that, but she hadn't wanted to push her luck by asking to be present when the king gave his friends and allies the news. Not when she'd been granted an exclusive in the search for Prince Lucas! That alone was going to be worth a small fortune in headlines.

And the only fly in the ointment was that she had to work with Duke Lorenzo.

Irritating man, she thought, grimacing. She didn't know how he'd developed a reputation as a flirt with the ladies. Granted, he had the Sebastiani looks—her heart had shifted in her breast just at the sight of him. Then he'd opened his mouth and ruined all her expectations.

That didn't, however, mean that she wouldn't be able to work with him. He had an attitude, but she'd dealt with worse. He might be a duke and come from a long line of royalty, but she was confident she could handle him. For the kind of headlines this story was going to generate, she could handle the devil himself.

"Speak of the devil," she muttered to herself as she spied Lorenzo making his way toward her through the crowded airport. Carrying a small suitcase in his hand, he looked like he owned the place, she thought, then had to grin ruefully. He was a Sebastiani. Maybe he did!

His green eyes narrowing at the sight of her, she wasn't surprised when he appeared to be less than pleased to see her. The only reason he was even associating with her at all was because the king had ordered him to. Lovely, she sighed. This was going to be just lovely. This was going to be worse than working with Deborah.

"Your Grace," she said by way of a greeting. "I'm ready when you are."

"Let's go, then," he said curtly, and motioned for her to follow him.

So much for common courtesy, she thought with a grimace as he led the way to the boarding gate the royal jet had been brought into. It was going to be a long flight. Hopefully, though, once they were on the plane, she wouldn't have to deal with him until they got to Denver. She'd been too excited to sleep during the flight over, and exhaustion was quickly catching up with her. Lorenzo would, in his search for the prince, no doubt hit the ground running when they reached Denver, so she was going to need all the rest she could get. Hopefully, the jet had a sleep cabin in the back she could take advantage of. She wouldn't mind using it—mainly to put more distance between herself and the duke.

"I hope you don't mind if I sit in the back and catch a few winks," she said as she followed him on to the lavishly appointed plane, trying not to gawk too much at the expensive furnishings.

"Don't be ridiculous," he retorted. "I can't talk to you when you're at the back of the plane. You'll sit with me."

"Your wish is my command," Eliza muttered under her breath, rolling her eyes. So this was what it was like to be royalty. No wonder so many of the children grew up to lead wild lives. They were spoiled rotten!

Lorenzo, to his credit, didn't take advantage of the flight attendant's offer to bring him food or drink immediately. "No, thank you," he told her with a charming smile he'd never once directed at Eliza. "We have a great deal of business to discuss right now. We'll have some wine later."

"As you wish, Your Grace," she said and disappeared behind a curtain at the back of the plane, leaving them seated comfortably in the expensive leather seats in the first cabin.

And just that easily, Eliza found herself flying in a private jet, seated next to one of the best-looking men in Europe. Any other woman might have let it go to her head, but she wasn't foolish enough to think that the duke had requested she fly in the same cabin because he wanted her with him. They were together for one reason and one reason only—business. It was his job to find Prince Lucas and hers to write about it. She'd be wise to remember that.

She told herself that wouldn't be difficult. He didn't like her—he was only tolerating her presence because he had to. And the feeling was mutual. That wasn't going to change, she assured herself, just because he fairly oozed charm when he smiled. Let him charm someone else. That wasn't what she was here for.

Still, once he settled next to her, buckled in, then turned the full force of his beautiful green eyes on her, her heart started to sputter and she wasn't nearly as indifferent as she would have liked.

"Tell me more about Willy," he commanded coolly as he pulled a small notebook out of the inside pocket of his suitcoat. "I need to know everything there is to know about the man. Do you think he really found the scarf? Or did he steal it? Is he capable of harming the prince? You said he fought in the Vietnam War. Does he suffer from flashbacks? Just how dangerous is he?"

He threw questions at her like she was some kind of underling, not even giving her a chance to answer one before he tossed another one at her. And that, on top of the heated words they'd exchanged at the palace, was too much, as far as Eliza was concerned. Settling into a more comfortable position, she leaned back in her seat and surveyed him with a jaundiced look in her eyes that he would have been wise to be wary of.

"Since we're going to be working together, Your Grace," she said silkily, "I think it's important that we begin as we mean to continue. I know you're the head of Montebello Intelligence, and I understand you're used to grilling people, but in the future, I would appreciate it if you didn't treat me as if I was some sort of suspect. For the record, I don't take orders well and I appreciate the word please when I'm *asked* to do something. I'm also reasonably intelligent. If you'll remember that, we'll get along just fine."

Just that easily, she put him in his place and made him feel like a jackass, all without breaking a sweat. He was the one with royal blood, but she was the one acting like a damn princess. And Lorenzo couldn't help but admire her for that. She'd had every right to tell him off—he'd acted like a jerk, and he didn't know why. There was just something about this tall, skinny American that really set his teeth on edge.

She was a reporter, he reasoned, and he'd yet to meet one that he liked. They were all a bunch of leeches. There wasn't a royal in the world who could make a move, however innocent, without a reporter somewhere jumping on the story and making money off of it. And he hated that. Other people were allowed their privacy and the right to occasionally do something stupid in public without it making headlines, but not a royal. Because of reporters like Eliza.

All right, so maybe he couldn't hold her responsible for what her cohorts did. He was still stuck with her, like it or not. He had to tolerate her, but that was it. He didn't have to like her ingenuity, didn't want to admire her tenacity, and sternly ordered himself not to find her Katharine Hepburn-type looks attractive in any way. He couldn't allow himself to forget that anything he said or did while he was with her could be splashed all over the front page. He hated that, but there was nothing he could do about it—the king had ordered him to accompany her back to Colorado. His objective was to find Lucas, hopefully alive, and he couldn't do that without Eliza.

And that meant he had to find a way to work with her. "Look," he sighed, "I'm sorry. I didn't mean to insult you and it certainly wasn't my intention to treat you like a suspect. I'm not happy with the king's orders, but I had no right to take that out on you. I won't do it again."

As far as apologies, it was much more than she'd expected. Pleasantly surprised, she said, "Thank you. I appreciate that." Now that peace was established, she was more than willing to cooperate. "I don't know what else I can tell you about Willy other than what I already have. He doesn't deliberately lie—he's just so suspicious that he's paranoid sometimes."

"But you believe him? You think he really found the scarf where he said he did?"

"Yes, I do."

"But you just said that he's paranoid sometimes. How do you know that he didn't find the scarf at the crash site and just imagine it was somewhere else? He doesn't sound very stable, if you ask me."

Eliza couldn't argue with that. There *were* times when Willy wasn't very stable. But she believed him, and she couldn't even say why. "I don't know how to explain him to you. After he found the scarf, he must have called me a dozen times at work. He was truly concerned that the king was going to accept the fact that the prince was dead and name a new successor to the throne."

"It wouldn't have mattered if he had," Lorenzo replied.

"Everyone knows that if Lucas showed up alive, even if it was years from now, that he would be the king's heir. He's his son. No one else could ever take his place."

"You and I know that, but Willy isn't always playing with a full deck. In his eyes, once the king named a successor, Prince Lucas would lose his place in line forever, and he couldn't let that happen."

Still skeptical, he could only shake his head in wonder. "And this is the man who's going to lead us to the prince. God help us all."

Eliza couldn't argue with that. Prince Lucas had been missing for a year, and what clues there were that might lead to his whereabouts had probably long since dried up and blown away. Every major law enforcement agency in the country had already looked for him, without success. If they were going to find him, they were going to need all the help they could get.

Lorenzo had never met anyone who could fall asleep so easily. After Eliza told him everything she could about Willy Cranshaw, she pulled her notebook computer from her satchel, busily typed her notes, then tucked it away again. Just seconds after that, she leaned back in her seat and was out like a light almost immediately. Not knowing her intentions until she dosed off, he felt guilty for not offering her a bed in the lounge at the back. Then, as he found himself studying her in spite of his best efforts not to, he was glad he hadn't.

Why did she have to be so pretty?

The thought slipped into his head uninvited, irritating him no end. He would have sworn he didn't care much for redheads, but there was something about her corkscrew curls that he found incredibly feminine and appealing— especially when they were piled on top of her head as they were now. He wanted to touch them to see if they were as soft as they looked—but he didn't dare.

Glancing away, he sternly ordered himself to ignore her. He might as well have told himself not to breathe. She'd forgotten to take off the small, hornrimmed glasses she wore when she worked, and they'd slipped down on her pert nose. He should have left them alone, but before he could stop himself, he found himself reaching for them.

Too late, he realized his mistake. When he gently lifted the glasses from her nose, she sighed in her sleep and turned slightly toward him, snuggling too close for comfort. The faint scent of her perfume drifted to his nose, teasing him. Swearing soundlessly, he clenched his teeth on an oath and carefully laid her glasses on the tray in front of her, then quickly turned his attention to a news magazine he retrieved from his briefcase. The words blurred before his eyes, but he didn't look at his companion again. It was just safer that way. And though he realized it might be even safer for him to move to another seat in the otherwise empty cabin, he couldn't bring himself to leave her presence. It was as if she held him there, by her side.

"Your Grace, we will be landing in Denver in approximately ten minutes," the flight attendant said.

Jerked awake by the softly spoken words, Eliza sat up with a start, only to frown when her gaze fell on the tray in front of her...and her glasses. She had no memory of taking them off, let alone laying them on the tray.

Suddenly suspicious, she glanced at her companion, but he never raised his eyes from his magazine. Had he taken them off for her? she wondered, only to dismiss the idea with a soundless snort. Not likely. He might have apologized for his curt behavior, but he'd admitted he wasn't happy about working with her. He would tolerate her, but she didn't expect him to be considerate. She'd probably removed her glasses herself and just forgotten about it.

And that was for the best, she assured herself. She didn't want any favors from him, didn't want any reason to like him. They didn't have to be friends for her to do her job—they just had to be civil. Then when they each returned to their very different worlds, they could part company without any regrets.

So she tucked her glasses back into her purse and didn't say a word, and neither did he. For the next ten minutes, the silence between them was deafening—until they landed and passed through customs. Then suddenly they realized there was a lot to do, and they hadn't discussed any of it.

"We need a rental car…"

"I need to call my boss…"

"I'll make sure the luggage is brought to the rental office…"

"I should have called Simon from Montebello. The paper might pay for the rental…"

"The king authorized me to pay for all expenses—"

Both speaking at the same time, they froze abruptly and only just then realized what the other had said. Frowning, Lorenzo said stiffly, "There's no reason to call your boss. I'm paying for everything."

His tone dared her to argue with him, and for a moment, Eliza had to struggle not to smile. If he thought Simon was going to object to him using his American Express card, he was in for a rude awakening. "I'm sure Simon will appreciate that, but I still need to call the office and check in. It won't take long."

"Then I'll collect the luggage while you're doing that and meet you at the rental car office."

His head high and his bearing regal, he strode off, and watching him, Eliza could well understand why King Marcus had considered Lorenzo as his successor. Confident and proud, he looked like he could take on the world with one hand tied behind his back.

Not, she reminded herself, that he was ever likely to be king. Not now that there was a good chance that Prince Lucas was alive. Was that a disappointment to him? she wondered. She'd have to ask him and include that in her story.

Her mind already working on the opening paragraph, she stepped over to the bank of phones against the wall and quickly punched in Simon's number. "Hey, LaGree," she teasingly greeted him when he answered with a rough hello. "I'm back and you're never going to guess what happened."

"It better be good, Red," he growled, "because you've got a column to file and a four o'clock deadline. Or did you forget that while you were having tea with the king and queen?"

"We never got around to tea," she chuckled, "but you don't have to worry about the column. Thanks to an exclusive the king granted me, I'm going to have enough material to fill the entire front page section."

"Get out of here! You got an exclusive?"

"Oh, I got more than that," she replied, grinning. "Duke Lorenzo flew back with me to talk to Willy and investigate where he found the scarf, and I'm going to be working with him during the search. Of course, this means I'll be out of the office for a while. I hope that's not going to be a problem."

"Are you kidding?! Damn it all, Red, I underestimated you! Listen, you follow this to the end, you hear me? Keep good notes and check in every couple of days so I'll know what's going on, okay? This is going to get you a Pulitzer,

Red. And if you pull this off and help find Prince Lucas, you deserve it.''

It wasn't often that he called her by her first name, and just that easily, he touched her heart. "Thanks, Simon," she said huskily. "Knowing you believe in me means a lot."

"You better believe I believe in you," he retorted. "Why do you think I didn't let Little Miss Priss steal this story right out from under you? She wouldn't know what to do with it if you handed it to her on a platter. And don't you worry about her while you're gone," he added. "She's happy in La-la land, and I plan on keeping her there as long as possible."

Her smile rueful, Eliza appreciated that, but they both knew Deborah would be a threat to her as long as her daddy owned the paper and she wanted to play Brenda Starr. "Maybe Brad Pitt'll fall for her and she'll never come back."

"We can only pray we get that lucky," he said dryly.

Grinning, she said, "I'd better go—I've got to meet the duke at the rental car office. Thanks again, Simon. I'll be in touch."

"Hey, who's paying for this?" he said quickly before she could hang up. "You didn't commit the paper to anything, did you?"

He suddenly sounded so worried that she couldn't resist stringing him along a little. "What do you think? I know how badly you want this story."

"Dammit, Red, don't do this to me!"

Laughing, she hung up.

She was still smiling when she reached the rental car office and found Lorenzo loading their luggage into the back of the Tahoe SUV he'd rented. "I thought we might need something rugged since we're going up into the mountains,'' he told her. "Were you able to talk to your boss?''

Grinning, she nodded. "He told me to take all the time I need.''

"Good. Then let's go.'' Always the gentleman, he opened the passenger door for her, then stepped around the vehicle and slid behind the wheel. Starting the motor, he put it in gear, then arched a brow at her. "Willy lives north of here, correct? In Boulder?''

"That's right,'' she said as he pulled away from the curb. "Turn right at the signal light.''

Without a word, he followed her directions, and within moments, they were on their way to Boulder. It seemed like she'd been traveling for a week, but as far as Eliza was concerned, they couldn't get there fast enough. There was, however, little point in hurrying. It was already late in the day. They'd have to wait until tomorrow to see Willy.

"When we get to Boulder, we might as well go ahead and get a motel for the night,'' she said as they left the city behind. "Willy doesn't like visitors after three, so I'll call him in the morning and set up a meeting for tomorrow.''

"But it's early yet,'' Lorenzo replied with a scowl. "Surely he can see us today. I wanted to head up into the mountains tomorrow to the campsite where he found the scarf.''

"You can't rush Willy, Your Grace,'' she replied. "He has his own rules when it comes to dealing with the outside world, and if we don't play by those rules, we can forget seeing him at all. I know it's frustrating, but it's his way or no way.''

Frustrated didn't begin to describe what Lorenzo was feeling. It had been a full year since Prince Lucas's plane had gone down, and now that a new lead had surfaced that might eventually point to his whereabouts, he couldn't even check it out. The Prince's safety was in the hands of a crazy old mountain man who wouldn't cooperate until he was good and ready.

And then, there was Eliza. From the moment he'd found her wandering the halls at the palace, he'd somehow lost control of everything. He'd ordered her shown to the door, but she'd still managed to finagle her way in to see the king and queen. When he'd wanted to fly to Colorado to interrogate Willy himself, she'd dropped the bombshell that the hermit would only talk to her. Because it was the king's wish, Lorenzo had been forced to endure her company, and now she was trying to control the investigation itself!

He wouldn't have it, dammit! He was the head of Royal Intelligence, and he wasn't going to allow a gossip columnist, of all things, to control how and where and when he did his job. And what the devil kind of perfume was she wearing, anyway? The fresh, light scent of hers drifted through the confines of the SUV, teasing his senses, teasing him. He told himself he was just tired—they'd been traveling nonstop for hours and they could both use some rest and a break from each other—but he knew it was more than that. He wanted to ignore her and he couldn't, dammit! And he didn't like it.

"We need to get something straight," he growled as they reached the outskirts of Boulder. "This is my investigation, and I'll run it as I see fit. You're just along for the ride."

He watched her eyes narrow, but to her credit, she merely said, "You think so, do you?"

"You're damn straight I think so. I know so! You're obviously very good at your job, but you're just a reporter. You have no experience in investigating—"

"Really?" she challenged, irritation glinting in her eyes. "Would you care to make a bet on that?"

Something in her tone warned him she wasn't the type of woman who made a bet unless it was a sure thing, but it was too late for him to backpedal now. "So now you're telling me you worked in intelligence? Yeah, right!"

Color seeped into her cheeks. "No one said anything about intelligence, Your Grace. I believe we were speaking about experience in investigating, and when it comes to that, I could tell you things about your own family that you probably don't even know."

"Like what?"

"Well, let's see," she said, considering. "If I remember correctly, you have a cousin on your mother's side who was arrested in Portugal last year for shoplifting." When his eyes widened in surprise, she added, "Apparently, this isn't the first time she's deliberately walked out of a store without paying for the merchandise she stuffed in her purse, but it is the first time a merchant actually dared to press charges. It took some fast talking on your part and a very generous contribution to the merchant's retirement fund to convince him to forget this ever happened."

Her smile more than a little smug, she said, "So, what were you saying about me not having any experience in investigating, Your Grace?"

Swearing under his breath, Lorenzo couldn't help but wonder how she'd dug this all up. He would have sworn he'd buried it so deep, the story would never see the light of day again. "Where the hell did you get your information?" he demanded. "There was no police report, and the merchant signed a settlement agreeing to keep the matter quiet."

"And he kept his word," she replied with a sassy grin. "He wasn't my source. I don't reveal them."

Torn between irritation and more than a little admiration—dammit, how had she found out about cousin

Louisa?—he warned himself he was going to have to watch himself with her. She was turning out to be far more interesting and intelligent than he'd anticipated. And it didn't help matters that she was so pretty. He'd always had a weakness for a woman with brains and looks, and he couldn't allow himself to think of her as anything other than a reporter…or he'd find himself in more trouble than cousin Louisa had last year in Portugal.

"Fine," he retorted. "Keep your sources to yourself. We both know this isn't about Portugal. The prince is obviously in trouble or he would have found a way to get in touch with the family by now. My objective is to find him—yours is to get the story. I don't have a problem with that. Just don't get in my way."

Eliza had no intention of doing that, but she wasn't going to stand around with in her hands in her pockets while he took charge and scared Willy off, either. Then they would lose the prince and the story!

"And just how am I getting in your way, Your Grace?" she asked archly. "Is it something I said? What I'm wearing? My hair?"

"Don't be ridiculous!"

"So it's not me, personally?"

"Of course not."

"Then there's no reason why we can't work together, is there?"

She'd neatly cornered him, and they both knew it. He scowled at her, and for a moment, she thought he was going to tell her exactly what he thought of her. Then a reluctant grin curled one corner of his mouth. "Very clever, Ms. Windmere. I can see right now that I'm going to have to watch myself around you."

"You certainly are," she agreed with twinkling eyes. "Don't underestimate me. You might live to regret it."

"I'll remember that," he promised. "And you'd be wise to do the same with me."

Blue eyes meeting green, they silently acknowledged mutual respect for each other's intelligence. It wasn't peace, but it was a start.

Eliza had often wondered what it must be like to be royal. She found out when Lorenzo pulled up before one of the most expensive hotels in town and flipped the keys to the valet. Before she knew it, she had her own private suite—with a Jaccuzi whirlpool and room service at her disposal—without Lorenzo even bothering to ask the price. He'd even tipped the bellboy to bring up her small overnight bag.

If she hadn't been so exhausted, she might have enjoyed staying in the lap of luxury. As it was, all she needed was hot and cold running water and a bed. Peeling off her clothes, she stepped into the shower and washed the dirt from what felt like three continents from her body. Fifteen minutes later, she fell in bed and was asleep before her head hit the pillow.

Dead to the world, she didn't know anything until the next morning, when there was a loud banging at the door. Startled, she jumped awake, her heart pounding. "What in the world—"

"Eliza?! Dammit, open this door! I need to talk to you!"

Not what in the world, but who, she thought with a groan. What was wrong with the man? It was barely eight o'clock in the morning and they weren't supposed to meet in the lobby until nine-thirty since she couldn't get in touch with Willy until after ten. So what was so important that he had to talk to her now?

Muttering curses under her breath—she and the Duke were going to have to get a few things straight!—she rolled out of bed, grabbed her robe, and marched to the door. Her green eyes blazing, she jerked it open and glared at him. "Do you have any idea what time it is? Do you even care that you're waking up everybody on this floor? What is wrong with you?"

"I'll tell you what's wrong," he growled. Snapping open the morning paper, he held it up right in front of her nose. "This! You've got some explaining to do, lady. Where would you like to start?"

Her eyes on the bold headline spread across the front page of the morning edition of the *Denver Sentinel,* Eliza hardly heard him. Prince Lucas Alive! she read with a sinking feeling in the pit of her stomach. Duke And Reporter Follow New Leads In Search.

And there, right below the headlines, was a very flattering picture of Lorenzo.

Chapter 4

"Well, hell," she sighed. This was just what they needed. They didn't have a clue what circumstances Prince Lucas was in or what was preventing him from getting in touch with his family, which was why the investigation had to be done quietly. And now with Lorenzo's picture splashed all over the paper, that was going to be impossible. "This is great. Just great."

And she knew exactly who to blame. Simon.

Oh, he'd claim he'd just picked up the story from the wire service, but she knew better. She'd been very careful to make sure that she'd told no one about the scarf except the royal family and Simon, and she'd bet the Pulitzer she one day hoped to win that the Sebastianis hadn't said a word to the press. They wanted their son back and they'd given her their word that she had an exclusive. They wouldn't have leaked the story.

That left only Simon. The crafty old buzzard had splashed the headline across the front page on purpose.

When the prince's plane had first gone down, the story had been firmly lodged on the front page for weeks. But when there was nothing new to report, interest in the prince's disappearance had grown stale. It had been months since there'd been any coverage about the search, and the public had a short memory. Simon knew that. Eliza could make a zillion agreements with the Sebastianis, but he was in the business to sell newspapers. And he was making damn sure he did that by stirring up attention about the prince again *before* she'd even written her feature, let alone turned it in for publication.

The only problem was, by plastering Lorenzo's picture on the front page and letting the world know he was coming to the States to take up the search, he may have sabotaged the search before they'd even begun.

She was, Eliza decided, going to kill him. The only question was how. If he blew this exclusive for her, she swore she'd be satisfied with nothing less than boiling him in oil.

"Well?" Lorenzo said. "What have you got to say for yourself?"

What could she say? "I didn't know anything about this, Lorenzo. You have to believe me. Evidently my boss thought he needed to generate a little interest in the Prince again."

"A *little* interest?" he choked. "With four-inch headlines? Dammit, every paper in the country's going to pick this up! Do you know what kind of problems that's going to cause?"

"It won't be that bad," she began.

That was as far as she got. "The hell it won't! The search is supposed to be on the Q.T. I realize that in your world, that's probably not in your vocabulary, but this isn't about you. It's about the prince, and we don't have a clue where he is or what kind of danger he could be in. Which is why

I wanted to keep the search for him quiet. Now that we wouldn't even be able to look for the campsite where Willy found the scarf without every Tom, Dick and Harry dogging our steps!''

He was furious, and Eliza couldn't say she blamed him. Finding the prince after all this time was going to be difficult enough without God knows who interfering with the search. "I'll call Simon right now and chew him out," she promised. "This won't happen again."

Silently cursing Simon for putting her in this position, she quickly punched in the number to his direct line. The second he came on the line, she let him have it with both barrels. "You're a dirty rotten scoundrel, LaGree. Do you have any idea what you've done?"

"Now, Red, don't get your girdle in a twist—"

"I don't wear a girdle!"

"Aw, c'mon, you know what I mean," he said, wheedling. "You want your Pulitzer, don't you? How're you going to get it if you don't advertise?"

"This isn't advertising, dammit, it's sabotage! A man's life is at stake. A prince, for heaven's sake! From now on, don't you dare publish anything else about the prince. Understood?"

If anyone else but Simon had been her boss, she probably would have been fired right there on the spot for speaking to him so, but he was a big enough man to admit when he was in the wrong. "All right, all right," he grumbled. "Quit your crying. I won't give away any more information that will put the prince in danger."

"Yes! As long as you keep the duke's picture out of the paper. He's not the story here, Simon. The prince is."

"Don't be ridiculous," he chided. "Duke Lorenzo would have been named the next king if Willy Cranshaw hadn't found the scarf. And now he's out searching for the man he could have replaced. Talk about ironic—of course he's part of the story! The readers are going to love this!''

Eliza knew he was right—there was nothing readers loved more than a tragic tale of what might have been—but that was beside the point. ''They can love it when the feature is published and without having the duke's picture splashed across the front page,'' she retorted. ''I mean it, Simon. He's not as well known as the rest of the family, and he wants to keep it that way. I want your word that there'll be no more pictures.''

For a moment, she thought he was going to argue, but he knew her well enough to know that she wasn't going to budge on this. ''Okay,'' he sighed grudgingly. ''No more pictures. I promise. Though I don't know what all the fuss is about,'' he muttered. ''There wasn't any harm done.''

''That's easy for you to say,'' she told him. ''You're not standing where I am.''

Hanging up, she turned to face Lorenzo. ''For what it's worth, he promised. I should warn you, though, that Simon has printer's ink in his blood. He lives and dies for a headline, and if he thinks he's got a good one, he's going to print it.''

It was the nature of the business, and they both knew it. ''You did what you could,'' he acknowledged. ''I can't ask for more than that.''

''I'll do what I can to see that it doesn't happen again,'' she promised. ''I have to check in with Simon on a regular basis, but I have no intention of telling him where we are or doing anything that will endanger the prince. This isn't just a headline for me, Lorenzo,'' she added quietly. ''I know he's your cousin and you care about him, but a lot of other people do, too. I'm one of them.''

There was no doubting her sincerity. His eyes searching hers, Lorenzo suddenly felt like a heel. From the moment he'd met her, he'd done nothing but give her a hard time. And he wasn't proud of that. Yes, she was after a story—what reporter wasn't?—but she wasn't one of those piranhas who sold her soul to the devil just to make the evening edition. If she had been, she wouldn't have cared less about the morning headlines, and she certainly wouldn't have stood up to her boss the way she had.

"I'm sorry I woke you up," he said gruffly. "I was just so mad when I saw the paper that I didn't even look at the clock. I guess I dragged you out of bed."

Since she was dressed in her nightclothes and her hair was still tangled from sleep, that was obvious, but Lorenzo regretted bringing the subject up the second the words were out of his mouth. With a will of their own, his eyes skimmed the blue nightshirt and robe she wore and he couldn't help but notice how touchable she looked in the morning. Her skin was soft, her cheeks flushed, her mouth bare of lipstick—

Suddenly realizing where his thoughts and his eyes had wandered, he swore silently and took a quick step back. "I just remembered that I have some calls to make," he said, taking another step back. "I'll meet you in the lobby at nine-thirty, just as we planned. Okay? We can eat breakfast at the diner across the street, then go see Willy."

He was gone before she could say a word, rushing out of her room like a man with a train to catch. Puzzled, Eliza caught sight of herself in the mirror and didn't have time to wonder what had lit a fire under the duke. If she was going to be ready by nine-thirty, she had to get moving.

Eliza was still brushing her teeth when the bellhop arrived at nine-fifteen to collect her bag, and she had to laugh. Lorenzo was making damn sure she met him on time in the lobby. Hurriedly packing the last of her things in her bag, she gave it to the bellhop, checked the suite to make sure she hadn't left anything, then carried her satchel— complete with her computer—down to the lobby herself.

"Why didn't you let the bellhop carry that?" he asked with a frown as he took the bag from her and escorted her outside to where the valet had brought up their rental. "That's why I sent him up."

"That's my livelihood," she said simply. "I don't trust it to anyone I don't know."

She didn't expect him to understand—he'd been born with a silver spoon in his mouth and couldn't possibly know what it was like to have to scrimp and save to buy something like a Notebook computer—but he didn't question her about it. Instead, he said, "I'll remember that," and opened the door of the SUV for her.

He'd done it before when they rented the vehicle at the airport, and this time, as before, the courteous gesture caught her off guard. She liked to think she was an independent woman who didn't need a man to open her door for her or carry her groceries or anything else for her. But he had a way of treating a woman that she found incredibly flattering. And he didn't even seem to be aware of it—his good manners were just ingrained.

Don't be too flattered, a voice in her head drawled. *He's way out of your league, and he doesn't like reporters. Remember that, and you'll get along just fine.*

Jerked back to reality, she felt heat climb into her cheeks as she realized where her thoughts had wandered. What in the world was wrong with her? Less than twenty-four hours ago, she'd wanted to shake the king for forcing her to work with the man, and now she found herself flattered that he'd opened the door for her? She had to be losing her mind.

Thankfully, she didn't have time to dwell on that. They reached the diner in a matter of moments, and once again,

Lorenzo was opening a door for her, only this time, it was to the diner. "A table for two," he told the hostess who greeted them with a smile. "Non-smoking."

"This way," the woman said, only to glance at him again and frown. "Hey, don't I know you? You look awfully familiar."

At his side, Eliza felt him stiffen ever so slightly, but his smile was easy when he said, "Sorry, but I've never been here before. You must have me mixed up with someone else."

"Oh. Sorry. It's just that I'd swear I've seen you before," she said. Then it hit her. "Oh, my God, you're that duke, the one who's looking for Prince Lucas! I saw your picture in the paper this morning."

Beaming, she said, "Oh, this is wonderful! I was telling my husband, Fred, not even an hour ago, that I bet someone kidnapped the prince and is hiding him out at Elk Canyon. It's a box canyon and you've really got to know where you're going or you'll lose all sense of direction.

"I could take you up there," she offered eagerly, her eyes shining at the sudden thought. "Of course, I'd have to take off from work, and I don't have any leave, so I'd need some kind of compensation, but we could work that out. I wouldn't be unreasonable or anything. I just want to help find the prince. 'Cause it's the right thing to do, ya know."

"I appreciate that," Lorenzo said with the inbred politeness that royalty always seemed to possess when it came to dealing with the public, "but I have some other leads to run down at the moment. If those don't pan out, I'll get back with you. Do you normally work the morning shift?"

With that simple enquiry, he dazzled her right out of her shoes. "Every morning," she said, beaming. "Oh, wow! Wait'll I tell Fred! He's going to drop his teeth!"

"I'm sure he will," Lorenzo said dryly. "Now...if we could have a table? We're really in a hurry."

"Oh, my gosh, what an idiot I am! I'm so sorry, Your Highness. Right this way."

Grabbing a couple of menus, she rushed them over to a booth next to the window, apologizing all the while and promising Lorenzo that he was going to have the best breakfast he'd ever eaten. "Your waitress will be right with you. Just ask for the special, and I promise you won't regret it."

Gracious, Lorenzo thanked her, his smile never wavering, but Eliza was starting to recognize that particular look on his face. He already had regrets, and she didn't doubt that if he had it all to do over again, he would have gone through a McDonald's drive-thru. As it was, just about everyone in the place was shooting him covert glances and whispering among themselves, and it was obvious that they, too, had seen the morning paper.

Coming to the same conclusion, Lorenzo swore softly, his expression grim. "I was afraid of this. It's that damn picture! How the hell am I going to conduct a search when the whole world is watching and offering their opinion?"

He didn't, thankfully, blame her, but Eliza wouldn't have blamed him if he had. If it hadn't been for her and her overzealous boss, he could have been well into the search and might have even found the prince before anyone knew what he was about.

"I'm sorry," she said quietly as soon as they'd given their order to the blushing young woman who rushed forward to wait on them and deliver two steaming cups of coffee to their table. "The damage is done. It won't do any good to retract the story—people have already seen your picture. They're going to recognize you unless you grow a beard or something. Of course, that takes time. It won't do you any good now.''

In the process of stirring cream into his coffee, he glanced up sharply. ''What did you say?''

Surprised, she blinked. ''About what? The beard? It's not going to do you any good today.''

''No,'' he said thoughtfully, ''but a disguise isn't a bad idea. I'll change my clothes, put on some sunglasses, even wear a hat. How do you think I'd look with a cowboy hat? I could get some jeans and boots and pass myself off as a cowboy.''

If he hadn't been so serious, Eliza would have laughed at the very suggestion that Duke Lorenzo Sebastiani pass himself off as a cowboy. He looked and dressed like he'd just stepped out of the pages of *GQ*. She didn't care what he wore, it wasn't going to change the sophistication that was as much a part of him as the green of his eyes.

''I don't know,'' she said doubtfully. ''Cowboys are a pretty rugged lot. It's more than just the clothes.''

''Are you saying I'm not rugged?''

Put on the spot, she said, ''No!'' But then she immediately changed her mind. ''Yes, that's exactly what I'm saying. You're a duke, for heaven's sake! Dukes and cowboys are as different as day and night.''

Lorenzo appreciated her honesty, but his title had been granted to him by the king in appreciation of his military service for Montebello. Just because he'd been raised by Marcus and Gwendolyn after his parents died and the palace had become his home didn't mean he was some kind of pampered royal who was afraid to get his hands dirty. He hadn't received any special treatment when he was in the military; he'd carried his own weight.

''We'll see,'' he said as the waitress arrived with a breakfast fit for a king. ''You just might be surprised.''

She had her doubts and she didn't make any effort to hide them, but Lorenzo wasn't worried. Digging into the ham and eggs and hashbrowns he'd ordered, he could already see himself dressed as a cowboy. A slow grin tugged at the corner of his mouth. His mission was a serious one, but he had to admit, this was going to be fun.

"The mall is the other direction," Eliza told him thirty minutes later when he pulled out of the diner parking lot and turned left. "I thought you wanted to get some western clothes."

"I do," he said. But instead of turning around, he drove slowly down the street, reading the signs of every business they passed. "Here we go," he said suddenly, grinning as he turned into the parking lot of a used-clothing store.

Eliza took one look at it and said, "You can't be serious."

"Oh, ye of little faith," he teased, and got out to open her car door for her.

The shop was everything he'd hoped it would be. Crowded and musty, it was packed full of everything from used Levi's jeans to old prom dresses from the fifties. And somewhere in all those old castoffs was his disguise.

"I can't believe you're doing this," Eliza said when he moved to a rack of used jeans and started going through them. "I thought you'd buy something new."

"And look like a drugstore cowboy? I don't think so. I want to look like the average John Wayne on the street, and I can't do that in new clothes." Glancing up from the jeans he was checking out, he arched a brow when he saw her smile. "What's so funny?"

"There was nothing average about John Wayne. That's why he was John Wayne."

He couldn't disagree with that. "Okay, poor choice.

Let's try for a hired hand who doesn't have two nickels to rub together. That means I need worn jeans and faded shirts that are frayed at the cuffs.''

"And something to drive around in besides a brand-new Tahoe SUV," she pointed out dryly. "It doesn't fit the image."

"Good point," he replied. "We'll take care of that later. Right now, let's work on the clothes."

With her help, it didn't take long to find exactly what he was looking for. The shop even had an old, scuffed pair of cowboy boots that were just his size. When Eliza looked aghast at the idea of him wearing someone else's used boots, he laughed. "Don't worry. I'm not going to ruin my feet. I just want to see how they look."

He disappeared into the small dressing area, only to emerge a few minutes later in his disguise. Settling the used and abused black Stetson hat he'd picked out on his head, he opened the dressing room door to find Eliza waiting for him outside. "Well?" he asked, spreading his arms wide. "What do you think?"

Stunned, she blinked, wide-eyed. "I don't believe it."

She'd always heard that the clothes made the man, but she'd never quite understood what the phrase meant until now. She'd covered the Sebastianis for years in her column, and during that time, she must have seen dozens of photos of Lorenzo in his military uniform tuxedos, and suits that came right out of Saville Row. And in each of those pictures, he'd always looked every inch the duke.

There was no sign of that man now. She didn't know how he'd done it, but even his posture had changed. With the scarred cowboy hat set low on his head, concealing his sandy-brown hair, the pointed old boots on his feet and the faded clothes molding his lean body, he looked like he'd just walked in off the range.

"Incredible," she said, amazed. "I never would have believed it if I hadn't seen it with my own two eyes."

Pleased, he grinned and tipped his hat back slightly, and just that easily, he changed the image again. He still looked like a hardworking cowboy, but now he had the look of a rogue, a flirt. With nothing more than a crooked grin, he set Eliza's heart pounding.

Shocked, she pressed a hand to her heart before she realized it, drawing a curious look from Lorenzo. "Are you all right?" he asked with a sudden frown. "What's wrong?"

"Nothing," she said quickly, and blushed to the roots of her hair. "You just surprised me. I never thought you'd be able to pull it off."

"I told you I could," he said with another grin that made her heart trip. "Now, what about you?"

She blinked. "I beg your pardon?"

"You can't dress like that when I look like I just walked off a roundup," he explained. "You're too citified. We don't look like we belong together."

Eliza wouldn't have described her black wool slacks and black and white sweater as *citified,* but she had to admit, he had a point. "I've got jeans in my suitcase. I'll change."

"You need a flannel shirt," he insisted, grabbing one off the rack. "And a sheepskin coat. It's cold out."

Eliza had never had a sheepskin coat in her life—the western style had never suited her. But even as she started to tell him no, she made the mistake of touching the one he held out to her. "Oh! It's so soft!"

"C'mon," he urged, grinning. "Try it."

Her eyes met his, and she couldn't resist the sparkle of fun she saw there. This was a side of him she hadn't even known existed. "Oh, all right. But I probably won't buy it.

After we find the prince, I'll have nowhere else to wear it.''

"So wear it to the grocery store," he said with a grin as he held it open for her to slip her arms in. "It's a used coat, Eliza. Have fun with it."

"Easy for you to say," she retorted sassily. "You look like the Marlboro man. I look like..." She glanced in the mirror and groaned "...a redheaded Olive Oyle being hugged by a sheep."

Any other man would have laughed, but Lorenzo was truly amazed that she thought she looked anything like Popeye's girlfriend. Did she truly not see how pretty she was?

"Why do you do that?" he asked in puzzlement, stopping her when she would have turned away and shrugged out of the coat. "Look at yourself." And not giving her time to object, he turned her back to the mirror, then stepped behind her, holding her in front of him with his hands on her shoulders.

"Look at you," he said again, this time huskily. "You're not skinny like Olive Oyle. You have the slenderness and grace of a young Katharine Hepburn. Can't you see it? Can't you see the passion and fire in your eyes? Look at your bone structure, the line of your throat. You're beautiful and you don't even know it. Look."

In the mirror, she watched as he pulled her fiery curls up off her neck, then cradled her face between his hands. His eyes met hers, and with nothing more than a look and the touch of his hands, he made her feel beautiful for the first time in her life.

And it shook her to the core.

Who was this man? she wondered wildly. How could he make her feel pretty when no one else ever had? For as long as she could remember, she'd been in that gangly stage where she was all arms and legs, angles and planes. Most girls outgrew that by the time they were sixteen. At twenty-seven, she never had.

He was a magician, she thought, dazed. A sorcerer with supernatural powers who painted images with words. Nothing had changed—she was the same person she'd always been—but when she saw herself through his eyes, images of the old Eliza Windmere fell away. And just that easily, she was pretty.

She wanted to laugh and cry and turn and throw herself into his arms. But she couldn't do any of those things. She didn't dare. Her heart was already pounding, her senses in a whirl, and it was all because of him. If she made the mistake of touching him now, she would be in serious trouble.

And that was the last thing she needed right now, she reminded herself. She wasn't looking for a man, especially one like Lorenzo. Not when her breakup with Robert was still an open wound. He'd been jealous of her job and the time she gave to it, and that had destroyed their relationship. And now, here she was, attracted to another man who didn't approve of what she did for a living. She wasn't going there again. She couldn't.

"I don't know that I'd go so far as to use the word beautiful," she said with a forced laugh as she took a step away from him, freeing herself from his touch. "But thanks for the compliment. Maybe I'll buy the coat, after all. It's really warm."

The magic mood shattered between them, she hurried to the checkout counter and could feel his eyes on her every step of the way. He let the moment pass, however, and she told herself she was relieved. Unfortunately, she'd never been very good at lying to herself.

True to his word, Lorenzo was nothing if not thorough. From the used-clothing store, they went straight to a used-car dealership and bought a ten-year-old pickup truck that looked like it had seen better days. It had a good motor, though, so they turned in the rented Tahoe without fear that they were going to break down in the middle of nowhere, then headed up into the mountains where Willy lived. Anyone seeing them in their new old clothes and the battered pickup would have never guessed that Lorenzo was a duke or she was a city girl who interviewed kings and queens and wrote for the *Sentinel*.

Smiling at the thought, she was just about to tell him how much she was enjoying going undercover with him when he ruined everything by saying, "When we reach Willy's, I want to do the questioning. I know you're friends and he trusts you, but he may know more than he realizes he does. He's going to have to talk to me."

Everything he said made perfect sense—to Eliza. It wouldn't mean a hill of beans to Willy. "If we were talking about an average man on the street, I'd agree with you. But as I've told you before, Your Grace, Willy dances to the beat of a different drummer. He doesn't have to do anything, and he knows it. He won't talk to you."

"Of course he will," he said stubbornly. "You said yourself how upset he was at the thought of the king naming another heir when his son was still alive. He obviously wants to help find Lucas. To do that, he's going to have to talk to me."

Eliza could have told him that Willy wouldn't even talk to her if she didn't call him ahead of time and make arrangements to meet him, but what was the point? His mind was made up, and Eliza only had to look at the stubborn set of his jaw to know that nothing she could say was going to make a difference. He was determined to do things his way. He'd find out for himself that wasn't going to work.

"Turn left at the next four-way stop," she told him. "Then just keep going straight for ten miles until we reach a dirt road. After that, it gets a little tricky."

Tricky was, in fact, an understatement. When they reached the dirt road that led to the box canyon where Willy lived, Eliza knew from experience just how easy it was to lose your way. Off-road drivers had carved out dozens of tracks that intersected the main road and it was very confusing.

Frowning, she leaned forward to study the terrain and said suddenly, "Turn left here...I think."

A quarter of a mile later, the road turned as rough as a washboard, just as it should have, and Eliza breathed a sigh of relief. "This is it. Watch the odometer. His house is exactly two miles from the cattle guard we're coming up on."

Because of the roughness of the drive, they were forced to go slowly, and it was another ten minutes before they actually reached the trees that surrounded Willy's house on all sides, completely concealing it from the untrained eye. When Eliza told him to pull over and park, Lorenzo looked around in confusion. "Here? I thought we were going to his house."

"We are," she said, nodding toward the trees. "It's back there."

When he lifted a brow in surprise, Eliza had to smile. Willy's cabin was only a hundred yards from the road, but from where they were parked, it looked like there wasn't another living soul for a hundred miles. "I told you he likes his privacy. C'mon."

Leading the way, she picked her way through the trees to a small log cabin that had to have been built by one of the original settlers in the area. Not quite plumb, it leaned to the left and had a front porch that appeared to be on the verge of collapsing. There were only two windows, which were dark and locked tight, and a formidable wooden door. Dark and dusty and less than welcoming, the place didn't encourage visitors any more than Willy did.

Knowing that, Eliza felt she had to try to talk some sense into Lorenzo one more time. "This isn't going to work, Your Grace. If you'd just listen to me…"

For an answer, he stepped forward and knocked loudly on the door. Not surprisingly, no one answered.

"Obviously, he's not home," he said, scowling.

"Oh, he's here," she said, and nodded to a metal loop on the door where it could be padlocked from the outside. "When he's not here, he padlocks the door."

"But there's no vehicle."

"Not that you can see," she replied. "He drives an old army jeep that he hides in the woods."

She didn't say another word, but she didn't have to. She'd made her point. Willy was home, and she knew him better than Lorenzo did. If he wasn't answering his door, it was because he was feeling threatened.

Glaring at the closed door, Lorenzo swore softly and shot Eliza a hard look. "I screwed up, didn't I? Don't answer that," he said quickly. "I know you told me he didn't trust outsiders. I just thought I could get him to talk to me."

"Why? Because royal blood flows through your veins? Trust me, Willy couldn't care less about that. In his eyes, you're a stranger. You could be the president of the United States, and he still wouldn't open his door to you."

"But he will for you."

She shrugged. "If conditions are right and he wants to."

Frustrated, Lorenzo knew he had no one but himself to blame for this little setback—she'd warned him that he needed her if he expected Willy to cooperate, but he hadn't believed her. As head of Royal Intelligence, he didn't have to go through someone else to get the information he needed. And he didn't like it, dammit, but what choice did he have?

His pride stung, he said stiffly, "Would you call him, then, and see what you can arrange? We can't even hope to find the prince without knowing where Willy found the scarf."

For an answer, Eliza pulled out her cell phone and punched in Willy's number. When she got a scratchy answering machine, she wasn't surprised. Willy always retreated when he was upset. Hopefully, he'd surface soon.

"Willy, this is Eliza," she said quietly when the machine began to record. "I apologize for intruding. Duke Lorenzo and I are leaving now, but it's very important that I speak to you. Please meet me tomorrow morning at nine at the waterfall. The duke will be with me, but I'm the only one you have to speak to, okay? Please don't let me down, Willy. We need your help."

She hung up and found herself face-to-face with a very irritated duke. "What the hell did you do that for?" he demanded. "I don't want to meet him tomorrow. What's wrong with today? It's not even eleven-thirty in the morning. We've got the whole damn day ahead of us."

"Willy needs time."

"We don't have time! Don't you get it? Thanks to your boss, the word is out that the prince is alive. And that means he's in danger. Do you know how many con artists, opportunists and outright thugs read the headlines this morning and saw this as their lucky day? They figured out—like we did—that the prince had to be in some kind of distress or he would have contacted his family by now. And they're going to go after him."

The thought sickened Eliza, but there was nothing she could do about it. "I'm doing the best I can, Your Grace," she replied. "If I could hold Willy's feet to the fire and make him talk, I would. But all we can do now is wait. Trust me. He won't talk until tomorrow."

If they were lucky. She didn't say the words, but she knew he heard them, nonetheless. His green eyes dark with fury, he struggled with his own impatience, and she knew exactly how he felt. She hated Willy's phobias, hated the way he called her with a press-stopping story he'd somehow stumbled across, only to retreat like a scared turtle when she needed more information. Sometimes, his tips paid off. Many times they didn't. She could handle that because she knew whenever she followed up a tip from anyone, there was always a chance it would fizzle into nothing. What drove her crazy, though, was the number of times Willy had left her cooling her heels. Patience wasn't her strong suit, and she could well understand Lorenzo's frustration.

To his credit, though, he knew when he was beat. Sighing in disgust, he said, "All right. It looks like we're going to play this Willy's way. We might as well go back to the hotel."

Chapter 5

They stayed at the same hotel they had before, this time in a suite with two connecting bedrooms, and Eliza spent the day working on the opening of her feature. It should have been easy, but she felt as if her entire career was on the line, and with good cause. Not only was Deborah waiting in the wings to take over her column, but no one else in the world had this story. She had to do it right. So she struggled with words and couldn't seem to find a place to start the story…until she shifted her focus to her meeting with the king and queen of Montebello. As she described the palace and the reaction of the prince's parents to the news that there was a good chance their son was still alive, she knew her readers would be more than satisfied with the story.

"I want to read that."

Lost in the quiet world she always retreated to in order to write, it was several long minutes before Lorenzo's words registered. When they did, she glanced up, startled, to find him scowling at her from the overstuffed chair from which he'd apparently been watching her for some time. Looking over the top of her glasses, she said, "I beg your pardon?"

"You heard me," he said flatly. "I want to read that. If there's anything that might be harmful to the prince, you'll have to take it out."

Her eyes narrowed fractionally. "Really? I don't remember anything in my agreement with King Marcus that gives you the right to censorship."

"That's because there isn't one."

"You're damn straight, there isn't one! I never would have agreed to it if there had been. This is the United States, Your Grace. We're real big on freedom of speech, not to mention freedom of the press, around here."

The citizens of Montebello were, too, but he only said, "It's my duty to protect the prince. If I say there's something in your writing that could be harmful to him, it's coming out. End of discussion."

She would have never deliberately placed anyone in danger with her writing, but what went into her column was for her and Simon to decide, not a fairy-tale duke who would be king. And it was high time he realized that.

"You think so, do you?" she taunted, arching a brow. "Well, take that!" And with a single key stroke, she sent the beginning of the feature in an e-mail to Simon.

Later, she realized it was her red hair that got her into trouble. The spark of temper that went along with that hair had been her cross to bear all her life. It had just flared like a match. She knew they were both under a great deal of strain, knowing the prince was out there somewhere, in possible danger, and they couldn't discover where because her informant wasn't in the mood to cooperate yet. She felt guilty and frustrated…and resentful that Lorenzo thought so little of her just because she was a reporter.

Stunned, Lorenzo couldn't believe her defiance. No one had ever challenged him so openly before! Outraged, he stormed over to her, so frustrated that he stupidly thought there had to be a way he could retrieve the e-mail. "Give me that!"

"No! What are you doing? Let go!"

Jumping to her feet, she grabbed her computer and clutched it to her chest even as he reached for it, and for a second, they acted like two children fighting over a favorite toy. Then his fingers accidentally brushed against her breast and everything changed. In a heartbeat, awareness flashed between them like heat lightning.

Drawing in a sharp breath, Lorenzo froze. He was, he liked to think, a man who knew women. But in that instant, he felt like a sixteen-year-old who'd experienced the kick of sexual attraction for the first time in his life and didn't have a clue what to do about it. With a will of their own, his eyes dropped to her lips, which had parted in a soft gasp, and his mind blurred. All he could think about was kissing her.

And it was all her fault. That soft, fresh scent of hers was driving him crazy. He'd dreamed of her last night, replayed in his sleep that moment in the used-clothing store when he'd helped her into the sheepskin coat and turned her in front of the mirror so she could see how pretty she was. He should have kissed her then. He'd wanted to, but the store clerk had watched them with an eagle eye, and the time hadn't been appropriate.

But now they were alone and he could already taste her….

Need clawing at him, he reached for her…and saw his own need reflected in her eyes. And just that quickly, the fog of desire misting his brain cleared. What was he doing? he wondered wildly, stiffening. They didn't even like each other! The only reason they were working together was because they were being forced to. And she was a reporter, for heaven's sake! How had he allowed himself to forget that? God only knew what would end up in her column if he was stupid enough to drop his guard with her.

That brought him back to his senses as nothing else could, and with a softly muttered curse, he abruptly stepped back. "I'm sorry. I don't know what I was thinking of rushing you like that. I'm just going crazy sitting around here twiddling my thumbs, and then when you sent that e-mail, all I could think of was getting it back. If anything happened to the prince because of something you wrote—"

"It won't," she said hoarsely, her heart pounding crazily. He'd almost kissed her, she thought, dazed, then told herself she had to be mistaken. She had a real talent for pushing his buttons. He was furious with her—why would he want to kiss her? Her imagination was just playing with her mind and her lonely heart, and if she wasn't careful, she was going to make a complete fool of herself.

Focus on what's important here, a voice in her head said sternly. *If you want hearts and flowers, pick up a romance novel!*

The story, she reminded herself, drawing in a calming breath. This was the biggest story of her life. Nothing else mattered but that. If the nights were long and she ached to feel a man's arms around her again, holding her close, that was something she would just have to deal with.

"It was just the opening of the feature on the prince," she said stiffly. "It was harmless."

"Then why didn't you let me read it?"

"Because I don't have to." It was as simple as that. "If we're going to work together with any degree of success, you're going to have to trust me. I know you don't like reporters, and we both know how badly I want this story, but not at the expense of anyone's life, especially the prince's. That's not who I am, Your Grace. If something happens to him before you find him, it won't be because of me.''

For a long moment, he just stared at her with those probing, all-seeing eyes of his, and she was afraid that he would somehow see how much she regretted that he hadn't kissed her. But she didn't flinch, and something he saw in her steady gaze must have finally gotten through to him. The stiff set of his shoulders relaxed, and in his sigh, she finally heard acceptance.

"You're right," he said gruffly. "I've been acting paranoid just because you're a reporter and that's not fair to you. You've done nothing but be upfront and honest, and I owe you an apology." Holding out his hand, he said, "I'd like to start over, this time as partners instead of adversaries. What do you say? Do we have a deal?"

She'd never been one to hold a grudge, especially when an apology was so sincerely delivered. Relieved, she smiled and shook his hand and tried not to notice how nice his fingers felt when they closed around hers. "Deal."

The next morning when they left to meet with Willy, there was no question that Eliza would do the talking. Lorenzo no longer had a problem with that. He'd set his ego aside and made peace, and as he drove over the rough terrain to their meeting place, he thanked God that he had Eliza along. They'd taken so many turns and twists on dirt roads that were little more than faint deer paths that he was completely turned around. That wasn't to say he couldn't find his way back to town if he had to—he had a compass and a damn good memory. But it would take him a while.

"This is it," Eliza said when the terrain turned to almost pure rock. "We stop here and walk the rest of the way."

Glancing around, Lorenzo frowned. There was no sign of another vehicle. "We're early. Willy doesn't appear to be here yet. Do you think he's coming?"

"If he is, he's here already. He would never take a chance of walking into something he's not sure of. If he decided to meet with us, he got here hours ago so he could check the place out. C'mon, I've got something special to show you."

Puzzled, Lorenzo stepped out of the truck, only to glance around in surprise as she joined him. "What's that noise?"

"The waterfall," she said with a grin. "Willy likes to meet here so he doesn't have to worry about anyone over-hearing us."

In his travels, Lorenzo had seen everything from Niagara to Angel Falls in Venezuela, but when he followed Eliza through the trees to the foot of a waterfall that appeared out of nowhere, nothing had ever touched him quite like the falls that cascaded over the canyon wall six hundred feet above them. He didn't even know the name of the river that crashed to the rocks below to kick up a haze of icy mist, but it had a rugged, untouched beauty that left him awestruck. They were miles from anywhere, in the middle of a mountain wilderness that appeared untouched by man. Who else had seen this besides himself, God, Willy and Eliza?

"Like it?" Eliza asked, grinning.

"It's magnificent." And just the place for a meeting, he realized. The roar of the falls did, indeed, drown out all sound that was more than a foot or two away. No wonder Willy insisted on telling Eliza his secrets there. It was as safe as a soundproof room.

The thought had hardly registered when he glanced past

Eliza and saw a middle-aged man of medium height cautiously approaching them. Stoop-shouldered and scruffy, his beard, mustache and shoulder-length hair gray with age, he looked right past Lorenzo and focused on Eliza. This was, Lorenzo knew without a doubt, the infamous Willy Cranshaw. Dressed in camouflage, from his boots to his waterproof jacket and skull cap, he would have blended into the terrain if Lorenzo hadn't been watching for him.

Eliza turned then and spied him, too, and grinned. With nothing more than that, Willy's entire demeanor changed. He grinned back at her, and for a short while, at least, his blue eyes were free of suspicion and he seemed happy to see her. Then his gaze once again shifted to Lorenzo, and the wariness was back, transforming his entire body. There wasn't the slightest doubt in Lorenzo's mind that the older man would have scurried off into the woods like a scared rabbit if he'd so much as looked at him wrong.

"Hey, Willy," Eliza said, drawing his attention back to her. "I'm glad you could make it."

"I like your new clothes," he said shyly. "They look good on you. Are you going to buy a ranch?"

"Not unless I win a million bucks in the Publisher's Clearinghouse sweepstakes," she retorted with a chuckle. "But, thanks. I like them, too. Duke Lorenzo helped me pick them out. He thought it might be safer for the prince if we disguised ourselves a little."

"So you're undercover? Like the CIA?"

"Not quite," she replied, smiling, "but close enough. The duke doesn't want anyone else to find the prince before he does and possibly hurt him. That's why I need to ask you a few questions for him, if that's all right."

"I dunno," he mumbled, ignoring Lorenzo completely. "Depends on what you want to talk about. You don't think I hurt the prince, do you?"

"Oh, no!" she assured him. "Thanks to you, his family knows he's alive. No one is blaming you for anything. But we do need to know exactly where you found the scarf. There may be other clues at the campsite that tell us more about the prince and where he may have gone when he left there."

Hesitating, Willy cocked his head at her. "You're going to put this in your story, aren't you? All about your search for the prince? Are you going to mention me? Will my name be in the paper?"

Expecting the question—he asked her the same thing every time he gave her a tip—she shrugged. "That depends on you. I know how you value your privacy, and I wouldn't want to do anything to destroy that. I can either mention your name or just refer to you as an unnamed source. The choice is yours."

When he considered his options, Eliza couldn't help but feel sorry for him. There was a part of him that longed for fame and fortune, but the war in Vietnam had scarred him, and as much as he yearned for publicity, his fear of people—and the government, in particular—sadly ruled his life. Not surprisingly, he said, "I think I like the sound of an unnamed source."

"That's fine," she replied easily. "But in the meantime, where did you find the scarf, Willy? We can't do anything until we know that."

"I just want to make sure I'm not going to get in trouble," he hedged, shooting Lorenzo another wary look. "I don't like the law, and if they find out I was hunting without a license up on Walnut Ridge, they're going to send someone after me."

"No one will know except you and me and the duke," she promised. "And we're not telling anyone. You know you can trust me, Willy. And the duke has no reason to wish you harm. He's very appreciative of your help. Because of you, the king and queen now know there's a good possibility that their son is alive. You gave them hope. Now help us find the prince. Where's the campsite? Up on Walnut Ridge?''

Nodding, he said, ''It's on the backside of the ridge, about a mile straight north from where the forest service road forks. You can't miss it. It's back in a stand of aspen not too far from Elk Creek.''

''And where did you find the scarf at the campsite? Was it just laying on the ground by the deserted campfire or what?''

He shook his head. ''It was hanging on a dead tree branch a few feet away from the campsite. I think it got caught there when the prince got scared for some reason and ran away.''

Out of the corner of her eye, Eliza saw Lorenzo roll his eyes, but he thankfully didn't say anything. If he had, Willy would have shut up like a clam and scurried back into the woods. ''Why do you think he was scared, Willy? Was there some sign that he might have been in some kind of distress when he abandoned the campsite?''

''Not that I could tell,'' he replied honestly. ''But the creek's not that far from the campsite…or where the prince's plane went down. I figure he wandered alongside the creek after he crashed and eventually built himself a campsite on the ridge. Some of the people looking for him had to figure the same thing.''

It made sense. After the prince's plane had finally been found, the FBI and local police had scoured the woods for several miles in every direction of the vicinity of the crash, searching for Lucas. It was the others, however, the fortune hunters and nutcases who had been lured to the crash site by the false rumor of a reward offered by a Hollywood gossip magazine, that worried Eliza the most. If any of them had decided to follow the creek in search of him, they might have surprised him into running. The question was, where would he have gone from there?

Glancing over at Lorenzo, she expected him to be at least somewhat impressed with Willy's theory, but judging from his set expression, he was reserving judgment. Disappointed, she told Willy, "You might be right, but we won't know until we see the campsite. Tell me more about the scarf and the log it was caught on. Where was it in relation to the campfire?"

"On the north side," he said promptly. "Maybe about ten yards away. If he was trying to get away from someone, that was the easiest way to go. It's rough country up there. There are cliffs on either side, and the creek's impossible to cross."

"So you think he went north?"

He shrugged. "He didn't have much choice if someone was trailing him from the south. It's the only way out."

As far as theories went, it was as good as any other, and only time would tell if he was right. Sensing Lorenzo's impatience to get on with the search, Eliza said, "Well, I guess we'll find out, won't we? Thanks for your help, Willy. We couldn't have gotten this far without you."

"I know what it's like to be missing," he said simply. "It's the loneliest, scariest feeling in the world."

There'd been a time in Vietnam when he'd been missing in action and on his own in the jungle, and the shadows of that still lingered in his eyes, decades later. For a long second, he just stood there, reflecting. Then he quietly turned and disappeared into the trees.

Staring after him, Eliza couldn't help but feel sorry for him, but there was nothing she could do for him, nothing he would *let* her do for him...except give him the space he needed. So she didn't call him back, but turned to Lorenzo instead. "Well, what do you think? Could the prince have headed north?"

"Maybe," he said with a shrug. "Maybe not. It's too soon to tell. I prefer to make my own conclusions once I've investigated the campsite."

Personally, Lorenzo didn't put much stock in anything Willy said. The man obviously had problems. He didn't seem quite in touch with reality, and if Lorenzo hadn't seen Lucas's scarf with his own two eyes, he never would have believed it was found by the old man. Did the abandoned campsite even exist? He hoped so. They'd find out soon enough.

They started the search at the spot where Lucas crashed his plane into the side of the mountain. The last time Lorenzo had been there, it had looked much different. The crash had only happened days before, and the shock had still been fresh. When Lorenzo had seen the wreckage for the first time, he'd sworn he could smell the prince's pain and horror as he'd realized he was going down. In spite of the fact that Lucas's body hadn't been discovered in the wreckage, Lorenzo had felt little hope that he would be found alive.

Time, however, had a way of healing all wounds. The fuselage and debris that were all that was left of the small plane had blended into the mountainside, and the snow nearly covered that. Anyone seeing the site for the first time would have thought the crash happened decades ago instead of just last year.

And this time, Lorenzo really believed Lucas had somehow managed to survive the crash. Oh, he hadn't changed his opinion about Willy, but he knew his cousin. He loved life and wouldn't have let go of it easily. If anyone could survive not only a plane crash, but the wildness of the Rocky Mountains in the dead of winter, it was Lucas.

"Where is the forest service road Willy mentioned?" he asked Eliza as she stood solemnly beside him, surveying the scene. "How would you get there from here on foot?"

Considering a moment, she frowned. "I'd head northeast as long as I could, then cross the creek and head north. I don't think the prince could have made it any other way if he was hurt. It's too rugged."

"Then let's try that," he said.

Surprised, she said, "You don't want to drive from here to the forest service road and start the search there? That's closer to where the scarf was found."

"But we aren't positive that the prince is the one who actually dropped the scarf at the campsite where it was found," he pointed out. "It could have been anyone— which is why I need to see if it would be possible for a man who walked away from a plane crash to make it from here to there on foot."

She hadn't thought of that. "Then I guess we'll leave the truck here and come back for it."

They started off through the woods, heading northeast, as she had suggested. Within minutes, they'd left the crash site behind and were completely surrounded by the forest. Following Lorenzo as he took the lead, Eliza tried to imagine what it must have been like for the prince after the crash. He had to have been dazed, probably hurt, and in all likelihood, he hadn't had a clue where he was or how far he was from civilization.

It must have been quite frightening, she thought with a shiver, especially when nightfall had approached. Darkness came early in the winter in the mountains, and he'd been all alone. Eliza liked to think she was pretty gutsy, but just thinking about that gave her the willies. There were wolves in the mountains. And bears…

Sure she felt the touch of eyes on her, she glanced over her shoulder, but there was nothing there. Nothing but trees. Goosebumps racing up her arms under the soft sheepskin of her coat, she moved closer to Lorenzo.

She hadn't thought he noticed, but suddenly, he, too, was examining the trees around them, his narrowed eyes missing little as he studied their surroundings. "Is something wrong?" he asked quietly.

Caught letting her imagination run away with her, she felt a blush sting her cheek. "I was imagining what it must have been like for the prince to find himself all alone up here," she admitted with a grin. "Then I got to thinking about wolves and bears…"

"And suddenly you could hear one sneaking up behind you," he guessed with a chuckle. "Don't worry, we're not going to be anyone's dinner. Whatever bears are in the region are hibernating, and the wolves are probably just as scared of you as you are of them. They won't bother you."

Logically, she knew that. But when they started through the trees again, she made sure she was just a few steps behind Lorenzo.

They crossed the creek at its narrowest point, then began the slow climb up to Walnut Ridge. It was a fairly steep hike, but not as difficult as it would have been if they'd taken a path to either the east or west. And even though the prince had probably been hurt after the crash, there was no question that he could have made the climb if his injuries weren't too severe.

"I don't know how the hell he walked away from that crash," Lorenzo said with a frown as they broke through the trees and reached the forest service road, "but he always was a lucky devil. I think he could have easily made it this far. But why didn't he call home, dammit? Or at least call for help? He had his cell phone with him."

"He must have been confused," Eliza said, "and who can blame him? You saw what the crash did to his plane. He couldn't have been thinking clearly."

Lorenzo agreed. He could well understand Lucas's muddled thinking after he'd plowed into the side of a mountain. But that didn't explain his continued silence. It had been a year since the crash, dammit! Where was he? Was he still walking around in a daze or had he somehow fallen into the hands of someone who meant him harm and wouldn't let him call his family?

Frustrated, the questions he had far outnumbering the few speculative answers he had, he said, "The answer has got to be here somewhere. C'mon. Let's find the campsite."

Given Willy's oddities, Lorenzo hadn't put much stock in the directions he'd given them, and with good reason. The man had refused to even look him in the eye! But when they headed due north, just as the old hermit had instructed, it wasn't any time before they came to the stand of aspen he'd told them about. And there in the middle of the trees was a small circle of stones that could only be the remains of a campfire.

"This must be it!" Eliza said excitedly. "Listen! You can hear the creek."

Cocking his head, Lorenzo caught the gurgle of a small creek in the distance. Eliza was right. This had to be the place where Willy had found the scarf. "I'll be damned," he said softly, impressed. "I didn't think the old geezer had it in him."

"I knew he wasn't lying," she replied, then sighed in relief. Suddenly realizing that she'd given herself away, she grinned ruefully. "Okay, so maybe I had a few doubts. Sometimes it's hard to know with Willy."

Having now met the old man, Lorenzo could well understand that, but at least he appeared to have told the truth this time. And if they were lucky, there would be a clue somewhere in the vicinity that would tell them why Lucas had left and where he might have gone.

Surveying the area, however, he didn't see signs of much life. It was a stark place for Lucas to take refuge. The aspen, naked of their leaves in the dead of winter, offered little protection from the weather, and the snow seemed to collect in unusually high drifts on the east side of trees. When the north wind blew, it was colder than hell.

"What was he doing here?" he murmured to himself as he began to inspect the campsite. "He apparently traveled five miles from where he crashed and stopped here long enough to at least make a firepit and start a fire. Why? Was he just too tired to go on or what?"

"Maybe it was getting dark and he didn't have any choice," Eliza suggested. "If he was going to survive the night, he had to have a fire."

"Or some other kind of shelter," he replied, his green eyes speculative as he slowly turned a full three hundred and sixty degrees and tried to imagine why Lucas had stopped here, of all places. Then his eyes landed on a dead tree that had fallen at an awkward angle at the base of a snow covered hill. Located just a matter of feet from the firepit, the tree should have lain flat at the base of the hill but it didn't. And it was that, Lorenzo decided, that bothered him. What was under that tree?

"What are you doing?" Eliza asked when he suddenly grabbed a stick off the ground and poked through the branches of the fallen tree. When he met no resistance, he started to smile. "What?" Eliza said in confusion. "What's so amusing?"

"The tree's covering the entrance to some kind of small cave," he told her, grinning, and proved it by pulling the decomposing tree away from where it lay. There, jutting out from the side of the hill, was a small rocky opening that appeared to be the entrance to a shallow cave.

"I knew it!" he said, pleased. "I bet the cave wasn't covered when he found it, so he dragged the tree over the opening to conceal it so he'd be safe."

Stepping closer, he knelt down at the opening and peered inside, only to feel his heart stop in midbeat when he saw the contents of the cave. There on the ground was a red thermal blanket that was identical to the ones carried on all of the king's aircraft. The queen had insisted that all blankets be red in case there was ever a crash—the blankets would be nearly as effective as a flare when they were spread out on the ground to flag down rescue planes.

"What is it?" Eliza asked quietly when he turned to stone. "Did you find something?"

"This," he said huskily, and pulled out the blanket. "It's from Lucas's plane. I'm sure of it."

Protected from the weather all these months, it was clean and dry and neatly folded, as if the prince had just left it. And that made little, if no, sense. Glancing around, Eliza scowled. Damn, she hated it when things weren't logical!

"It seems like he would have stayed here until help came for him," she told Lorenzo with a frown. "The man had a blanket and cave to keep him safe from the elements, a firepit and plenty of firewood to warm him, not to mention water from the creek to drink. It was the middle of winter, he couldn't have known where he was, but he still walked off and left the safest place he'd found. Why? What possessed him to do such a thing? The authorities had dogs and helicopters looking for him all over these mountains. You know he had to at least hear the helicopters. Why didn't he spread the blanket out in the clearing? Somebody would have found him.''

He shrugged, worry darkening his eyes as he looked around. ''I don't know. Maybe he was so shaken from the crash that he wasn't thinking clearly and didn't realize anyone was looking for him.''

''Or something spooked him,'' she said. ''Think about it. Why else would he have left the blanket? He thought to dig it out of the wreckage of the plane, but then he walked off without it when he left here. I can't think of any reason why he would do that unless he was scared and he left in a hurry.''

His brows knit in a frown, Lorenzo didn't like the sound of that, but he had to agree that there was little other reason for Lucas to abandon the cave. Unless, he was out in the surrounding woods, searching for food, and wasn't able to make it back to camp for some reason. He could have fallen and broken a leg or hit his head and knocked himself out. In the dead of winter, that would have been a costly mistake.

No! he told himself fiercely. Lucas wasn't dead! He couldn't be. Not when they were so close to finding him. There had to be another explanation.

''I want to look around,'' he told Eliza hoarsely. ''Just in case.''

He didn't say just in case of what, but he didn't have to. If he'd learned anything about Eliza over the past few days, it was that she wasn't a slow-witted woman. ''Let's spread out,'' she suggested. ''We can cover more territory. I'll meet you back here in a half hour.''

Moving to opposite sides of the campsite, they began the search with grim expressions. Later, Lorenzo couldn't have even said what he was looking for…except a body. Thankfully, they didn't find one. They didn't find anything, in fact, and Lorenzo had just about resigned himself to the fact that he might never know what had led Lucas to abandon the campsite when he inadvertently stumbled across a deer stand half-hidden in some trees about a quarter of a mile from the camp.

"It had to be hunters," he told Eliza when they met back at the campsite. "He heard the guns and must have thought someone was shooting at him."

"So he took off."

Lorenzo nodded grimly. "He wouldn't have gone south, that's where the hunters were."

"And the cliffs on either side of the creek made it impossible for him to go east or west. He had no choice but to go north."

"Just like Willy said," he retorted. "Crafty old goat. I bet he knew about that deer stand all along."

Eliza shrugged, a rueful smile curling the corners of her mouth. "I wouldn't put it past him. Willy doesn't always feel the need to share everything he knows."

"Now you tell me," Lorenzo retorted, but he couldn't complain. Willy had put them on the right path to finding the prince, and he owed him for that. There was no question that the king and queen would reward him for his help if he would let them, but for now, he couldn't worry about Willy. Half the day was gone, and he had a feeling they had a long way to go before they tracked down Lucas. By mutual agreement, they headed north.

For a while, they made good time. Hurrying to keep up with Lorenzo's long stride, Eliza didn't notice that the terrain had become progressively rougher until she unexpectedly stepped in a hole. Between one heartbeat and the next, she went down.

She didn't remember crying out, but suddenly, Lorenzo was there, his handsome face lined with worry. "Are you all right? What happened? Here, let me help you up."

"I stepped in a hole," she said, dazed. She struggled to her feet, only to wince, and in the next instant, he'd swept her up off her feet and set her head spinning. "Lorenzo! What are you doing?"

"Making sure you didn't break your ankle," he growled, and carried her over to a nearby log. Setting her down, he immediately dropped down to a knee in front of her and began gently tugging off her right boot and sock.

Eliza told herself there was nothing personal in his touch—he would have done the same for anyone. Then his hand closed around her bare ankle, and just that easily, he set every nerve ending in her body tingling. Startled, she gasped softly…and drew his eyes to her.

"Does that hurt?" he asked huskily.

He knew it didn't—she could see the awareness in his eyes, the same awareness that now had her heart thundering in her breast—but she only shook her head. "No," she choked. "It's just a little tender. I'm sure I'll be fine."

He frowned at that. "Maybe we should call off the search for the rest of the day."

"No! I appreciate the offer, but it's not necessary. Really," she insisted when he hesitated. "I'm fine. Look."

She wiggled her foot, testing her ankle. Under his hand, Lorenzo felt the delicacy of her bones, and in spite of himself, he was fascinated. Because she was such a tiger when it came to her job, he tended to forget just how delicate she was as a woman…until he touched her. Then he found himself wanting to run his hands over her. Just once, he told himself, he wanted to see how soft she was.

Don't even think about going there, a voice in his head

growled. *Not unless you want the story to end up on the front page.*

That brought him back to his senses as nothing else could, and with a hastily swallowed oath, he jerked his hand back and handed her her sock. "If you're sure. Tell me if it starts to hurt you."

Rising to his feet, he vowed he wasn't going to touch her again. But as soon as she'd pulled her sock and boot back on and they continued moving north, he couldn't stop himself from reaching out to help her whenever they reached a rough spot. And with every touch of their hands, he found it harder and harder to let her go.

When they finally reached the end of the narrow valley and stumbled onto a road, Lorenzo was torn between relief and frustration. He didn't have to touch her anymore, but they'd come to the end of the trail. Once Lucas reached the road, he could have gone anywhere.

Chapter 6

The town of Lightning, Colorado, might have only been fifty miles from Boulder, but it was as far from the city as Jupiter was from the sun. With a population of three hundred, there was no hotel, no sophisticated restaurants, nothing that would appeal to royalty. The local café wasn't open for dinner, but the bar next to the town's only motel was. Divided by the two lane highway that went right through the middle of the town, Lightning was little more than a wide spot in the road. It couldn't even claim a traffic light.

When Lorenzo pulled up in front of the motel, Eliza half expected him to suggest that they drive on to the next town before stopping for the night. The Lightning Bolt Motel was little more than an old-fashioned motor court that must have been there since the forties. A neon sign blinked in the office window, the parking lot was full of potholes and what little paint there was on the long, narrow ranch-style building was faded and chipped. To put it bluntly, the place looked like a dump.

But Lorenzo didn't even blink twice at the sight of the place. "I'll check in," he said as he cut the engine. "There's no use both of us going in. You can stay in the car and rest."

Exhausted, Eliza could have hugged him for that. After they'd lost the prince's trail when they'd come to the two-lane highway, they'd hiked back to the truck, retraced their route, then discreetly checked the towns up and down the highway in either direction, stopping at local restaurants, gas stations and hotels to see if anyone favoring a candid picture of Lucas had come through there during the past year. It was a tedious exercise in futility, and not surprisingly, no one had been able to help them.

Logically, they had both known finding the prince wasn't going to be easy, not after so much time had passed since the crash, but the enormity of what they were up against hadn't hit them until they kept running into one brick wall after another. The prince could be anywhere. For all they knew, he'd left the state of Colorado and could be sunning himself on the beaches of Florida…or Hawaii, for that matter. *If* he was even in the United States. At this point, there was no way to know.

They'd set themselves an impossible task—they were looking for a needle in a haystack—but Eliza knew Lorenzo was as dedicated as she to finding the prince. *That* wasn't the problem. It was the realization that they were going to have to spend a lot more time together than either of them had anticipated.

Hours after she'd nearly twisted her ankle, she could still feel the touch of his hand on her. And he'd touched her countless times since. Every time they came to a stump or the creek or rocky ground when they were hiking through the woods, he'd held out his hand to her, his eyes had met hers, and something had passed between them that still had the power to make her heart turn over in her breast.

"Stop thinking about it," she told herself sternly, but she couldn't. Her imagination was a blessing and a curse at one and the same time. With no effort whatsoever, she only had to close her eyes to feel his hand slide slowly up her calf to her knee, then her thigh—

The driver's door opened with no warning and Lorenzo slid behind the wheel. "Okay, we're all set," he began, only to stop when he noticed her face. "Are you okay? What's wrong?"

Mortified by her thoughts, she quickly glanced away, pretending to study the long line of empty rooms and the equally empty parking lot. "Nothing. I'm just tired. I guess you didn't have any problem getting two rooms."

"The clerk said we could take our pick," he replied, "so you're in three and I'm in nine. Unless you'd rather switch. They're the same."

"Three's fine," she replied as he pulled up before her room. "You don't have to get out. I can get my bag."

She might as well have saved her breath. He was out of the truck before she was and pulling her small suitcase from behind the seat, where they'd stored the luggage. "No problem," he assured her. "Here, let me get your door for you, too." And before she could stop him, he unlocked the door to her room for her and escorted her inside.

There was nothing redeeming about the room, other than the fact that it was clean, but Eliza hardly noticed. In the small room, which was barely bigger than the full bed and dresser it held, Lorenzo stood so close she could smell the woodsy scent clinging to his skin and clothes. Long after he left to go to his own room, she knew the scent of him would linger to tease her senses.

"It's not much to look at," he said, surveying the room,

"but the clerk assured me the beds are new and the linens are clean. If you're half as tired as I am, you'll sleep like the dead."

"I'm sure I'll be fine, thanks," she replied.

They agreed to meet at the truck at nine the following morning, and with a soft good-night, Lorenzo left to go to his own room. Watching the door shut quietly behind him, Eliza knew she was in trouble when she wanted to call him back. Suddenly lonely, she told herself they were spending too much time together. A break would do her good.

But even as she acknowledged that she needed some time to herself to get her head on straight, she knew she couldn't just sit in her room the rest of the evening and watch TV. She needed a distraction, something, anything, to get her mind off Lorenzo. Glancing out of the room's narrow window, she found herself studying the bar next door. The bright neon sign in the window advertised food and live music. She and Lorenzo had had an early dinner, but that had been nearly an hour ago, and she hadn't eaten much. Her stomach rumbled at the thought of some nachos, and she welcomed the distraction. Grabbing the key to her room, she shut the door behind her and headed for the bright lights across the parking lot.

It was Friday night, and Eliza wasn't surprised that the place was packed—nothing else in town was open. The parking lot was full of pickups, and inside, cowboys and their girls occupied every table. "It's a twenty-minute wait," the harried hostess told Eliza as a party of six walked in right behind her. "Sorry I can't promise you anything sooner, but we're shorthanded tonight, and it's Friday."

That was all she needed to say. "I know what you mean," Eliza told her with a smile. "I'll wait at the bar."

She'd wanted a distraction, and she'd gotten one. As she

took one of the few empty seats at the bar, she took in the sight and sound and smell of the place and its clientele for her story. She wanted to remember everything for her readers.

"White wine," she told the bartender when he was finally able to take her order.

"Put that on my tab," the cowboy sitting next to her said, shooting her a bold grin. "A lady shouldn't have to pay for her own drink."

She saw the leer in his eyes and swallowed a groan. This wasn't what she needed tonight. She was tired, she just wanted her wine and an order of nachos, and to be left alone. In the scheme of things, she didn't think that was too much to ask.

"Thanks," she said shortly, "but I can buy my own drink." Turning her attention back to the bartender, she lifted a brow at him. "How much do I owe you?"

If she hadn't been so tired, she would have noticed the cowboy was more than a little inebriated and, consequently, handled the situation differently. But she never saw the alcoholic glaze in his eyes—or the spark of anger that flared there at her words—until it was too late. The second the bartender took her money and walked away, her unwanted companion was leaning close and letting her have it with the sharp edge of his drunken tongue. "What's the matter, Red? My money not good enough for you? Is that what you're saying? 'Cause if it is, I don't like your attitude, little girl. You hear me?"

Oh, she heard him, all right. How could she not? He had her pinned in her seat, trapping her there, and suddenly, her heart was slamming against her ribs in fear. She might have been slender, but she'd never thought of herself as little—until she found herself being glowered at by six feet four inches of very angry cowboy.

They were surrounded by people, she told herself. Nothing was going to happen to her in a crowded bar. But everything about the cowboy was threatening, and no one so much as glanced her way. The bartender was occupied at the other end of the bar, and everyone else was involved in their own conversations. Given the chance, he could have snapped her in two, and no one would have noticed until it was too late.

"Look," she said quickly, "I didn't mean to offend you. It's nothing personal—"

"She's with me," a familiar male voice said suddenly from behind her. "Have you got a problem with that?"

Eliza had never been so glad to see anyone in her life. Glancing back over her shoulder, she smiled broadly. "Lorenzo! Thank God!"

She knew she must have lit up like a Christmas tree at the sight of him, and the cowboy didn't like it one bit. Giving Lorenzo a hard glare, he growled, "Who the hell are you?"

"Her fiancé," he lied without missing a beat. And just to be sure the cowboy understood, he laid his hand on Eliza's shoulder, claiming her as his.

For one heart-stopping moment, Eliza was sure the man was going to belt him. His dark eyes narrowed dangerously, and even as she watched, his hands clenched into fists. But then the bartender made his way back to their end of the bar, another couple waiting for a table took seats on the other side of them, and the cowboy thought better of causing any more trouble. Backing off, he muttered, "You can have her, man. She's too skinny, anyway. I like my women with some meat on their bones."

Weak with relief, Eliza waited only until the man had turned and walked away before she burst out laughing and threw herself into Lorenzo's arms. "Thank you! I was so scared! Did you see the size of his hands? I thought he was going to snap me in two like a toothpick.''

"What did you say to him?'' he asked with a grin, chuckling as he returned her hug. "For a minute there, I thought we were both toast.''

"I don't know what he was so bent out of shape about. All I did was insist on buying my own drink. Geez! You'd have thought I insulted his family name or something.''

"If that's his usual way of picking up a woman, no wonder he's alone,'' Lorenzo retorted. "Are you all right?''

She laughed, feeling foolish. "Yeah, he just caught me off guard. I just came in for some nachos, and the next thing I know, a man's trying to take my head off.''

"Eliza, your table's ready,'' the hostess said over the speaker system that was wired into the bar and hostess area. "Table for Eliza.''

"Finally!'' she sighed, relieved. Completely forgetting the fact that she'd wanted some time away from him to get her head on straight, she smiled and said, "Would you like to join me? We can split an order of nachos...or something else, if you like. I lost my appetite, so it doesn't matter to me.''

"Nachos sound great—if you're sure you want company,'' he added. "After dealing with that jerk, I wouldn't blame you if you wanted to be alone for a while.''

"Oh, but you didn't do anything! And if I hadn't been so tired, I would have handled him with one hand tied behind my back.''

Lorenzo didn't doubt that. If there was one thing he'd discovered about Eliza during the time he'd spent with her, it was that the lady was nothing if not self-sufficient. She carried her own bags, had no trouble taking the lead and never, ever, played the helpless female. A randy cowboy wouldn't present any more of a problem for her than a flat tire. She'd deal with both, then go on her way.

And he liked that about her. The women he knew cringed at the thought of breaking a nail. None of them would have been caught dead traipsing through the mountains like he and Eliza had all day. They were too delicate for that, too cool to sweat. Not Eliza. She'd thrown herself into it with enthusiasm and never once complained. And she had no idea how much he admired her for that.

Still, he should have politely turned down her invitation. He hadn't come into the bar in search of her—he'd wanted a drink to help him get her out of his head. Considering that, spending more time with her was not a wise thing to do. He should have said thanks but no thanks, and left her to his own devices while he ordered a double scotch. Instead, he heard himself say, "Lead the way."

"Great! I hope you don't mind jalapenos. I like my nachos spicy."

Two steps behind her as they followed the hostess to their table, Lorenzo had to grin at that. Why wasn't he surprised? She liked hot peppers, driving fast and doing whatever was necessary for a story. Whatever else the lady was, no one would ever accuse her of being a Milquetoast.

They arrived at their table then to discover it was located in a dark, intimate corner of the bar, away from the noise of the music and the conversation of the other customers. Lorenzo took one look at it and stiffened. Suddenly, splitting an order of nachos had become something else entirely, and he didn't know how the hell it had happened.

He didn't say a word, but he didn't have to. Eliza wasn't any happier with the situation than he was. Frowning at the candle in the middle of the table, she muttered, "This is a bar, for heaven's sake, not a romantic hideaway. We need another candle," she told their waitress when she suddenly appeared with menus. "It's dark back here."

The waitress could have told her that bars were supposed to be dark, but she only shrugged. "I'll see what I can do. What else can I get you?"

"Nachos," Lorenzo said. "And another glass of wine for the lady, and a beer for me."

She didn't even write it down. "It's coming right up," she promised, then grabbed a candle from a nearby table where four young cowboys sat eating greasy burgers and drinking beer. Not missing a beat, she set the candle down in front of Eliza and moved on to the next customer. The cowboys didn't so much as sputter in protest.

Her blue eyes twinkling, Eliza grinned. "I like her style."

"She reminds me of you."

That caught her by surprise. "Really? How? We don't look anything alike."

Since the waitress outweighed her by a good forty pounds and was a bleached blonde with a Dolly Parton hairdo, Lorenzo could understand her confusion. "Not in looks," he explained. "It's her attitude. She doesn't let the cowboys around here make anything off of her. You don't have any problem standing up for yourself, either. I heard how you spoke to your boss that morning he published the news that Lucas was alive. I was surprised he didn't fire you."

A rueful smile curled the corners of her mouth. "Simon wouldn't do that. He might want to tar and feather me, but trust me, he's not stupid enough to let the competition snap me up. Anyway, right's right and wrong's wrong, and he screwed up. Not that he would admit it," she added. "There's no fun in that."

"It sounds like the two of you bicker like an old married couple."

"Oh, we're worse than that," she laughed. "His wife said so!"

Chuckling, Lorenzo could just imagine them arguing over her column. She might gripe about Simon, but there was no question that she was fond of him…and that the editor brought out the best in her. Lorenzo had read her column. She was good.

"Your office must be a pretty wild place then," he said as the waitress set the nachos they'd ordered in front of them. "How'd you get into writing? And about royalty, of all things?"

"Fairy tales," she replied simply. "I've loved them since I was a little girl. When I discovered I had a way with words, it just seemed natural to write about the only people living modern day fairy tales."

"Just because we live in palaces doesn't mean life's a fairy tale," he said. "The prince's plane crash is a fine example of that."

"Fairy tales are full of tragedy," she said with a shrug. "They just end with happily ever after."

"And you think that's how the prince's story is going to end? All tied up with hearts and flowers and pink ribbons?"

He wasn't the first person to react to her love of fairy tales with cynicism—she encountered it all the time. With him, as with the others, she merely smiled. "Time will tell, won't it?"

She hadn't meant to reveal so much of herself, but talking to him was so easy. As they munched on nachos and the waitress brought them fresh drinks, she told him about the screenplay she one day hoped to write, and he opened up about the years he'd spent in the military and how much he enjoyed being in charge of Montebello's Royal Intelligence. From there, the conversation moved to their childhoods, their hopes and dreams, and where they each wanted to be when they were fifty. And somehow, time just seemed to slip away.

Eliza would have sworn they'd been there just a little over an hour when she glanced at her watch and saw that it was going on eleven. Shocked, she set her wineglass down with a thump. "Oh, my God! Look at the time!"

"Don't panic," Lorenzo laughed. "You're not going to turn into a pumpkin at midnight."

"Cute," she retorted, wrinkling her nose at him. "I've still got to write my notes for today and check in with Simon. He's going to kill me for calling so late."

"He'll get over it," he assured her as he rose to his feet. "But it is getting late."

When he reached into his back pocket for his billfold, Eliza knew she only had to let him pay and the evening would have been a date. She was horrified to discover that she'd never wanted anything more. "No!" she said quickly when he tossed down a twenty to pay the entire tab. "I'll pay for mine."

She watched his eyes narrow and knew he knew exactly what she was doing, but he didn't argue. "That's fine. We can go dutch." And picking up his twenty, he exchanged it for a ten.

Eliza added her own ten, then followed him outside. Her heart thundering, she half expected him to insist on walking her to her motel room door, but she could just imagine what would happen if he did. He'd open the door for her, check inside to make sure her room was safe, and somehow or other, they'd end up in each other's arms.

Just the thought of him touching her, kissing her, left her weak at the knees. How long had she wanted him to kiss her without even knowing it? she thought, stunned.

"...if that's okay with you."

Lost in her thoughts, she didn't realize he'd spoken until he looked at her expectantly. Brought back to their surroundings with a blink, she wanted to crawl in a hole. "I beg your pardon?"

"I'll watch you from here," he said, coming to a stop in the parking lot midway between their two rooms, "to make sure you make it to your room without any problems. If that's okay with you."

"Oh, no...I mean, yes! That'll be fine." Disappointed, she forced a smile and was thankful he couldn't see her blush in the poorly lit parking lot. "Then I guess I'll see you in the morning. Good night."

She could feel his eyes on her all the way to her room, but Eliza never looked back. She didn't dare. Her key clutched in her hand, she slipped inside and quietly shut the door. A split second later, she called Simon. They might argue like cats and dogs, but when she needed advice, whether it was business or personal, she could always trust him to say the right thing.

"This better be good, Red," he growled the second he came on the line and recognized her voice. "I was really sawing wood."

"I'm sorry," she said, stalling for time. Because she needed to think of some excuse why she had been too distracted to call in. She couldn't very well tell her boss she was in over her head with a certain devastatingly handsome duke.

Slouched on her couch and feeling sorry for herself because her boyfriend, Derek, had dumped her for no reason, Ursula Chambers stared at the TV with a jaundiced eye and paid little attention to the local news anchor, who read the lead story with an irritating nasal drawl. So what if some missing prince was believed to be alive, she thought sourly. She missed Derek. And she still didn't know why he'd walked out. They were good together, dammit! If he'd resented it when she joked around with his buddies, he should have told her he didn't like it, and she would have stopped. She wasn't a mind reader. But had he opened his mouth? Hell, no! He'd shut up like a clam and hadn't talked to her for days, then the next thing she knew, he was packing his things. It wasn't fair!

Frustrated and starting to get angry, she grabbed the phone and was just about to punch in Derek's number to give him a piece of her mind when her eyes fell on the TV screen and a picture of the missing prince that flashed there. Confused, she frowned. What the devil was the reporter talking about? The man in the picture wasn't a prince. He was her sister's ranch hand, Joe.

"Prince Lucas has been missing since his plane crashed in the mountains near Boulder last winter," the reporter said. "New evidence, however, has been recovered that leads authorities to believe the prince may be alive. The investigation has been reopened, and a search is expected to be underway shortly."

Confused, Ursula told herself she shouldn't have had that second drink after dinner. Her eyes were playing tricks on her. But even as she tried to convince herself she was seeing things, pictures didn't lie. Unless Prince Lucas of Montebello had an identical twin brother, he and Joe, the ranch hand her sister had been all lovey-dovey with a couple of weeks ago when Ursula had dropped in to see her, were one and the same.

Unable to take her eyes off the television screen until long after the news anchor had gone on to the next story, Ursula just sat there, stunned. Then it hit her. Her big break had arrived.

"My God! My sister's hiding a prince—at my family ranch no less. This is it! I'm going to be rich!"

Laughing, she jumped up from the chair and danced a jig. She could see it now...her picture all over the papers and flashing on every TV screen in America. And the headlines—oh, they were going to be beautiful! Struggling Actress Finds Prince! She'd be a hero! Every producer in Hollywood would be kicking himself for not recognizing her talent when he'd had the chance. And she'd make them pay for that when they finally came knocking on her door, she promised herself smugly. Oh, yes, they'd pay.

And so would the king and queen of Montebello. What would they pay to have their only son back? They had to have billions. Just thinking about how grateful they would be made her weak at the knees. She would be invited to the palace, to balls and parties and fancy soirees. Hell, they might even ask her to move to Montebello and live with them! If she played her cards right, she could be sitting pretty for the rest of her life.

Oh, this was going to be good, she thought, purring in delight. Everyone who'd ever slammed a door in her face was going to regret it—she'd make sure of it—starting with Derek. The jerk! She'd loved him—and trusted him to make her a star. Then he'd walked out on her, and she'd lost her lover and manager at one and the same time. She'd been devastated, but had he cared? Hell, no! He'd laughed in her face and told her she would never be anybody. He was going to regret that.

Then there was the family. Oh, she supposed Jessica was sympathetic enough, but everyone else had snickered at her dreams of being a famous actress and made fun of her behind her back. And she'd hated them for that. For as long as she could remember, she'd been sick of being poor, sick of trying to get ahead and getting nowhere. She'd left home at eighteen because she couldn't stand it anymore, because Hollywood was the dream factory of the world, and she wanted the life that Julia Roberts and Meg Ryan had. She could act as well as they could—she knew she could!

But she never got the chance. Her parents had died before she could even land her first part—small though it was. Without an agent, the only steady job open to her was waiting tables. Then she'd met Derek and he'd promised her he would make all her dreams come true. But the only part he ever got her was a bit in a porno flick, and what good was that when she couldn't even brag about it to anyone, least of all her goody-goody sister?

He'd failed her and so had everyone else, and when she was finally forced to return to Colorado and her hometown of Shady Rock because she didn't have a dime to her name, she'd been so bitter and disillusioned that she hadn't come out of her apartment for days. That was weeks ago, and nothing had changed. All she'd been able to see ahead of her were days and weeks and months of blandness and poverty for the rest of her life.

Until now. Now she was going to have the last laugh.

Anticipation glinting in her blue eyes, she whirled around, looking around her messy apartment for her purse. She had to go to Jessica's, had to see for herself that Joe and the prince were one and the same man. She didn't understand what the prince was doing hanging around her sister—or why he didn't seem to want to be found—but she didn't care. As soon as she verified he was her man, she was calling King Marcus of Montebello. By the time she got through talking to him, she was going to be richer than Cleopatra!

Already spending the money in her mind, she had just found her purse and was in the process of digging for her car keys when there was a knock at her door. "Damn!"

she swore. If that was old lady Baker from next door, there to complain because her TV was too loud again, she was going to tell her off. Let her go to the apartment manager— she didn't care if they threw her out on her ear. She was about to come into money!

Prepared to tell the old goat exactly what she thought of her, she stormed across to the door and jerked it open, only to gasp, "Jessica! What are you doing here? I was just on my way out to the ranch to see you."

"Oh, Ursula!" her sister sobbed. "I need your help. Joe left me!"

"What?!"

Caught up in her own misery, Jessica didn't even notice that her sister paled at her words. Her heart hurting and tears flooding her soft, wide blue eyes, she stumbled into the apartment like a wounded animal and fell into Ursula's arms. "I don't know what happened," she sobbed. "One second, everything was fine, and the next, we were arguing and he walked out."

"What do you mean *he walked out?*" she demanded, awkwardly patting her. "He'll be back, of course. He just needs some time to cool off. You'll see. Leave him alone tonight, and by morning, he'll be ready to kiss and make up."

"No, he won't," she sniffed, pulling back to wipe her eyes. "He's gone to find himself."

Her heart breaking, Jessica knew she shouldn't have said any more. Joe was entitled to his privacy, and even though he'd only met Ursula once, he hadn't trusted her from the moment he'd first laid eyes on her. He'd asked Jessica to keep his secret to herself, and she should have done that. But she dissolved in tears just at the thought of never seeing him again, and she had to talk to someone. And even if

they weren't all that close, Ursula was her sister, and the
only family she had left now that her parents were gone.

"What do you mean he's gone to find himself? Where?"
she asked sharply. "What do you know about Joe, Jess?
And don't start crying again, dammit! This is important.
Has he gone home?"

"I don't know," she sniffed. "He doesn't know where
home is."

Ursula had never had much patience with emotional dis-
plays, and when Jessica saw her start to scowl, she cried,
"It's true! He has amnesia. That's why he jumped at the
chance to work for me when he came to the ranch all those
months ago. He had nowhere else to go!"

Ursula had heard her fair share of tall tales, but this one
was over the top. The man was a prince, for heaven's sake!
His family was rolling in dough, and as King Marcus's only
son, he stood to inherit a lion's share of that. A man didn't
just forget that. Not unless he was crazy or something, and
from what she'd seen of Joe the only time they'd met, he
was a far cry from crazy. So what kind of scam was he
trying to pull? Whatever it was, he had to know he wasn't
going to get away with it. She'd make sure of it, she vowed
grimly.

"Let me get this straight," she said with a frown. "He
doesn't know who he is, but he's gone to find himself. How
the hell is he going to do that, Jess, if he doesn't know
who he is?"

Tears still streaming down her face, she couldn't answer
that one. "I don't know!" she cried. "I just know he's
gone, and I don't know where. And I never got to tell
him—"

When she broke off abruptly, Ursula pinned her with a
hard look that would brook no opposition. "You never told

him what? Tell me, Jess. You might as well. You know I'm going to find out anyway.''

She'd always had a way of getting secrets out of her little sister, and they both knew it. It only took another chiding look for Jessica to cave in like a stack of dominoes. Hugging herself, she blurted out, "I'm pregnant! And Joe doesn't know."

Stunned, Ursula just looked at her. Then her condition— and its repercussions—registered, and with a shriek, she swept Jessica into her arms. "Honey, that's wonderful!" If they didn't have the prince, they had his heir! And that sweet, adorable baby that was destined to be king would be her nephew! "When did you find out? Why haven't you told me? Here, sit down. We have to make plans!"

Hustling Jessica over to the nearest chair, she plopped her down in it, then grabbed a footstool for her to rest her feet on. "Can I get you something? Are you drinking plenty of milk? We want the baby to have strong bones. When's he due?"

"I don't even know if he is a he," her sister replied. Frowning in confusion, she looked at Ursula like she'd suddenly grown two heads. "This wasn't the reaction I expected from you. I thought you'd be upset with me...especially now that Joe's taken off. How am I going to run the ranch and have a baby? There's so much to do around there already. I can't do everything by myself."

Far from concerned, Ursula only laughed. "Don't you worry about that, honey. Trust me, you're going to be well taken care of—Joe's family will see to that."

"His family? What are you talking about? I told you he has amnesia. He doesn't even know what his real name is, let alone who his family is."

"He may not," her sister retorted slyly, "but I do." Snatching up the morning newspaper, she opened it to the front page and wasn't surprised to find Prince Lucas's picture there for all the world to see. "Look," she said, pushing the paper at her. "You fell in love with the prince, Cinderella! His real name is Prince Lucas Sebastiani of Montebello."

Not even looking at the picture, Jessica laughed. "Right! And I'm Queen Elizabeth. Stop fooling around, Ursula."

"I'm not joking. Look!"

With the picture shoved right under her nose, she had no choice but to look at it. Humoring her, she said, "Okay, so he's a prince—"

Her gaze dropped to the smiling man in the picture, and between one heartbeat and the next, her world turned upside down. Though the beard was gone and the face younger and less care- and weatherworn, she couldn't deny the resemblance. Stunned, she gasped, "Oh, my God, that's Joe! How—"

"No," her sister corrected her, "that's Prince Lucas. Read the article, Jess."

Her blood roaring in her ears, Jessica tried to read the article that accompanied the bold headlines, but all she saw was the prince's name before her gaze was tugged back to the man in the picture. Joe. It had to be him. There couldn't be another man in the world who had that same engaging smile and twinkle in his eye. But he wasn't a prince. How could he be? He was just a drifter who'd showed up at the ranch one day looking for work.

"I don't understand," she said huskily, glancing back up at Ursula in confusion. "How can this be?"

"He crashed his plane into the side of a mountain somewhere outside of Boulder last year, and he's been missing ever since. He must have hit his head, sweetie."

"And all this time, he's been wandering around, trying

to find out who he is. My God, that's so sad! I've got to
find him!"

She would have struggled up from her chair and hurried
out to her truck to begin immediately looking for him, but
Ursula moved lightning quick to stop her. "Oh, no you
don't! The prince can take care of himself. You've got
other more important things to do—like taking care of
yourself and the baby. I think you need to go to Montebello."

"What?!"

"It's the only logical thing to do," she retorted, already
picturing where *she* would live in the royal palace. She
might even find herself a royal husband! "The king needs
to know that he's about to become a grandfather. I'll go
with you to tell him. He can see that you're taken care of—
after all, you're the mother of his grandson. Then when his
son is found, he'll make sure he does the right thing and
marries you."

"Oh, no! I would never use the baby to force a proposal
out of Joe," she said, horrified. "He doesn't even know
I'm pregnant."

"He'll know soon enough when we find him."

"No! If he loves me, he'll come back to me without
knowing about the baby."

"But the baby could one day be king of Montebello,"
she pointed out. "You have to tell the king!"

Her heart bruised and aching, Jessica didn't care two
cents about that. It was Joe she cared about, Joe she loved.
She desperately needed him to return that love, and for the
last few months, she'd convinced herself that he did. She'd
seen the emotion in his eyes, felt it in his touch, tasted it
in his kiss. But he'd left without ever saying the words,
and that hurt.

"The only thing I care about is Joe," she cried as tears

once again welled in her eyes. "What if he never comes back?"

But even as she cried out in pain, memories stirred, and suddenly, she had a vague recollection of Joe talking about his duty to himself and others. And just that easily, she knew Ursula was right. He *had* left her to go back to his real life! And he hadn't said a word about who he was. Why? Because he was afraid she would want something from him or his family.

Hurt, her pride stung, she wiped away the last of her tears and squared her shoulders. He didn't have to worry about her trying to contact him, she thought grimly. It wasn't going to happen.

"If that's the way he felt, then I'm glad he's gone," she said coldly. "He's obviously not the man I thought he was."

"So make him pay for that. Call the king."

"No."

Jessica didn't turn stubborn very often, but when she did, there was no budging her. Frustrated, Ursula swore silently. They could both live high off the hog if she'd do the right thing and inform the royal family of her pregnancy, but she had to turn all stubborn and noble on her, dammit! She'd let her get away with it now, but not for long. This was the opportunity of a lifetime and she wasn't going to let Jessica or anyone else blow it for her!

Chapter 7

He couldn't get her out of his head.

Tossing and turning and unable to sleep, Lorenzo tried to blame it on the bad bed, the groaning heater that barely kept the room warm and the eighteen-wheelers that raced by on the highway that seemed to be right outside his door, but a man could only lie to himself so much. It wasn't the accommodations that were interfering with his sleep, or the traffic on the highway or even whoever was snoring in the room next door and rattling the walls. It was *her,* and there wasn't a damn thing he could do about it.

Disgusted with himself, he rolled out of bed, dragged on his jeans and a flannel shirt and stepped out onto the wooden porch that ran the length of the one-story building. It was well past midnight and colder than hell and he hadn't bothered with shoes, but the freezing silence of the night was a welcome distraction. With his shoulders hunched, his hands buried in the pockets of his jeans and his toes curled under, he stared out at the all-consuming darkness of the night and tried to focus on Lucas. Where was he? Was he all right? Why hadn't he called the family? Didn't he realize everyone was worried sick about him? Or had something—or someone—prevented him from calling?

It was that that worried Lorenzo the most, but there was little he could do for Lucas right now except continue the search first thing in the morning…with Eliza. Just that easily, his thoughts circled back around to her, and with a will of their own, his gaze traveled to the end of the porch and her room.

Swearing, he didn't want to notice that her lights were out or imagine her in bed. He didn't want to remember her smile or the way her blue eyes danced when she laughed or the softness of her skin when he touched her. He didn't want to be able to recall every single conversation they'd ever had or admire her sharp wit and pretty smile. And he damn sure didn't want to dream about her every time he closed his eyes. But he did, and it was slowly driving him crazy.

It had to stop, he thought grimly. He had to stop thinking of her as anything other than a reporter he was forced to work with. Because if he didn't, he was going to do something stupid…like give in to the need she stirred in him so effortlessly. And he didn't have to reach for her, didn't have to kiss her, didn't have to make love to her, to know that if he made that mistake once, he would have a hard time walking away from her. Then, he really would be in trouble.

Promising himself that wasn't going to happen, he deliberately tore his gaze from her darkened window and went back inside. And this time when he went to bed and closed his eyes, he focused on the progress report he planned to make to the king on the search for Lucas. When he finally fell asleep, Eliza was nowhere in his thoughts.

In the dark of the night, however, when his defenses were done, she slipped into his dreams again and played havoc with his senses. By the time an icy cold dawn broke on the horizon, he was hot and bothered and more than a little irritated. And it was all Eliza's fault.

Given the chance, he would have avoided her the rest of the day if the opportunity had presented itself. But they still had the most difficult part of the search ahead of them—canvassing every town and village and wide spot in the road they came to until they found Lucas. And he'd have a hard time doing it without Eliza's help. Damn, that rubbed against the grain.

Meeting her at the truck at nine o'clock, he greeted her with a scowl. "I don't know about you, but I'm not interested in breakfast this morning. If you're hungry, I suggested you grab a candy bar or something from the gas station. We need to get on the road as soon as possible."

At his curt tone, Eliza lifted a delicately arched brow, but all she said was, "I could use a cup of coffee. There's a pot in the motel office. Would you like some?"

"No."

He didn't bother to soften his tone or so much as thank her for being considerate. "Somebody obviously got up on the wrong side of the bed," she said coolly. "What's the matter? Didn't you sleep well?"

"I slept just fine," he retorted. "Go get your coffee. We're wasting time."

She stiffened at that, outraged. "Whoa, Your Royal Highness! We're not going anywhere until we get a few things settled. I don't know what your problem is this morning, but you're not going to take it out on me. Understood? I didn't do anything—"

"The hell you didn't," he growled. "You *are* the problem!'' And before she could guess his intentions, he reached for her and dragged her into his arms.

It was the wrong thing to do. Before his thoughts blurred and his mind shut down, he knew that. But the second his mouth covered hers, the thing that he knew was so wrong for him had ever felt so right. How long had he been aching to kiss her? To give in to this gut-wrenching need that was like a fever that never went away? It seemed like weeks, months, and he'd only known her a matter of days, dammit!

She did this to him, he thought, groaning at the taste of her, the feel of her. This was all her fault. If she hadn't had those snapping blue eyes of hers, he could have found a way to resist her. If her smile hadn't been so full of fun and mischief, she wouldn't have caught him off guard. And then there was those fiery-red curls of hers. Her hair had a life all its own and constantly tempted him to touch. What else could a man with any blood in his veins do?

But it was the feel of her slender body in his arms, the sweet heat of her mouth as she kissed him back that drove him crazy. They were standing in a parking lot in the middle of small-town Colorado, in full view of anyone who cared to drive by, and all he could think of was how much he wanted to make love to her. Just once before they found the prince. Was that too much to ask?

It was the thought of Lucas that finally brought him back to his senses. One minute, he was kissing her like there was no tomorrow, and the next, he suddenly realized what he was doing. Swearing under his breath, he abruptly put her from him, cursing himself for being a fool. Had he lost his mind? Lucas was God knew where, possibly in serious trouble, and it was his job to find him. And all he could think of was Eliza. If the king ever found out about this, he'd have his head, and he couldn't blame him. He had a job to do, and it was high time he did it!

"Get in the truck," he said roughly. "I'll get your coffee for you." And without giving her a chance to argue, he turned and strode to the office of the motel, where free coffee and doughnuts were provided for the guests.

Later, Eliza never remembered opening the door to the truck and sliding into the cab. Thankfully, she wasn't expected to drive. Her head reeling and her heart still slamming against her ribs, she just sat there, dazed. She'd never met anyone who could make her feel this way with just a kiss, and as her head started to clear, she readily admitted that she was shaken. In spite of the fact that she loved fairy tales and writing about the royals, she liked to think of herself as a woman who had her feet squarely on the ground. She was practical and pragmatic, and not one of those dreamy-eyed women who were constantly looking for their soul mate. As far as she was concerned, there was no such thing as Mr. Right. Love was based on physical attraction and chemistry, and she'd always believed that you could find that with any number of people.

But there was something about Lorenzo that just felt so right.

Suddenly feeling like crying, she readily admitted he scared the hell out of her. He wasn't driving all over Colorado with her because he liked her—he just needed her help finding Prince Lucas. Once they located him, she was crazy if she thought Lorenzo was going to stick around to be with her. He'd be gone so fast, it'd make her head swim. And if she was stupid enough to let herself fall in love with him, all she'd have to show for their time together was a possible Pulitzer and a broken heart.

"Remember the story," she muttered to herself. "That's the only reason you're in this. Concentrate on that, and you'll do just fine."

That should have been easy. She readily admitted she

was ambitious. She wanted a Pulitzer, and she was willing
to do whatever it took within the law to get one. But when
Lorenzo returned with her coffee a few minutes later and
slipped behind the wheel of the pickup, it wasn't thoughts
of the story that made her heart skip a beat. It was Lorenzo
and the brush of his fingers against hers when he handed
her her coffee.

Still, she acted as if the kiss had never happened when
she sipped her coffee and sighed in contentment. "Mmm.
That's good and strong, just the way I like it. So…now
what? Do we keep searching towns to the north or move
out in circles from where the scarf was found?"

If he was bothered by the fact that she made no reference
to the kiss they'd just shared, he gave no sign of it. Starting
the truck, he pulled out of the parking lot and headed north.
"We know he headed north from the crash site to where
he camped, then north from there until he reached the road.
I don't think he'd turn back south at this point and retrace
his steps. And west only takes him deeper into the mountains. He could go east, of course, but my gut says north."

Eliza had always been one to follow a hunch. She'd
learned a long time ago that her instincts very seldom let
her down. "North it is, then. Maybe today we'll get lucky."

For a while, it seemed as if they had, in fact, stumbled
onto a bit of luck. A clerk at the rancher supply store in
the first town they reached frowned at the picture Lorenzo
showed him of Prince Lucas and said, "Doesn't look like
anyone I know but I can't swear to it. Maybe this is the
fella that was staying at the old Barlow place last winter. I
never saw him myself, but I heard folks talking about a
drifter holing up there for a while. Of course, he's moved
on now, but this could have been him."

Eliza exchanged a look with Lorenzo and told herself
not to get too excited. The clerk hadn't actually identified

the prince from his picture. "Where exactly is the Barlow place? We need to talk to the Barlows."

"Sorry, but you're out of luck there," the older man chuckled. "Dennis Barlow and his wife, Sarah, died twenty years ago in a fire. The place has been empty ever since."

"Someone must own it," Lorenzo said with a frown. "We'll talk to them."

"Sure. Their daughter, Martha. But she lives in New York City. She hasn't been back home since her parents died. She just lets the place sit empty."

"And you don't know anyone else who saw this drifter?"

"Nope."

"Then how did anyone even know there was someone staying there?"

"They saw some lights and thought it was a ghost," he said with a crooked grin. "Some folks have been saying for years that the place was haunted. When the lights appeared on the anniversary of the night Dennis and Sarah died, everybody got spooked and kept their distance."

"So no one ever went and checked out who was staying there?" Eliza asked. "Not even the sheriff?"

"Whoever it was wasn't hurting anything," he said with a shrug. "The place was already half-burned down and barely standing. And like I said, folks around here thought it was a ghost, at first. By the time everyone calmed down and realized that was crazy, whoever was staying out there had moved on."

So there was no one who'd actually seen the drifter, no one who could even tell them anything at all about him. For all they knew, it could have been a woman. "We'd still like to look at the place," Eliza said, "just to see if my brother left any clues about where he was going. He had a breakdown last year and wandered off, and we've been looking for him ever since. He's not taking his medication, you know, and he's manic-depressive. That's why we have to find him. He could do anything.''

It was a wild tale and just outrageous enough to be plausible. Lorenzo hadn't been comfortable with it at first, but they'd had to have some explanation of why they were looking for a missing man, and they couldn't just go up to a stranger on the street and ask if they'd seen Prince Lucas. Not only would people think *they* were crazy, but word of that kind of activity was bound to get back to all the fortune hunters who'd sat up and taken notice when Simon had announced on the front page of the *Sentinel* that the prince was alive and a new search for him was underway. So Eliza had come up with the idea of a sick, confused, lost brother, and so far, everyone had swallowed it whole.

The clerk was no exception. ''Man, that's rough. No wonder you're worried.'' Quickly giving them directions to the abandoned Barlow property, he warned, ''There's a No Trespassing sign at the gate, but don't pay any attention to it. The sheriff put it up because some teenagers started hanging out there, and he was afraid someone would get hurt.''

Encouraged for the first time in days, they thanked him for the information, then immediately headed for the Barlow place. Following the directions he'd given them, they turned off on a side road on the north side of town and followed it until they passed over a creek and spotted a gate with a No Trespassing sign. Sitting well back in the trees were the remains of what had been the Barlow's home.

Eliza took one look at it and could understand why the locals had thought it was inhabited by ghosts. Even in the bright light of morning, the place looked spooky. It might have burned years ago, but the charred remains of what appeared to have once been a cozy cottage stood like a memorial to its dead owners. Half the roof was nothing but blackened rafters open to the sky, and the walls that still stood had been vandalized years ago. All of the windows had been broken or shot out, and the front door stood wide open, silently welcoming anyone brave enough to step inside.

Eliza didn't consider herself a superstitious person, but she took one look at the place and shivered. If a house could put off bad vibes, this one did. "If the prince really stayed here, I can see why he left after only a few days. This place gives me the willies."

Lorenzo grimly agreed. "He would have never stepped foot in the place if he was thinking clearly. Obviously, he's in worse shape than I realized."

"*If* he stayed here," Eliza pointed out. "We don't know for sure that the drifter really was the prince."

"Let's check it out," he said and stepped through the front door.

The inside of what was left of the cottage was even more depressing than the outside of the building. Smoke- and water-damaged remnants of the Barlow family's past had been untouched by time in the two rooms that had managed to escape the fire. Pictures hung on the wall just as they had the night the fire broke out. There were still dishes in the kitchen cabinets and clothes in the closet. If ashes from the fire and dust from the past twenty years hadn't covered everything in sight, it would have looked as if the owners of the house had just stepped out for a while.

"Lucas could have stayed here for a while," he said as he inspected the living room and noted the soundness of the roof and walls. "He could have built a fire in the fireplace and slept on the couch. After sleeping in caves and wandering around in the mountains after the crash, this must have looked damn good.''

Moving to the windows to check the condition of the curtains, he didn't realize he'd disturbed some of the insects who called the house home until he felt something scurry across the back of his neck. Swearing, he slapped at it blindly. ''Damn!''

Surprised, Eliza glanced up from the debris she was inspecting on a desk in the corner. ''What is it?'' she asked, concerned. ''Did you hurt yourself?''

''It's just a spider,'' he retorted, slapping at the back of his neck again. ''I think I got it.''

She shuddered, a grimace of distaste wrinkling her brow. ''Nasty things. Are you okay?''

''I'm fine,'' he assured her. ''It just surprised me. Did you find anything interesting?''

Regretfully, she shook her head. ''It doesn't look like anyone has been here for years.''

Lorenzo had to agree. ''Maybe it was just some kids playing tricks on the locals,'' he said as he moved to the fireplace and squatted down to see if he could tell how long it had been since a fire had been lit. ''They probably got a big laugh when everyone started talking about ghosts.''

Reaching for a nearby andiron, he poked at the charred logs there only to stiffen at the sight of a half-burnt matchbook. ''I'll be damned,'' he swore softly. ''He *was* here! Look! This is a matchbook from a nightclub in Paris. Lucas was there just two days before the crash!''

It wasn't much evidence, but it was a sign they were on the right track, and after running into one dead end after another for the past two days, they were both thrilled. ''At least we know he was here,'' Eliza said, relieved. ''The question is, where did he go from here?''

''North,'' Lorenzo said without hesitation. ''I don't

know if he was following the North Star or what, but I know he went north. Maybe he was confused and had his coordinates mixed up when he crashed. He might have thought he was south of Denver, and he was trying to find the city. Whatever the explanation, I think we'll find him if we just keep heading north.''

Encouraged, they spent the rest of that day and the next two days doing exactly that, and neither was surprised when no one they spoke to could remember a man matching the Prince's description coming through that part of the country any time over the course of the past year. Lucas had kept to himself when he'd found the Barlow place, and Lorenzo could only suppose that he hadn't sought help because he was afraid. He couldn't imagine why he would be frightened, but that was the only reason he could think of for not going to the authorities. If he was still afraid when he left the Barlow place and moved on, then he was probably still avoiding people as much as possible. Tracking him wasn't going to get any easier.

Discouraged and bone tired by midafternoon of the third day of fruitless searching, his back and shoulders stiff with tension, he studied the sky in front of them and said, ''I don't like the looks of those clouds. It looks like we've got some bad weather brewing. Why don't we stop for the day?''

''It does look like we're in for a blow,'' she agreed. ''And I'd just as soon not get caught out in the middle of nowhere if a blizzard's going to hit.''

So he checked the two of them into another small motel in another nameless Colorado town and didn't even care that the days and nights were starting to blur into one. A throbbing headache taking up residence in his head, he carried Eliza's suitcase into her room and said, ''You're on your own for dinner. I'm not hungry.''

Surprised, she frowned. "Are you all right? I saw a steak house when we drove into town. I thought I'd check it out later. You're welcome to join me."

"No, thanks," he retorted, rubbing at the pain that knitted a deep groove between his eyes. "I've got to write up a report for the king, then I'm going to take a shower and turn in early. You're welcome to use the truck, though." Pulling the pickup keys from his pocket, he tossed them to her, only to draw in a quick breath when a sudden hot pain flared in his shoulder.

"What's wrong?" Eliza asked, frowning when she noted how pale he'd suddenly become. "Did you pull a muscle or something?"

He felt like hell, but it wasn't his nature to complain. His mother had died when he was nine, leaving him with his father, Antonio, who had always been an indifferent parent at the best of times, and downright cold when more was asked of him than he wanted to give. He'd had no patience with a grieving child and had drilled into Lorenzo that a man didn't show weakness. That was a lesson that Lorenzo had never forgotten. Even after his father died and he went to live with Marcus and Gwendolyn at the age of thirteen, he'd kept his feelings to himself.

"I'm fine," he said shortly. "I'm just a little stiff from driving so long. A hot shower will help."

"Maybe," she said, studying him worriedly. "Are you sure you haven't hurt your shoulder or something? Maybe I should take a look at it. I drove as much as you did today, and I'm not stiff."

"So you handle stress better than I do," he retorted. "I'm fine, Eliza. Quit worrying."

That was easy for him to say—he obviously didn't realize just how bad he looked. There was a dullness in his eyes and, in spite of his paleness, a flush to his cheeks that concerned her. But it was the stiffness with which he held himself that worried her the most. Something wasn't right.

"I'm not worried," she lied. "But if your muscles are so tight, you're in pain and you obviously need a massage. Sit down and I'll rub the kinks out for you."

"That's not necessary."

"So humor me," she retorted. "Take your shirt off." Not giving him a chance to argue, she pushed him into a chair and whipped his long sleeve polo shirt over his head, only to freeze at his groan of pain. "What is it?" she asked in alarm when every drop of blood drained from his face. "What did I do?"

"My shoulder," he said hoarsely. He tried reaching behind him, but even that was too painful.

Alarmed, Eliza rushed around behind him, only to gasp at the swollen, angry wound located just out of his reach near his right shoulder blade. "My God, it looks like some kind of insect bite! Do you remember something biting you?"

"No, but I could have picked up a tick or something in the woods."

Eliza had seen tick bites before, but never one that looked like this. Infected and hot, it had angry red streaks that radiated out from the center of the bite. "I bet this is from that spider that was crawling on your shoulder at the Barlow place," she said, suddenly remembering the way he'd slapped at his neck and shoulders to kill it. "Why didn't you say anything?" she scolded. "Spider bites can be nasty."

"I just thought I scraped against something in the woods," he replied. "It didn't really start bothering me until this morning."

Hurriedly unzipping her suitcase, she dug through her things for the disinfectant and antibiotic cream that she never went anywhere without. "And you didn't say a word," she said, shaking her head in disgust as she doused a cotton ball with disinfectant. "No wonder you look sick. Sit still. This could hurt."

Holding her breath, she gently pressed the cotton ball to the wound, barely touching him for fear of hurting him. But even that was too much. Sucking in a sharp breath, he stiffened, then before Eliza could even guess just how much pain he was in, all the air seemed to hiss out of him. Without another sound, he crumpled to the floor.

"Lorenzo! Oh, God!" Horrified, she dropped to her knees beside him and carefully rolled him to his side. Clammy with sweat and burning up with fever, he was as pale as the snow that had started to fall outside. "I'm sorry," she choked, patting his face to try to bring him around. "I didn't mean to hurt you. Wake up, Lorenzo. You've got to wake up!"

For a moment, she thought he was dead. Out cold, he didn't move so much as a muscle. Then he groaned low in his throat and slowly opened his eyes, only to frown when he found himself lying on the floor. "What happened?"

He spoke barely above a whisper, and that scared her even more. He was a strong man. She'd never seen him so helpless. Tears welling in her eyes, she brushed his hair back from his forehead. "You passed out," she said huskily. "You're really sick. We've got to get you to a doctor."

To his credit, he tried to stand when she helped him up. But he was a big man. Lean, but well-muscled and well over six inches taller than her, he outweighed her by at least sixty pounds. When he leaned on her for support, she was barely able to help him the three steps to the bed before he passed out again.

Her heart thundering in her breast, Eliza couldn't remember the last time she'd been so scared. She tried rousing him, but he just lay there. Alarmed, she quickly called the motel office. "I need an ambulance!" she cried the moment the clerk answered. "Call 9-1-1!"

"The closest ambulance is twenty miles away in Valley View," the woman replied, "but Doc Stevens is just down the street. His office is right next door to the video store. Do you want the number? I've got it right here."

Afraid his receptionist would put her off, or worse yet, put her on hold, she said, "No, I'll go myself. Thanks."

Eliza didn't know if he made house calls, but she didn't care. In this instance, she would refuse to take no for an answer. Grabbing her coat and the keys, she checked only to make sure Lorenzo was still breathing before she ran for the door.

Dr. Albert Stevens's office was right where the clerk said it was, but it wasn't until Eliza hurried inside and found the waiting room empty that she realized it was already after five o'clock. Horrified that the doctor had already left for the day, she rushed over to the sign-in desk and banged on the frosted glass, praying all the time, "Please, please, let him be in."

"We're closed," the elderly receptionist said the second she slid open the window. "If you'd like to make an appointment, you can call in the morning."

"I can't wait until morning," Eliza snapped. "I've got a sick friend down at the motel who's suffering from a spider bite. I need a doctor now!"

"But Dr. Stevens is a gynecologist!"

"I don't care if he's a damn dentist," she roared, losing her cool. "My friend is seriously ill. Is Dr. Stevens available or not?"

"He's available," a middle-aged man said as he stepped into the waiting room. Already wearing a wool coat and hat, he had his medical bag in his hand. "Lead the way, Miss…"

"Eliza," she replied, not standing on ceremony. "We're at the Silver Moon Motel. Room three."

She didn't wait to see if he followed, but turned and hurried out to the truck, which she'd left running in the parking lot. Thirty seconds later when she braked to a screeching halt in front of her room, Dr. Stevens was right behind her. "I think the spider bit him a couple of days ago, but neither one of us realized it until this afternoon when his shoulder really started to bother him," she told him quickly as she jerked open the door and the doctor strode over to where Lorenzo lay on his stomach on the bed. "When I tried to clean it with some disinfectant, he passed out."

"I'm not surprised," the older man said as he examined the wound. "This is quite a nasty bite. I'm going to have to lance it."

Eliza had been afraid of that. "Don't hurt him."

"I'll make sure he won't feel a thing," he assured her with a half smile, and pulled a sedative from his bag.

Less than fifteen minutes later, it was all over. The bite had been thoroughly cleaned and bandaged and Lorenzo was given a shot of antibiotics. He hadn't been unconscious throughout the entire procedure, but the wound was deadened, as the doctor had promised, and he didn't feel a thing. Still, he was exhausted and fell asleep before the doctor finished writing out a prescription for a ten-day supply of antibiotics.

Handing the prescription to Eliza, he warned, "This isn't something he's going to get over quickly. He's going to need plenty of rest and fluids, and you need to make sure he takes the full course of antibiotics. Aspirin should bring his fever down. If it doesn't, call me." Jotting his home number down on the back of his card, he handed it to her. "I'll drop by in the morning to check on him. If you need me before then, don't hesitate to call."

Giving her shoulder a reassuring squeeze, he walked out without even asking for payment. Relieved, Eliza would have cried, but she didn't have time. She had to get to the drugstore to fill Lorenzo's prescription before he woke up. Slipping back into her coat, she grabbed the keys to the truck and hurried out.

The next twenty-four hours passed in a blur for Lorenzo. A black cloud of pain weighed heavy on his brain, and even though he slept, he couldn't seem to get comfortable. Fire burned in his shoulder like a hot poker, and when he wasn't dripping in sweat, he was chilled to the bone. One minute he was shivering under the covers and the next, he was kicking them off. The sun went down, then came up again, and it seemed like only minutes had passed.

And then there were the dreams. He dreamed of spiders and dark forests and Lucas running out of a burning house. But it was Eliza who haunted him. She was there when he finally slept, there when he found the strength to open his eyes, there when the fire in his shoulder raged out of control. She shoved pills down his throat and nearly drowned him with water and juices, and then when his defenses were down and he couldn't seem to control his thoughts, she stepped into his fantasy and made love to him. It was enough to drive a man crazy.

Hot, frustrated, exhausted, he tossed and turned and hated being out of control of his own body. And when his fever finally broke and he could barely lift his head off the pillow, Eliza was once again there. Even with his eyes closed, he would have known her touch anywhere. She stroked his brow, tucked the covers around him, and sat so close beside him on the bed that he could smell the sweet and spicy scent of her.

And in his weakened condition, he could no more resist her than the tides could resist the pull of the moon. Reaching for her hand, he enclosed her fingers in his. "How long have I been out of commission?" he asked faintly.

"A day and a half. The doctor has been here twice."

He'd thought it had only been hours since he'd passed out. Stunned, he swore weakly. "Damn spider! I should have killed it when I had the chance. Help me up."

Eliza couldn't believe he was serious. "You've got to be kidding! Where do you think you're going?"

"Back to work."

"Don't be ridiculous! You're weak as a kitten—"

"I don't care," he retorted, struggling to sit up without her help. "Lucas could be in trouble. We've got to get back on the road."

He had that stubborn set to his jaw, the one she'd come to know only too well since they'd met. He'd made up his mind, and nothing she could say was going to change it. So she didn't even try. Instead, she stepped over to the drapes and pulled them open to reveal the whiteout conditions outside.

"We're in the middle of the worst blizzard in a century," she told him, "so you can relax. We're not going anywhere and neither is the prince if he's anywhere in the state of Colorado. The governor's shut down every highway in the state."

Chapter 8

Trapped, there was nothing Lorenzo could do but accept the fact that for the time being, at least, they weren't going anywhere fast. Outside, a frigid north wind howled like a banshee while the storm raged and the snow piled up in ten-foot drifts. From where he lay on the bed, he could see that the entire world had ground to a halt. Anyone crazy enough to step outside was asking for trouble.

And he had enough of that, as it was. His trouble, though, had curly red hair and a touch that was guaranteed to drive a man slowly out of his mind. And she didn't even seem to realize what she did to him. She puttered around the room—her room; he'd never made it to his own—picking up towels and glasses, and he realized just what she'd done for him during the past two days. She'd fed him and nursed him and bathed him with cool cloths to bring down his fever, and even though she didn't touch him now, he could still feel her hands on him. And that, more than anything, shook him to the core.

In the past, he'd never let anyone take care of him. Whenever he'd been sick—and that was rare—he'd turned away the women who wanted to coddle him and play nursemaid, preferring to take care of himself. And now he knew why. It was…unsettling. And far too intimate.

If he'd had his wits about him, he would have insisted on going back to his own room. It would have been the right thing to do. His fever had broken, and while there was no question that he was still very weak, he didn't need her hovering over him, waiting on him hand and foot. He might be tired, but he could take care of himself.

He knew that, accepted it, and still stayed right where he was. Later, he knew that would worry him, but right now, he couldn't find the strength to do what was wise. His defenses were down, and he didn't want to be alone. Honesty forced him to admit that he enjoyed her touch and wanted more. Thankfully, he didn't have to be concerned about things getting out of hand. He couldn't even sit up without her assistance. Nothing was likely to happen.

"I guess we're stuck here then," he said gruffly. "Have you heard how long the storm's expected to last?"

"It should blow itself out by tonight, but it could be another couple of days before the snowplows are able to clear the roads…especially up here in the mountains. The road crews will work on the interstate highways and cities first."

Staring out the window at the blowing snow, he felt the cold all the way to his bones. "I wonder where Lucas is."

"He's a survivor," she reminded him. "Anyone who can walk away from a plane crash is smart enough to find shelter from a blizzard. Wherever he is, I'm sure he's fine."

Lorenzo had to agree. In spite of the fact that Lucas was a prince and had grown up behind the protective walls of the palace, he'd already proven that he was no lightweight when it came to surviving in the wilderness. He would have seen the storm building, just as he and Eliza had, and found a safe place to wait it out.

"The king will have heard about the storm and be worried since I passed out before I could send him a progress report on the search. I need to call him."

"The local lines are down because of the storm," she informed him with an apologetic smile. "And the cell phones aren't much better. I tried calling Simon while you were sleeping, but all I picked up was static. It probably won't improve until the weather clears."

And there was no way to know exactly when that was going to happen. "So I guess there's nothing to do but rest."

"And eat," she said. "I wasn't able to get much down you over the last day and a half. Are you hungry? I could make you some soup. It's nothing fancy—just canned chicken noodle—but you need something mild after being so sick."

He would have sworn he wasn't hungry, but at the mere mention of food, his stomach rumbled. Grinning sheepishly, he said, "I guess that answers your question."

Relieved that he was finally willing to eat something, Eliza hurriedly opened a can of soup she'd bought at the small grocery store across the street from the motel, then heated it on the two-burner cooktop in the room's kitchenette. Almost immediately, the scent of the cooking soup filled the room, and her own stomach reminded her that she hadn't eaten much herself over the past thirty-six hours.

Quickly filling a mug for him, she carried it over to the bed. "I thought it would be easier if you sipped it from a mug," she said as she sank down onto the edge of the bed beside him and handed him the thick, old-fashioned coffee mug that she'd found in the cupboard of the kitchenette. "Careful. It's hot."

Not surprisingly, his hands weren't quite steady. Lightning quick, she reached to help him and covered his fingers with hers. And just that quickly, her pulse was skipping. Startled, she told herself to get a grip. She'd been touching the man for the past day and a half. He was sick—he couldn't even hold a cup for himself. Considering that, the last thing she should have been thinking about was what his closeness did to her.

But she couldn't draw a breath without taking in the scent of him. And when her eyes met his as she helped him lift the mug to his mouth, something happened to her heart. It seemed to turn right over in her breast. Time slowed, then stopped altogether. And all she could think of was that they were alone, possibly for days, and all she wanted to do was crawl into bed with him.

The strength of the need caught her by surprise, and given the chance, she would have jumped up from the bed and put as much distance as possible between them. But he needed her help to eat, and she was left with no choice but to hold the mug for him while he sipped the soup. Her hands trembled slightly, but if he noticed, he made no comment.

"Thanks," he said huskily when he finally finished the entire mug of soup. "I hadn't realized I was so shakey."

"You should regain your strength quickly now that your fever's broken and the antibiotics are starting to work," she said stiffly. "By this time tomorrow, you'll probably feel a hundred percent better."

"I hope so," he said, then was caught off guard by a yawn. "How can I be sleepy?" he groaned. "I just woke up!"

"So now you get to sleep again," she retorted, her smile

not quite reaching her eyes. "The more you rest, the quicker you get back on your feet."

When he only scowled, she grinned. "Don't look at me like that, Your Grace. You're human, just like the rest of us, so quit your crying. It's time for a nap."

His royal genes showing, he scowled at her and managed to look just as intimidating as the king did when he wasn't happy, but she was right, and they both knew it. With an irritated sniff, he turned on his side, presenting her his back, and closed his eyes. Within thirty seconds, he was sound asleep.

Afraid she would give in to the need to lie down with him, Eliza hurried over to where she'd set up her computer on the room's only table. She hadn't been able to write anything while he was so sick, and Simon was probably having a fit wondering what was going on. Now that she no longer had to hover over Lorenzo, maybe she could get some work done.

But when she sat down to write, she found her gaze continually going to Lorenzo. He'd rolled over onto his stomach in his sleep and turned his face toward her. How many times had she touched him over the past day and a half? Watched him? She'd been so worried about him that she'd done nothing but sit and stare at him when he was sleeping to make sure he was still breathing. And now that the danger was past, she was still watching.

Did he have any idea just how easy he was on the eye? she wondered, then had to laugh at herself. Of course, he did! She kept abreast of his activities for her column, just as she did the rest of the royal family, and there was no question that he was a favorite with the ladies. He'd been known to date seven different women in as many days, and then there were the groupies. More than a dozen had tried to break into the royal palace over the years just to be with him, and whether he was interested or not, that had to go to a man's head.

He could, no doubt, have any woman in the world he wanted—which made him the last man she wanted to have a crush on. But she couldn't take her eyes off him…or forget the taste of him, the feel of his arms around her. She tried to tell herself it was just because she'd been so concerned about him that she'd gotten used to touching him, caring for him, and it was only natural that she was attracted to him. But then the irritating voice of reason that resided in her head reminded her that he'd kissed her before he'd become sick, and she'd melted at his touch even then.

All right, she reasoned. So she'd let her emotions get out of hand. Being snowed in hadn't helped matters. Once the weather cleared and Lorenzo was back on his feet and they picked up the investigation again, she'd be fine. In the meantime, she had to keep her distance or she was going to find herself in over her head.

To her credit, she tried. Deliberately turning her attention back to her computer, she kept her eyes trained on the screen and didn't once look toward the bed for the next two hours. When he woke up from his nap, she didn't rush over to check to see if his fever had returned, but stayed where she was and tried to make sense of what she'd written. The first paragraph was little more than gibberish, however, and it didn't get much better after that. Groaning, she hit the delete button.

"Problems?" Lorenzo asked quietly from the bed.

"Nothing that can't be fixed," she said shortly, scowling at the screen. "Some days, the words come slower than others."

"You're probably tired after taking care of me," he replied. "Maybe you should take the next couple of days off.

We've been working long hours. A break will do you good.''

She agreed, but that didn't mean she could take any time off. They were snowed in, for heaven's sake! She didn't even want to think what would happen if she didn't have her work to distract her from this crazy attraction she had developed for him. "I can't," she replied. "You don't know Simon. He gets a little paranoid when he doesn't hear from me. Knowing him, he's already called out the national guard. If I don't have more done by the time the phone lines are open, I'm going to be toast.''

She turned her attention back to her computer, and he thankfully let her return to her work and didn't try to continue the conversation. And for a few minutes, she was actually able to string several decent sentences together. Then Lorenzo tried to get out of bed.

"What are you doing?" she cried when he pushed to his feet and stood there swaying like a reed in the wind. Jumping up, she rushed to his side, scolding him all the while. "If you need something, you should have asked me to get it for you. Get back in bed right this minute before you hurt yourself!''

"I need to take a shower," he said, ignoring her, and taking a step toward the bathroom.

If she hadn't been there, he would have fallen flat on his face. He stumbled, then staggered against her, and in the next moment, they were in each other's arms. Startled, they both froze.

How long they stood there, blue eyes staring into green, Eliza couldn't have said. It seemed like seconds, eons. Her heart slamming against her ribs, she should have moved. It would have been the smart thing to do. But there was something in his eyes, a heat, a spark of emotion that seemed to steal the breath right out of her lungs. Transfixed, she couldn't think, couldn't breathe, couldn't look away.

Later, she never remembered when he moved. One second, they were staring at each other like they'd never seen each other before, and the next, his arms were tightening around her, drawing her closer. A heartbeat later, his mouth was on hers.

Her head swimming, Eliza clung to him and felt as if she'd suddenly walked into a dream. He'd kissed her before. She'd thought she'd know what to expect, how he would make her feel. But this was different. This was magic.

Softly, slowly, as if he had all the time in the world, he wooed her with a tender kiss, brushing her mouth with his over and over again and melting her bones one by one. It was sweet, wonderful, and oh, so tempting. Her heart thundering in her breast, she moaned softly and sank into him, aching with need.

Their relationship was about to change forever—she felt it and she knew he did, too. He held her as if he would never let her go, and when she kissed him back hungrily, he groaned and slanted his mouth over hers, taking the kiss deeper, then deeper still.

Holding her, running his hands over her slender curves, he couldn't seem to stop touching her. He'd forgotten how soft she was, how delicate. Her skin felt like rose petals, and when she kissed him like he was the only man in the world, all he wanted to do was pull her down to the bed and make love to her until they were both too weak to move.

Just once, he told himself. But even as he tried to convince himself that once was all it would take to get her out of his system, he realized it was too late for that. He didn't know how it had happened or when, but she stirred something in him that no one ever had. He dreamed of her, ached for her, and in the dead of night, his body gave him away and he reached for her.

Which was why, he decided, he wasn't making love to her today or any other day. But damn, letting her go was the hardest thing he'd ever done! He loved the feel of her, the enticing womanliness of her that she seemed so unaware of. Given the chance, he could have done nothing but hold her for hours...but that would have tempted him past bearing.

So he put her from him abruptly, while he still could, and they both felt the loss. For a long moment, they both just stood there, stunned by what had passed between them. Lorenzo's pride refused to let him be the first to look away, but when she glanced away, he found little satisfaction in the victory. "I have to take a shower," he said huskily, and headed for the bathroom on legs that weren't quite steady. This time, she made no effort to stop him.

How Lorenzo managed to take a shower without losing his balance when he was still weak as a baby, Eliza never knew. Afraid he would fall, she wanted to help him, but she didn't dare. Not after that kiss. Her heart was still pounding like a drum ten minutes later, and that was reason enough to keep her distance.

Still, she couldn't concentrate on her writing as long as he was in the bathroom, so she finally gave up in defeat and just sat there at the table and listened for the sound of him hitting the floor. It never came. Instead, he jerked open the door without warning and caught her staring. "If you're waiting for the shower, it's all yours," he growled. "I'm going back to bed."

Watching him stalk across to the bed, Eliza thought, no man had a right to be so good-looking when he'd just been flat on his back with a fever that morning. It just wasn't fair. The shower had brought some color back to his cheeks, and he'd taken the time to shave. Bare-chested, his pajama bottoms riding low at his waist and his damp hair curling from the shower, he was the stuff fantasies were made of.

Turning his back on her, he crawled into bed, clicked on the television, and proceeded to ignore her. Obviously, he was more than a little irritated with her, she thought, and couldn't imagine why. She wasn't the one who had initiated the kiss or ended it—he was. And now he was sulking like a little boy. Lifting her eyes from her computer to study him quietly, she suddenly found herself fighting a grin. Who would have thought a duke—and the man who had come a heartbeat away from being named heir to the Montebellan throne—would pout?

Amused, she promised herself the day would come when she would tease him about that. In the meantime, she should be thanking him for keeping his head because she certainly hadn't. If he hadn't stopped when he had, they would be in bed together right now, and that thought sobered her as nothing else could. He could steal her heart. From the very beginning, she'd known she was susceptible to him, but she hadn't realized just how vulnerable she was until he'd kissed her the way he had. Something had shifted in the region of her heart, and she didn't think she would ever be quite the same again.

And that shook her to the core. She couldn't allow herself to get any ideas about him. Not now, not ever. He was a duke, for heaven's sake! There was no place for an American reporter in his life.

An unexpected pain squeezed her heart, and she was horrified to feel tears burn her eyes. She never cried! When Robert had walked out on her because she wouldn't quit her job and spend more time with him, she hadn't shed a tear. Growing up, she'd watched her mother fall apart every time she and her father had a fight, and she'd decided she wouldn't be that kind of woman. She was stronger than that, tougher. She wouldn't give anyone the power to reduce her to tears.

Keeping that promise to herself hadn't been all that difficult. Until now. Shaken, she didn't know how Lorenzo had brought her to this with only a few kisses. However he'd done it, he wouldn't do it again, she thought grimly. From now on, their relationship would be strictly professional. Stiffening her spine, she returned her attention to her work. Later, she couldn't have said what she'd written, but she didn't care. Her eyes didn't once stray to Lorenzo.

The rest of the day and the next passed in much the same way. They only spoke to each other when they had to, and when it came time to go to bed, she moved to his room, which was right next door, and slept there. As Lorenzo progressively grew stronger, he didn't need her help to get in and out of bed or to make it across the room to the bathroom, and if he noticed that she didn't rush to help him anymore, he didn't say anything. Telling herself that was fine with her, Eliza refused to acknowledge that she missed those moments when she'd touched him so freely.

Outside, the storm finally blew itself out, but only after dumping a record amount of snowfall all over Colorado. As soon as the highway department trucks were able to start clearing the roads, they were out in full force, but the task the road crews had ahead of them was a daunting one. With so much snow to clear, they couldn't move quickly.

Trapped in two connecting rooms, there was nothing Eliza and Lorenzo could do but wait. It wasn't easy. They were both aware that if the prince was in a more populated area, where the roads were probably cleared first, he could already be on the move…while they sat twiddling their thumbs in small town U.S.A. Impatient, disgusted, they watched TV for reports on the roads and tried to ignore the sense of urgency that pulled at them.

By the time the highway department finally opened the road for travel all the way to the Wyoming state line, the strain of forced confinement was taking its toll. Skirting around each other like two snapping turtles who'd gotten up on the wrong side of the bed, they were barely speaking to each other when they threw their things in the pickup and checked out. Things only went downhill from there.

"With this storm, we're not going to be able to check every wide spot in the road," he said stiffly as he pulled out of the motel parking lot and headed north out of town. "A lot of places will be snowed in for weeks. Our best bet will be to stop at the police department in every town we come to. If a stranger matching Lucas's description has been through there within the past year, the sheriff's probably going to know about it."

Eliza couldn't believe he was serious. "What makes you think that? The sheriff couldn't tell us who was staying at the Barlow place back in Gatesville. Granted, all sheriffs aren't created equal, but Prince Lucas isn't exactly announcing his presence to the authorities. In fact, from where I'm standing, it looks like he's gone out of his way to keep a low profile. He won't go anywhere near the sheriff."

His mouth pressed into a flat line of annoyance. "I think I know Lucas a little bit better than you do," he retorted, staring straight ahead at the walls of trees that lined the highway for miles. "And I am in charge of the investigation. I have to do what I think is best."

He didn't have his nose in the air, but he didn't have to. He'd used that same superior tone when Eliza had first met him, and she didn't like it any better now than she had then. She might write a gossip column, but she wasn't some ditsy bimbo who couldn't find her head from a hole in the ground. He hadn't gotten this far in the investigation by himself—she'd been right there with him every step of the way. She was damn good at what she did, and if he respected nothing else about her, he had to respect her skills as an investigative reporter.

"You do that, Your Grace," she retorted, calling him by his title for the first time in days, "and you're going to drive right by him and not even know it. But don't let me stop you," she said with a sniff, lifting her own nose in the air. "I'm just a lowly peon, far below you in rank—"

"I never said that!"

"Not in so many words, no," she agreed. "But then again, words aren't always necessary, are they? As you just pointed out, this is your investigation."

He didn't deny it. "Yes, it is. Finding Prince Lucas is my responsibility, not yours."

"Then I guess I'm just along for the ride. I'll try not to get in your way. If you want my opinion, I'm sure you'll ask for it."

For a moment, she thought she saw regret flash in his eyes, but he only shrugged and returned his attention to his driving. "That's your choice."

Hurt, she shut up like a clam and looked out the window and watched as they passed one ranch, then another, without ever slowing down. She never said a word.

She didn't, in fact, speak to him for the rest of the day. Whenever they reached a town and he stopped at the sheriff's office and local hospitals, she stood at his side and asked her fair share of questions as the candid picture of the prince was passed around, but she didn't speak to Lorenzo personally. And he didn't seem inclined to speak to her. The set of his jaw getting more rigid as the day went on, he only spoke when it was absolutely necessary.

Later, she couldn't have said how long her silence would have lasted, but Fate stepped in at the end of the day, catching them both off guard when they hit another dead end in another small, one-horse town in the middle of nowhere. There was only one motel in town, and it only had six rooms. When they stepped into the tiny office to see about getting two rooms, the clerk, who had to be eighty if he was a day, shook his head regretfully. "Sorry. I've only got one left."

Startled, Eliza said, "But we need two rooms!"

"Then you'll have to drive to Rosebud, but you're not going to have any better luck there," he warned. "The power company brought in crews from Boulder to repair all the downed lines from the storm, and they've booked every hotel room within a hundred miles. If you want two rooms, you might find them on the other side of Cheyenne, but not here."

Cheyenne was an hour and a half away—there was no way they could drive that distance tonight. Not when they were tired and hungry and just wanted to stop. They exchanged a look and realized they had no choice. "We'll take it," Lorenzo said flatly.

Their room turned out to be little more than a broom closet. The full-size bed took up most of the floor space, leaving only enough room for a walkway around it and a small dresser that held the TV. When Lorenzo stepped inside and she followed him in, they both froze. They wouldn't be able to turn around without bumping into each other. Neither one of them wanted to think about what would happen when they shared the bed.

"It's just for one night," Lorenzo said coolly.

If he wasn't shaken by this, Eliza was determined she

wouldn't be either. ''We're both adults,'' she replied easily. ''I'm sure we can both handle the situation.''

It should have been easy—after all, they were both exhausted and barely even speaking to each other, she reasoned. They'd go to bed, then to sleep, and continue the search tomorrow as if nothing had happened. There was no reason to make a big deal out of it.

For a while, at least, Eliza actually believed that logic would prevail. She was convinced she had her emotions under control, so when he suggested they have dinner together at the family-owned restaurant down the street, she accepted. After all, she had something to prove. She could be as blasé as he.

But when they settled at a table for two at the restaurant and their waitress brought the hamburgers they'd ordered, Eliza couldn't summon up much of an appetite. She found her thoughts straying to later, when Lorenzo would actually slip into bed with her, and her heart started pounding dully. After only three bites, she set her burger down and pushed her plate slightly away.

Lorenzo didn't appear to be any hungrier than she, but he lifted a brow at her. ''Is something wrong with your burger?''

''No, I'm just tired,'' she fibbed. ''It's been a long day.''

''I can ask for a takeout box,'' he offered. ''You can take it back to the room if you like.''

Her heart jumped at the idea of returning to the room early. ''No, that's not necessary,'' she assured him quickly. ''I don't want to ruin your meal. Take your time. There's no hurry.''

He took her at her word and didn't, thankfully, rush, but it only took so much time to eat a hamburger. All too soon, they were headed back to the motel, and Eliza was as nervous as a virgin on her honeymoon. ''I'm going to take a

bath and wash my hair,'' she said the second he followed
her into the tiny room and shut the door. "It could take a
while."

"No problem," he said easily. "I'm going to call the
king and see if I can get through."

He stood across the room from her, yet she could have
reached out and touched him. And he would be even closer
when they crawled into bed together. Her mouth going dry
at the thought, she said hoarsely, "Then I'll just get my
things and give you some privacy."

In the time it took to blink, she grabbed her nightgown
and robe and hurried into the bathroom. Her heart pounding
crazily, she told herself she was acting like an idiot, but
there didn't seem to be anything she could do about it.
Filling the tub, she slipped into the steaming water and
began to wash her hair.

She'd warned him she would be a while, and she hadn't
been kidding. After she'd washed and rinsed her hair, she
lounged in the hot water until it cooled, soaking away her
tension. Then she painted her toenails and waited for her
hair to dry. It wasn't until she found herself applying her
favorite scented lotion all over her body that she realized
that Lorenzo might think she was going to all that trouble
for him.

Mortified, she groaned. She always put lotion on after a
bath—she did it without even thinking about it—but Lorenzo had no way of knowing that. They'd never shared a
room before. And there was nothing she could do about it
now. Except take another bath, and that seemed a little
ridiculous. If he got any ideas, she'd just explain that her
bath habits had nothing to do with him.

Confident that she had it all worked out, she pulled on
her gown and robe, then drew in a calming breath. When
she opened the bathroom door, she wanted to think she

looked cool and collected. Inside, however, her nerves were in a knot, and if Lorenzo had listened carefully, he would have heard her knees knocking.

She needn't have worried that he'd noticed. He'd finished his phone call, and even though he'd told her to take her time, she had taken far too long and he was obviously waiting. "Sorry," she mumbled.

"No problem," he assured her, and stepped around her to get to the bathroom. A split second after he shut the door, the shower sprang on, and with a muttered curse, Eliza quickly slipped out of her robe and crawled into bed. If she planned to be asleep before he came to bed, she didn't have any time to waste. Her heart thumping crazily, she switched off the light on her side of the bed, which was farthest from the bathroom, and turned her back on the rest of the room.

Sleep was, of course, impossible. Her nerves wound tighter than a broken clock, she lay as stiff as a board and listened for the shower to go off. When it did, her heart stopped dead in her chest.

Later, she knew she was going to laugh about this. She was twenty-seven years old, for heaven's sake, not sixteen! There was no reason to be acting like this. Lorenzo was a duke and a gentleman. He wasn't going to force himself on her.

Not that she'd ever thought he would, she quickly assured herself. He wasn't that kind of man. No, the problem wasn't Lorenzo. It was her own desire.

Shocked by the direction of her thoughts, she should have gotten out of bed right then and there and made a pallet on the floor. But it was too late for that. Before she could move, the bathroom door was jerked open and the scent of him drifted to her nostrils, teasing her senses. The bed sank down behind her, and in the next instant, he turned off the light on his side of the bed, plunging the room into darkness and stealing her breath at one and the same time.

In the hushed silence, Eliza was sure he had to hear the thundering of her heart. It was loud enough to wake the dead and she felt like it was going to pound right out of her chest. But if he heard it, he gave no sign of it. He sighed and turned over into a more comfortable position. A moment later, he relaxed and seemed to drift easily into sleep.

Her every nerve ending on alert, Eliza couldn't have said later how long she lay there, not daring to move so much as a muscle. It could have been just minutes—it felt like hours. She was convinced she'd never be able to relax enough to fall asleep, but it had been a long day and she was tired. The tension gripping her slowly eased, and with a soft sigh, she, too, shifted into a more comfortable position. A heartbeat later, she was out like a light.

Beside her, Lorenzo knew the minute she fell asleep. Keeping his head turned away from her, he didn't dare turn toward her. When she'd stepped out of the bathroom in a baby-blue flannel robe and gown, he'd taken one look at her and forgotten his own name. With her face bare of makeup, her red hair curling damply around her shoulders, and the clean fresh scent of lotion teasing his senses, she'd never looked more beautiful. He'd known then, even as he hurried past her to take a cold shower, that it was going to be a long night, and he'd been right. Lying beside her, sharing the bed that was hardly bigger than a sardine can, was much, much worse than he'd anticipated. All he wanted to do was reach for her. He didn't dare.

Silently swallowing a groan, he resigned himself to staying awake all night. If there'd been a chair to sit in, he would have gladly taken it rather than the bed, but the room was sadly lacking in amenities. The only place to sit—or lie—was the bed. Deliberately, he forced his thoughts away from Eliza and the sweet sound of her breathing to the sound of the television next door. If he listened carefully, he could hear every word and sound effect of the first *Star Wars* movie.

Concentrating on the audio to the movie, he never knew when he fell asleep. One moment, he was listening to the sounds of a battle in space and the next, he was asleep. When he woke hours later, the TV next door had been turned off and Eliza was in his arms.

Somewhere in the back of his brain, an alarm bell rang, but he never heard it. Every thought, every nerve ending, every one of his senses was focused on Eliza. It seemed like he'd been waiting forever to hold her like this, and he hadn't even known it until now. Snuggled against him, her breath a soft caress against his neck, she felt like a dream in his arms. Closing his eyes, he drew in the womanly scent of her and slowly ran his hands over her, learning her curves, the dips and valleys, every sensuous line of her body. And with each stroke, each touch, each caress, he slowly went out of his mind.

A wise man would have known when to stop, and he'd always considered himself smart when it came to women. But surrounded by the darkness, the real world seemed very far away, and he couldn't see the harm. Not when she felt so wonderful in his arms. Need fisting his gut, he ached to kiss her. Giving in to impulse, he leaned down and found her mouth in the dark.

Dreaming of Lorenzo making love to her, Eliza sighed in her sleep and pressed close, her body sweetly humming at his kiss. He had wonderful hands, she thought sleepily. He knew just how to touch her to make her float.

Then his fingers brushed her breast and lingered, gently

cupping her through her gown, and she abruptly came awake to discover this was no dream. "Lorenzo!"

"Make love with me," he rasped softly, tightening his arms around her and coaxing her with a long, drugging kiss. "Feel what you do to me. Don't say no."

Her body already crying out for his, she couldn't find the strength to say no. Not this time. Not when she ached for him, longed for him, with every fiber of her being. Cocooned in darkness, they were the only two people in the world, and when he reached for the buttons to her gown, then swept it over her head even as she tugged at his pajama bottoms, nothing had ever felt so right.

With a murmur of need, she surged back into his arms, loving the hard, lean, muscular length of his body against hers. Skin to skin, mouth to mouth, they moved together, always touching, exploring, teasing each other until they were both breathless. And with each caress, each slow stroke of hands and mouth and tongue, the fire that burned between them only blazed hotter.

Her breath tearing through her lungs and her heart racing, Eliza hadn't been able to stop herself from imagining more than once what it would be like to make love to him. From the few times he'd kissed her, she'd known he was a sensuous man—he would know how to pleasure a woman. But she hadn't expected such…caring. She felt it in the gentleness of his touch, tasted it in the passion of his kiss. And it destroyed her.

"Lorenzo!"

"I know, sweetheart," he groaned when the need he'd built in her threatened to consume her. "Just let go. It's all right. I've got you."

Kissing her again, he surged into her, filling her, and just that easily, he pushed her over the edge. With a cry, she shattered.

Feeling her come undone beneath him, Lorenzo groaned. No woman had ever matched his passion so perfectly. She moved, drawing him closer, and that was all it took to destroy what was left of his control. Burying his face against her neck, he pressed his mouth to the sweet pulse that pounded there and lost himself in her.

Chapter 9

Eliza woke the next morning to the sound of Lorenzo shaving in the bathroom. Regret sinking in her stomach like a lead weight, she buried herself in her pillow and groaned. She'd lost her mind last night. That was the only explanation. Lorenzo had touched her, kissed her, and every ounce of common sense she possessed had flown right out the window.

How could she have been so stupid? she wondered. He was a duke, for heaven's sake! Royalty! He rubbed shoulders not only with his famous relatives, but every other royal family in Europe. He'd been to Monaco and Buckingham Palace and dined with the president! She didn't even want to think about the famous women he'd dated—movies stars and models and the daughters of tycoons. What would a man like that want with a woman like her?

Granted, she reasoned, he had made love to her. But she refused to let herself hope that that meant something. The search had thrown them together for days now and there was no doubt that there was a spark of attraction between them. Considering that, it was only natural that they turn to each other in the middle of the night.

But all they'd shared was sex, she told herself firmly. That's all it could be, all it was ever going to be. As a little girl, living in the tiny town of Deer Creek, Colorado, she'd dreamed of kings and queens and castles in the air. She did not, however, live in a fairy tale. Her feet were firmly grounded in reality, and she knew it was only a matter of time before Lorenzo returned to Montebello. When he did, he wouldn't take her with him. He wouldn't marry her. He wouldn't even have a relationship with her after their quest for Prince Lucas came to an end. He might be attracted to her now, but when it came to having a serious relationship, he would chose a blue blood, a woman whose background was similar to his, someone who lived the life of a royal and didn't just write about it.

She should have remembered that last night. She wouldn't forget it again.

The electric razor abruptly went silent in the bathroom, and she realized suddenly that he was going to step into the bedroom any second and find her still lying in bed like she was waiting for him. Horrified, she jumped up and grabbed her robe, and not a second too soon. He opened the bathroom door just as she finished belting her robe. Startled, they both froze, and when their eyes locked, every touch, every kiss, every memory of the night was there between them.

Her heart pounding, Eliza hadn't meant to even speak about the hours they'd spent in each other's arms. The sooner she was able to put it out of her mind, the better. But the second her gaze met his, she knew that she wasn't going to be able to pretend that last night never happened. Everything had changed between them—she could feel it in her heart and see it in his eyes. If she didn't do something right now to turn back the clock to yesterday, she was going to find herself back in his arms again...and back in his bed. And when he returned to Montebello, she'd be left with a broken heart.

She couldn't let him do that to her, she thought, hugging herself. He wasn't Robert. He had touched her in a way no one ever had. He could make her cry.

"We need to talk," she blurted out. "About last night."

Lorenzo couldn't have agreed more. He'd thought he could control the need she stirred in him, but he'd thought wrong. When he'd woken with the sun to find her in his arms, all he'd wanted to do was kiss her awake and make love to her all over again.

For the life of him, he didn't know how she'd done it. He wasn't one of those men who took every woman he dated to bed, but he'd made love to his fair share of women over the years, and there was always a part of his heart that he'd kept in reserve...until last night. She'd lit a passion in him unlike anything he'd ever known before, and hours later, he was still reeling from it.

"All right," he said quietly. "What about last night?"

He had to give her credit. Obviously this wasn't easy for her, but she didn't beat around the bush. Instead, she looked him right in the eye and said, "It was a mistake. It can't happen again."

He should have been relieved. He didn't want her or any other woman messing with his emotions. He'd been there and done that in the past, and he didn't care to repeat the experience. Oh, one of these days, he supposed he would fall in love again, but not now. Right now, he was committed to finding Lucas, and he didn't have a clue how long that would take. Before it was all said and done, the search could take him just about anywhere, and there was a good possibility that Eliza could be with him every step of the way. Considering that, getting romantically involved with her could turn into a disaster. It was better if their relationship remained strictly professional.

Knowing that, however, and having the woman who had rocked him back on his heels admit that she didn't want to repeat the experience were two different things. Right or wrong, what they'd shared last night had been incredible, and having it classified as a mistake stung his ego...and his heart. And he didn't like the feeling at all.

For no other reason than that, he told himself he was grateful to her. If he needed an excuse to back off, she'd just given it to him.

"I agree," he said coolly. "I'll make sure it doesn't happen again." By never touching her or kissing her again, he silently vowed. Then he wouldn't be tempted.

Eliza should have been relieved. This was what she wanted—a strictly platonic relationship—and he didn't seem to have a problem with that. So why did she suddenly feel so hurt? He'd only agreed to what she'd insisted on.

Confused, the crazy urge to cry again stinging her eyes, she stiffened her spine and quickly changed the subject. "Good. Now that we've got that settled, I need to get dressed and call Simon, then we can get to work."

"When we checked in, I saw a sign in the office that said there is fresh coffee and doughnuts in the lobby until ten o'clock each morning. I'll go get us some."

He was gone before Eliza could tell him she wasn't hungry, but she couldn't complain. Taking advantage of the privacy, she quickly called Simon.

"Well, it's about damn time!" he growled the minute he recognized her voice on the other end of the line. "Where the hell are you?"

"Still looking for my prince," she said sweetly. "I had

a few minutes, so I thought I'd call and check in. Did you get the e-mail with my column?''

She would have sworn she sounded like her usual self, but something in her tone must have given her away. ''The column was great,'' he assured her. ''Now tell me about you. What's wrong?''

''Nothing!''

''Yeah, right. You might be able to fool that duke you're running around with, but personally, I'm not buying it. What's wrong, Eliza?''

If he just hadn't called her by her name, she might have been able to shrug off his questions and change the subject. She could handle the Simon who was as rough as a corn cob on the outside. But when he let down his guard and showed his softer, caring side her defenses crumbled every time.

''It's nothing I can't handle,'' she said quietly.

''It's the duke, isn't it?''

She should have known she couldn't keep anything from him—he'd always been as sharp as a tack—and her silence told him everything he needed to know. ''I knew it,'' he growled. ''You fell for him, didn't you?''

''I did not!''

She might as well have saved her breath. ''Dammit, Red, what were you thinking? He's a duke! A damn blue blood, for God's sake! He probably sleeps on silk sheets and has a butler who lays his clothes out for him every morning!''

Eliza had to laugh at that. Somehow, she just couldn't see Lorenzo letting anyone pick out his clothes for him. ''He's a military hero in Montebello, not some namby-pamby duke who has a houseful of servants to cater to his every whim.''

''Oh, that's going to make me sleep better tonight,'' he retorted sarcastically. ''Didn't anyone ever tell you you have to watch the war heroes? They're the worse ones. They go through women like Sherman through Georgia.''

Fighting a tremulous smile, Eliza felt the sting of tears in her eyes and was thankful he couldn't see her—he'd be shocked that she'd turned into such a crybaby. ''I'll try to remember that,'' she said huskily. ''But just for the record, I haven't fallen for him.''

''See that you don't,'' he said gruffly. ''He'll break your heart and that'll sour you on the royals, and then what good will you be to me? I need a columnist, dammit, and you're the best one around!''

Grinning, she wasn't surprised that sentiment gave way to the bottom line—the newspaper. With Simon, every subject always came back to the paper and the next day's edition. ''Nothing's going to interfere with my writing, La-Gree, so don't lose any sleep over that. I'll be in touch.'' She was still chuckling when she hung up.

When Lorenzo returned with coffee and doughnuts, neither of them had much appetite. Making quick work of the abbreviated breakfast, they checked out of the motel ten minutes later and once again, they began the search. And just as Lorenzo had promised himself, he didn't touch her again, let alone kiss her.

He should have been pleased with himself. But keeping his mind on his work wasn't easy. Every time they stopped to question local residents about strangers coming through town over the course of the past year, he couldn't help but admire her skill in working with people. Damn, she was good! She pulled information out of them they didn't even know they had, learning where abandoned houses and barns were in the area and who the local busybody was who kept track of everyone who passed through town. Every town had one, and Lorenzo wouldn't have even thought to search

out such a person. But she did, and even though Mildred
Hinkle, the old woman who was the town's biggest gossip,
couldn't give them any concrete information they could
use, Lorenzo couldn't find the strength to worry that they'd
run into another dead end. He couldn't take his eyes off
Eliza.

She had a way of smiling that just turned him inside out.
And she wasn't even looking at him! She chatted with old
lady Hinkle like they'd known each other all their lives and
didn't even seem to know he was in the same room. And
he didn't care because he could watch her to his heart's
content. Lord, she was beautiful! He only had to look at
her to remember the feel of her skin under his hands and
mouth....

Suddenly realizing where his thoughts had wandered, he
tried to reel them back in, but he was fighting a losing
battle. He couldn't forget last night, couldn't forget what it
was like to hold her and kiss her and make love to her until
he was too weak to move. He wanted her. More than he
had before he'd made love to her. And there wasn't a damn
thing he could do about it. He'd promised himself he
wouldn't touch her.

And it was driving him slowly out of his mind.

How he got through the rest of the day without reaching
for her, he never knew. They didn't talk about anything but
the prince and where to take the search from there. She
made no reference to last night, and unlike him, she appeared to have put it out of her mind completely. She didn't
brush up against him, didn't sit too close to him in the
truck, didn't give him so much as a single intimate look.
And that only made him want her more.

By the time they stopped for the night and once again
found another motel, he didn't know if he wanted to shake
her or kiss her. Thankfully, he didn't have a chance to do

either. There was no shortage of rooms at the Pine Tree Motel. They wouldn't be sharing a room tonight.

"You go ahead," he said huskily when she suggested they share a pizza at the pizza parlor across the street. "I'm not really hungry. I was thinking about turning in early."

Not sure if she was relieved or disappointed that he wouldn't be joining her, Eliza forced a smile. "Then I guess I'll order a small and bring it back to my room so I can work while I eat. If you change your mind, there will be plenty."

He wasn't going to change his mind and they both knew it, and that was probably for the best, Eliza told herself as she wished him good-night. Everything had changed between them last night. She'd had to fight the need to move closer to him all day, and as she carried her luggage into her room and he headed to his own room six doors down, she couldn't believe how much she already missed him. She wanted to call him back before he shut the door, closing her out for the night, but she did have some pride. If he didn't want to be with her, she certainly wasn't going to push herself on him.

But as she shut the door to her own room, she'd never been lonelier in her life. The room could have been in any small town in America and had little to recommend it other than cleanliness. But it wouldn't have mattered if it had had a Jacuzzi hot tub and a big screen TV with Surround Sound technology, she still would have had little interest in the place. All she could see was the bed…and remember last night.

Her appetite now non-existent, she decided to skip dinner altogether and have a bath instead. But thirty minutes later, after a long, leisurely soak, she dreaded the thought of crawling into bed alone. If she was able to sleep at all— and that was highly doubtful—she knew she would dream of Lorenzo, and she didn't think she could take that right now. So she grabbed her computer, instead, and set it up on the small table in the corner. An hour later, she finished adding the last of her notes to her file on the search for the prince. Then she switched her attention to the novel she was secretly writing. Long after the clock on the bedside table had struck midnight, she was still working. At that point, she would have worked on her grocery list if it would have kept her out of that lonely bed.

"I think we've lost him."

Climbing back into the truck after talking to everyone they could think of in another small town they couldn't even remember the name of, Lorenzo swore softly. Once again, they'd struck out and hit a dead end. Normally, he wouldn't have let that bother him. They'd run into a lot of dead ends since they'd begun searching for Lucas—one more was nothing new. If they drove farther down the road, they'd probably run into someone who had a vague recollection of someone matching Lucas's picture passing through town last year. They just had to be patient.

But they'd been patient for the past three days, and they had nothing to show for it. And it was getting damn frustrating. Up until three days ago, he'd been convinced that Lucas was still heading north. Now he wasn't so sure.

Reading his thoughts, Eliza said, "Do you think he might have headed west, instead? Or have we just missed him? Considering how much territory we're covering, it would be easy to do."

She had a point. Until now, the search had been limited to the small towns and villages on the state highway that Lucas had stumbled across after he'd left the campsite where Willy had found his scarf. Since they'd obviously lost his trail, he'd turned off the highway somewhere. The question was...where?

"After going north all this time, I can't imagine why he would suddenly change course," he said as he started the truck and headed out of town. "It's not like he came to the end of the road and had to go another direction."

"Maybe we haven't missed him at all then. If he was hitchhiking and caught a ride with a long-distance trucker, he could be in Montana, for all we know. We just haven't caught up with him yet."

"If he stayed on this road," he pointed out. "If he went along for the ride with someone, he could be in Key West, Florida. Until we pick up his trail again, there's no way to know for sure."

If they picked up his trail.

Eliza didn't say the words out loud, but she didn't doubt that he heard them, nonetheless. And she was just as worried as he was. They had to find the prince's trail soon, or she was going to be in serious trouble. She wasn't on vacation—she had a job to do, and up until now, Simon had been filling her column with backup material she kept on hand for just such an occasion. But that was running out, and Simon's patience wasn't inexhaustible. If the prince wasn't found soon, he would start pressing her for facts about the search to tantalize the readers. He would want headline material, evidence he could splash across the front page that Prince Lucas really was out there somewhere, lost in the mountains of Colorado, and right now, she wasn't giving him that. She couldn't. Not without blowing her exclusive and putting the prince in danger.

And then there was Deborah to worry about. She would be back from California by now and was, no doubt, already whispering in her daddy's ear that she could have found Prince Lucas if she'd just been given the chance.

Eliza could just hear the little blond bimbo now. *She's costing the paper money, Daddy. While she's out running up and down the highway with a duke, the Gazette is eating our lunch with real news stories. Fire her, Daddy. You know I can do her job. I was born in this business. I've got your blood in my veins.*

Fuming, Eliza almost called Simon to tell him she was doing everything she could, but her common sense assured her that wasn't necessary. He wasn't any happier about having to baby-sit the owner's ditsy daughter than she was. He tolerated her because he had to, but he didn't have any problems standing up to little Miss Muffet. He'd distract her with other assignments and do everything he could to protect Eliza's job for her.

Time, however, was running out and she knew it. If they didn't find the prince soon, she would have to return to Denver and let Lorenzo continue the search without her.

When her heart lurched at the idea of returning to the paper, she tried to tell herself she hated to give up the story and go home empty-handed. But she wasn't fooling anyone, least of all herself. For the first time in her life, she didn't care two cents about a story. It was Lorenzo she didn't want to give up.

"So what do you think?"

Caught up in her thoughts, she blinked. "About what?"

For the first time in days, a smile curled the corners of Lorenzo's mouth. "Obviously, I lost you for a few minutes."

"Sorry," she said, wrinkling her nose. "I was thinking about...work."

"So was I," he replied. "I know it might be a waste of time, but I don't like to change the course of an investigation until I'm sure I've checked everything. I think we should continue heading north for the rest of the day."

"And if we don't pick up the prince's trail again?"

"Then we backtrack to where we lost him and start over again, this time in a different direction."

That, unfortunately, would take more time than she had to give before it could possibly yield results, but that wasn't his problem. "I agree," she said, and didn't have a clue how she managed such a cool tone when her heart was breaking. "After all this time, one more day's not going to make that much difference and you want to cover your bases."

So it was decided. They headed north, and Lorenzo didn't have a clue that this would be the last day they spent together if they weren't able to pick up the prince's trail. And it was better that way. If she had to leave, she didn't want any long goodbyes.

As they passed through one small town after another, they left no stone unturned. They questioned everyone they came into contact with, from gas station attendants to grocery store clerks to a group of old men who met at one town's local café every afternoon for coffee and gossip. They even visited hospitals and doctors' offices in case Prince Lucas had sought out medical attention. But no one remembered anyone passing through town who matched the prince's description.

Always the optimist, Eliza tried to hold out hope that they would get a break, but as the day wore on, it became more and more obvious that that wasn't likely to happen. One town gave way to another, then another, and they were left with no choice but to keep going north.

By the time they reached the small town of Shady Rock, the sun had already sunk behind the mountains and early twilight was quickly darkening the winter sky. Tired, discouraged and sick at heart, Eliza said, "It looks like this is the end of the road."

"We tried," he said simply. "Let's check out the businesses that are still open, then find a place to stay."

The town, such as it was, appeared to be already closing up for the night, but a few of the shops and offices that lined the main street were still open. Knowing they were running out of time, they parked and quickly split up so they could cover more territory.

"I'll take the west side of the street," she said, and hurried across to the small dress shop on the corner.

The bell on the glass door rang merrily as she stepped inside, drawing the attention of the older woman who was just closing out the cash register at the old-fashioned counter. Glancing up with a friendly smile, she said, "Good afternoon. Come on in. Is there something I can help you with?"

"I hope so," Eliza replied, returning her smile. "I'm looking for my brother." Giving her the story she and Lorenzo had come up with, she added, "I know he was probably in Valley View last winter, but I lost track of him after that. I was hoping he might have come through Shady Rock."

Pushing her glasses farther up her pert nose, the clerk frowned. "Well, let me think, dear. My memory's not what it used to be, but I'm not senile yet. Well, not completely, anyway," she added with twinkling eyes. "Oh, by the way, I'm Sally Tucker. And you are?"

"Uh…Carol. Carol Jones," Eliza said, improvising.

Smiling, Sally confided, "I enjoy talking with people much more when I know their name. Now…what does this brother of yours look like?"

"He's six foot two, athletic, with dark brown hair and blue eyes," she replied promptly, then grinned as she embellished the story. "He's my big brother—I always thought he was a pain—but my girlfriends thought he was a hunk. If you ever saw him, you wouldn't forget him. He looks like Prince Charming.''

That wasn't far from the truth, and for a moment, Eliza was afraid she'd gone too far and the older woman had connected the missing Prince Lucas with the missing "brother" she was looking for. She frowned consideringly, then she said, "You know, it seems like I do remember hearing that someone like that passed through town some time back.''

Already focusing on what she was going to say if the clerk asked her if she was looking for Prince Lucas, it was a long moment before Eliza actually heard her. When she did, her heart stopped in midbeat. "I beg your pardon?''

"I didn't see him myself," she warned her, "but Charlie Johnson's wife, Mary, was in here one day buying a new dress for church, and she kept going on and on about a man who'd come into her husband's store looking for work. She said if she'd been twenty years younger and thirty pounds lighter, she would have gone after him in a heart-beat...Charlie or no Charlie. Not that anyone believed her," she chuckled. "Everybody in town knows she thinks Charlie hung the moon.''

"What about the man she was talking about?" Eliza said hoarsely. "Did he find a job?''

"I don't know," she replied with a shrug. "I never did hear.''

Her heart pounding, she just barely swallowed a groan. "What about the woman you mentioned...Mary Johnson? Would she know? Where can I find her?''

"She's in Cheyenne right now, visiting her daughter, who just had a baby, but Charlie's the one you need to talk to." Glancing at the clock on the wall, she said, "His hard-ware store is just three doors down and he doesn't close until six. You should be able to still catch him if you hurry.''

Thrilled, Eliza impulsively hugged her. "Thank you *so* much, Sally! You don't know what this means to me!''

Laughing the older woman returned the embrace. "I hope it helps. Now, go on with you. You don't want to miss Charlie.''

She didn't need to say more. Promising herself she would come back to get her story—she was a wonderful character for her column feature—Eliza rushed outside.

Johnson's hardware store was right where Sally had told her it was, and the open sign was still in the window. Every nerve ending in her body tingling with excitement, Eliza cautioned herself not to find a place on her bookcase at home yet for her Pulitzer—this could all be a mistake. Sally had good intentions, but she didn't actually see the man Mary Johnson had raved about. It might not be the prince at all.

Her common sense accepted that, but her heart wanted nothing to do with logic. Already writing the story in her head, she pulled open the door to Charlie Johnson's hardware store and hurried inside.

If circumstances had been different and there was no prince to look for, no duke she was trying to keep in her life, Eliza could have spent hours in Johnson's hardware store. It was the kind of place that looked like it had been there for a century or longer. The wooden floors were scarred from years of abuse from booted feet, and the shelves that stretched up the walls to the twenty-foot ceilings were crowded with every conceivable tool and nail and pipe known to mankind. The place even smelled old.

But time was running out, and she was on a quest. Seeing no one at the front counter, she called out, "Hello? Is anyone here?''

"Back here!" a male voice called from the storeroom at the back of the store, and a few seconds later, a middle-aged man stepped through the open doorway. "Sorry to keep you waiting," he said with an easy smile. "I was just checking some inventory. What can I do for you, ma'am?"

"Actually, Sally Tucker suggested I talk to you. I'm looking for my brother—he may have passed through town a few months ago." Quickly giving him the made-up story of her lost brother, she said, "Sally thought he might have come in here looking for a job. He's tall, with dark hair and blue eyes. Here—I have a picture." Quickly digging it out of her purse, she handed it to him.

Not nearly as talkative as the dress shop clerk, Charlie frowned consideringly at the picture, and Eliza felt her hopes sink. Maybe Sally was wrong, after all. "I believe your wife was the one who told Sally about him," she added, trying to jog his memory. "Apparently, she thought he was the best-looking thing since Clark Gable, which is why I thought the man might have been my brother. He has that effect on people. He's really good-looking."

"Oh, yeah!" he said, a huge grin transforming his face as recognition hit him. "I remember! That was quite a while back. I didn't recognize him without the beard. He's a good-looking kid. Mary took one look at him and threatened to trade me in for a new model. I sent him out to the Chambers ranch. They were short on ranch hands at the time."

This was it! Eliza thought excitedly. She could feel it in her bones, and her bones never let her down! "So he got the job? Is he still working there? How do I get to the Chambers' place? I've got to find my brother!"

"Whoa, girl!" he laughed. "Don't go off half-cocked just yet. He got the job. He was in here last month collecting supplies. But you can't go driving out there tonight.

You'll never find it in the dark. The ranch entrance is set back from the road and hard to see if you don't know where to look for it.''

"Then I'll call—"

"Can't," he said with a shake of his head. "The telephone lines are still down out that way from the storm. They probably won't be fixed for another week or more."

Stuck, Eliza swallowed a groan. She couldn't believe this was happening! After the days and days of searching, they finally had a lead, and they couldn't follow up on it until morning! Resigned, she forced a crooked smile. "I guess I sound a little impatient, don't I? It's just that I've been so worried."

"Of course you have," he retorted. "He's your brother. But at least you know where he is now. He'll still be there in the morning. Here, let me write out the directions for you, then you can get a room at the Eagle's Nest Motel for the night, and drive out to the Chambers' place in the morning. Just remember to take it slow and easy or you'll miss the turn off."

"I will," she promised, carefully tucking the sheet of paper he'd written the directions on into her purse. "Thank you so much! I can't tell you how much this means to me!"

"No thanks are necessary," he said with a chuckle. "If this fella's really your brother, then I'm happy to help. Now get down to the Eagle's Nest and get you a room before they're all rented out. There's a dance in town tonight, and a lot of the ranchers in the area rent a room rather than drive back home when it's over."

He didn't have to tell her twice. "Then I'd better find the Eagle's Nest," she replied with a smile and hurried out to find Lorenzo.

She didn't have to look far for him. He'd already checked all the businesses on the east side of the street and had crossed to find her. "Well?" he asked as he approached her in the thickening twilight. "I struck out again. What about you? Did you have any luck?"

"As a matter of fact, I did," she said with a sassy grin. And with no more warning than that, she threw herself into his arms. "Oh, Lorenzo, I think I've found him!"

Giving him a fierce hug, she pulled back, so excited she couldn't stand still. "I can't believe it! Mr. Johnson, the owner of the hardware store, recognized him from his picture. He said he's working at the Chambers ranch. He was in town just last month for supplies."

"Let's go, then," he said and quickly took her arm to hurry her back to the truck. "Did you get directions? Was this Johnson character sure it was Lucas? What did he say about him? Is he all right?"

"He couldn't really tell me too much—just what I told you—but he was positive it was him," she said breathlessly as she hurried to keep pace with his long legs. "The only problem is we can't go out there tonight. Mr. Johnson said we'd never find it in the dark."

Stopping in his tracks, Lorenzo swore. "Damn! Are you sure? This is the first break we've had. I hate to wait."

"I know, but from the way Mr. Johnson described the entrance to the ranch, we really need to go during the day or we'd drive right past it. And we may not need to go out there at all," she said with a smile. "There's a dance tonight, and apparently all the ranchers in the area come into town for it. Who knows? We might just see Prince Lucas there."

"So you think we should go to this dance?"

"It wouldn't hurt," she said with a shrug. "We can check it out, see if he's there, and celebrate the end of the search. Because it's him, Lorenzo. He has a beard now, but

Mr. Johnson was sure it was him. We've finally found him!''

Lorenzo wouldn't believe it until he saw his cousin with his own two eyes, but he had to agree with Eliza. They had a positive picture I.D.! All their hard work and endless searching was about to pay off. "I'm not calling the king until I know for sure, but I think you're right. Lucas is close by."

"Then you'll go to the dance?"

Grinning, he nodded. "We could both use the break. And if Lucas isn't there himself, there might be other ranchers there who've seen him around."

"Then we'd better get over to the Eagle's Nest Motel and see about getting us each a room before they sell out. According to Mr. Johnson, they'll be in short supply tonight because of the dance."

She didn't have to say any more. Taking her arm, Lorenzo rushed her back to the truck.

Chapter 10

The Eagle's Nest was one of those small travel courts that had been built in the late forties and never progressed much beyond that. Carports separated the rooms, the bathrooms were all pink tile and the furniture was, amazingly, made of real wood. Separated from Lorenzo's room by their connecting carport, Eliza stepped inside her room and couldn't help but be charmed. She felt like she'd stepped back in time.

"I'll pick you up at seven," Lorenzo said as he carried her bag inside for her. "Unless you want to get something to eat beforehand."

"Oh, no," she said, her mind already jumping to what she had to wear. "We can get something later. I'll see you at seven."

Standing right where he was, Lorenzo lifted a brow at her in amusement. "Why do I have the feeling you're trying to get rid of me?"

"Because I am," she retorted, grinning at him. "I can't

remember the last time I went to a dance. I have to get ready.''

They both knew the dance would be a casual one—they could probably both go as they were, in their jeans and long-sleeved western shirts, and no one would look twice at them. But Eliza was as excited as a teenager who'd been invited to her first junior high dance, and Lorenzo had never seen her that way. She didn't have a clue how cute she looked.

''Then I guess I'll make myself scarce,'' he said with a grin. Giving in to impulse, he trailed a caressing finger over the curve of her cheek. ''See you later.''

It was the first time he'd touched her in days. Her body humming, Eliza pressed a hand to her cheek and couldn't have said how long she stood there, remembering the night they'd made love and her entire life had changed. Then she remembered the dance. She was wasting time.

Quickly grabbing the phone book and phone, she found the number to Sally's Dress Shop and punched in the number, praying all the while. ''Please be there. I need your help.''

She'd just about given up hope and was about to hang up when the dress shop owner suddenly answered the phone. ''Sally's,'' she said breathlessly. ''May I help you?''

''Sally! This is…um, Carol. I just talked to you about my brother…''

''Yes, dear, I remember. Was Charlie able to help you?''

''As a matter of fact, he was.'' Quickly giving her a rundown of what the hardware store owner had told her, she said, ''I know in my heart that my brother is at the Chambers ranch, but I can't drive out there until the morning. In the meantime, I need your help again. I was thinking about going to the dance at the VFW hall tonight, but I don't have a dress.''

"Then you called the right person. I was just about to walk out the door, but I don't have anything pressing to do at home except watch the evening news. C'mon over. I'd love to help you find a dress.''

"I'll be right there," Eliza promised and hung up.

She walked to the dress shop—it was only two blocks— and arrived to find Sally waiting for her. Grinning like a co-conspirator who'd just successfully robbed a bank, the older woman unlocked the door, glanced up and down the street, then motioned her inside. "This is going to be so much fun! So tell me what you want? Something long? Short? Frilly? Come and look! I have just the color for you."

Pulling her over to a rack where a dozen dresses of every conceivable color hung, she didn't wait for Eliza to pick out a dress, but chose one for her instead. "This is it," she said softly. "Trust me. You'll look beautiful in it."

Eliza took one look and hesitated. It wasn't the kind of dress she ever would have chosen for herself. First, it was red, and she never wore red—it always clashed with her hair. And the material was some kind of soft, clingy material that would hug her figure and make her look even thinner than she was. "Oh, I don't know, Sally. I was thinking of something more tailored. And I'm not sure about the color."

"I am," the older woman said, her smile understanding, "but we'll pick out some other things and you can try them all on and see which one you like best. Now how about this? You like blue, don't you? It goes beautifully with your eyes."

They made a whirlwind trip through the store, picking out a half-dozen dresses in six different colors and styles, then Sally rushed her to the dressing room. "You'll need shoes to match, and something for your hair. Oh, the blue is nice on you, dear. What do you think?"

Studying herself in the full-length mirror of the dressing room, Eliza frowned. It was a nice dress, but it was similar to something she had bought last year. This was her last night with Lorenzo and the only chance she would have to go out with him on a real live date. She wanted something special. This wasn't it.

"It's okay," she said with a shrug, "but not quite what I'm looking for. Let's try the green next."

One by one, she tried one dress after another, all except the red, and although they were all pretty, she didn't think any of them were eye-catching. And Sally knew it. Grinning, she didn't say a word, but simply held out the red dress to her.

"All right," she sighed, "I'll try it. But it's a waste of time."

Turning her back to the mirror, she stepped into the garment and pulled it up, smoothing the soft material over her hips as Sally zipped it for her. It did have a wonderful feel to it, she thought. If only it wasn't red! "I love the way it fits over my hips," she told Sally as she turned to face the mirror. "Do you have it in another color—"

Catching sight of herself in the mirror, she never heard the older woman's response. Stunned, she just stood there, unable to believe her eyes. She'd always been gangly and had never felt very comfortable in dresses. She was just too thin...which was why when she did have to wear a dress, she generally chose shifts and loose-fitting dresses so they would add a little weight to her slender frame. But there was nothing loose about this dress. Cut on the bias, it softly molded her breasts, hugged her small waist, then flared over her hips and fell to midcalf in a feminine swirl of soft red wool to highlight every curve of a figure she hadn't known she had.

"Oh, my," she said faintly, pressing a hand to her pounding heart. "It's beautiful!"

"No, you're beautiful," Sally corrected her with a smile. "When the cowboys at the dance tonight get a look at you, you're going to knock them right out of their boots."

Eliza wasn't interested in the cowboys—it was only one very special duke she wanted to impress—but that was something she kept to herself. "But it's red," she said, still stunned by the way the color flattered her skin.

"Yes, it is," Sally chuckled. "And it looks wonderful on you. I presume you're buying it."

"Of course!"

"Then let's see about your shoes. And before you leave here, I'm going to French braid your hair for you. Okay?"

Still reeling from what the dress did for her, Sally could have told her she was going to shave her head and she wouldn't have argued. "Whatever you say," she said with a grin and followed her to the small shoe department at the back of the shop.

Lorenzo knew he should have stuck to his disguise and worn jeans and a western shirt to the dance, but he figured the small town of Shady Rock wasn't too up on their royal watching. Besides, he wanted to wear his own clothes for a change. Especially tonight. He couldn't forget the sparkle in Eliza's eyes when she'd all but booted him out of her room so she could get ready for the dance. She'd been so excited, and he couldn't resist the need to make the night special for her. So he took a quick shower and shaved, then dressed in slacks, a dress shirt, coat and tie. If he was slightly overdressed, he didn't care. Tonight was their first real date—and probably the only one they would ever have—and he wanted it to be memorable.

Anticipating her surprise when she saw him and realized that tonight was going to be different from other evenings they'd spent together, he knocked on her door promptly at seven. When she didn't answer, he frowned and knocked again. "Eliza?" he called. "Are you ready?"

"Coming," she replied. "Just a moment."

A split second later, he heard her turn the deadbolt and was all set to tease her about running late for their big date. Then she opened the door.

With a single look, she stole the air right out of his lungs. He'd known she planned to primp for the dance—she'd all but told him so—but he'd never expected this. His heart slamming against his ribs, he couldn't take his eyes off of her. She wasn't a woman who fussed with her makeup and hair—most of the time, all her focus seemed to be on her work. In spite of that, he'd always thought she was pretty. But now…dear God, she was beautiful!

She'd done something with her hair, taming the wild burnished curls into a feminine braid that revealed the delicate lines of her throat and neck. Aching to kiss her where her pulse throbbed at the base of her neck, he swallowed…and made the mistake of dropping his gaze to her dress.

There wasn't anything the least bit suggestive about it. It was modest and sophisticated, with a scooped neck and flared skirt that revealed very little skin. Yet it was still the sexiest thing he'd ever seen. *She* was the sexiest thing he'd ever seen, he silently corrected himself. And she finally knew it—he could see the knowledge in her eyes—and that made her even sexier.

"You're gorgeous," he said huskily.

Warm color surged into her cheeks. "Thank you," she

said, flashing him a flirtatious smile. "So are you. I'm glad you didn't dress western."

"I wanted tonight to be special," he said simply, and held out his hand to her. "Ready?"

"For anything," she said with a grin, and placed her hand in his.

The VFW hall was little more than a metal airplane hangar with a wooden dance floor, but whoever had decorated it had done themselves proud. Thousands of twinkle lights hung from the rafters, setting the place aglow, and on the tables that were spread around the hall, chunky candles in hurricane lamps were the centerpiece for pine cuttings that added a wonderful scent to the night air. It was the music, however, that drew a crowd to the hall, and as Lorenzo and Eliza stepped inside, the dance floor was already packed; and it was just barely seven. Listening to the music coming from the country-western band on stage at one end of the dance floor, it was easy to see why. The band wasn't just good, it was fantastic.

Surprised, Lorenzo grinned. "I don't know what I was expecting, but it wasn't this. This is great!"

Eliza had to agree. She'd been afraid they would be overdressed—not that she would have changed her dress for anything!—but a majority of the couples present had dressed up. And the cowboys who'd worn jeans wore their best.

"I've got to remember all of this so I can include it in my story," she said, her sparkling blue eyes taking in everything at once. "My readers aren't going to believe this!"

The song the band was belting out changed then to a love song Shania Twain had won a Grammy for, and just that easily, the mood in the hall shifted and turned romantic. Lifting a masculine brow at her, Lorenzo said, "I believe they're playing our song, Ms. Windmere. Shall we?"

Eliza couldn't have resisted if she'd been offered her own column in the *New York Times*. Without a word, she let him lead her to the dance floor.

She loved music; she always had. And dancing. In her head, she was Ginger Rogers whenever she pictured herself stepping onto a dance floor. She could see herself in Fred Astaire's arms, dipping and swirling and gliding across the floor with a grace that was wonderful to behold.

In reality, however, she'd always been a little stiff.

She just couldn't seem to make herself let go, though God knows, she'd tried. And though she still loved to dance, she'd accepted long ago that she would never be as graceful as she longed to be on the dance floor.

Then she stepped into Lorenzo's arms and everything changed.

At first, she told herself that her heart was playing tricks on her. The lights dimmed, Lorenzo gathered her close, and she was floating. She was sure her feet didn't even touch the dance floor. Then she realized they were moving—*she* was moving!—as gracefully as a pair of swans gliding across an alpine lake.

Stunned, she stopped dead in her tracks, her eyes wide. "Oh, my God! I'm dancing!"

Lorenzo laughed. "Isn't that what we came for?"

"But you don't understand—I'm not any good at this!"

"Really?" he chuckled. "You could have fooled me." Still laughing, he pulled her back into his arms.

The evening that followed was like something out of Eliza's dreams. They danced nearly every dance, moving in perfect step in each other's arms, and when they weren't on the dance floor, they were still holding hands, still touching. All around them, people laughed and danced and swayed to the beat of the music, but they saw and heard only each other.

Breathless, her heart throbbing from his nearness, from the feel of his body brushing against hers, she couldn't remember the last time she'd been so happy. There was only tonight...and Lorenzo—the feel of his arms around her, the intoxicating scent of his aftershave, the way his hand held hers as if he would never let her go. It was perfect and magical, and neither of them spoke of tomorrow or the future. Nothing mattered but tonight and this evening they'd stolen for themselves out of time.

It couldn't, however, last forever. One hour turned into another, then another, and before they knew it, the band was announcing the last dance. Just that easily, the evening was over.

Her heart sinking, Eliza didn't want it to end. It was too soon. Tomorrow, their time together would be over, one way or the other. If they found the prince, he and Lorenzo would fly to Montebello immediately. If the man who was working at the Chambers ranch turned out to be someone else, Simon wouldn't allow her to continue with a search that was going nowhere, and she would have no choice but to return to Denver. She would go back to her life, Lorenzo would continue with his, and they'd eventually look back on this time they'd had together as if it was something out of a dream.

Sadness pulled at her, and to her horror, she felt tears sting her eyes. Glancing away before Lorenzo could see, she would have sworn she didn't make a sound, but somehow, he sensed the change in her mood. With a quiet, wordless murmur, he pressed a gentle kiss to the corner of her eye, then her ear. "Let's go back to the motel," he said huskily, and led her outside to the truck.

The night was cold, and sometime during the past three hours, a fine powder of snow had fallen, but Eliza never noticed as Lorenzo helped her into the truck, then joined her in the cab. With a flick of his wrist, he started the motor and turned on the heater. Then he was reaching for her.

It seemed like she had been waiting for this moment all evening. With every dance, every brush of his body against hers, the need inside her had burned brighter, hotter, until all she could think of was him and where he would touch her next. It had been soft, exquisite torture, seduction without a single kiss. And she'd loved it. But now she wanted, needed, more.

Turning into his arms, she kissed him sweetly, hotly, with all the pent-up frustration burning inside her, and when he groaned, she almost forgot that they were in a parking lot. "Lorenzo!"

"I know, sweetheart," he rasped, dropping a string of kisses down the side of her neck. "I hadn't planned to start this here, but you've been driving me crazy all night. Hey, where are you going?" he said when she would have moved across the bench seat to the far side of the cab.

"We're in a parking lot," she reminded him with a soft moan when he kissed her again.

"I know, sweetheart," he said roughly. "Don't worry. I'm not going to get us arrested. Just stay close while I drive us back to the motel."

How he managed to concentrate on his driving, Lorenzo never knew. She was all he could think of. Even as he drove, he couldn't let her go. His right hand covered hers, their fingers linked, and they sat hip to hip, thigh to thigh, all the way to the motel.

Without a word, Lorenzo walked her to her door, and when she held out her key to him, there was no question that he was staying the night. Unlocking the door for her, he followed her inside and shut the door. A heartbeat later, they were in each other's arms.

How long had he wanted her? He couldn't even remember when it had begun. From the moment he had first met her, she'd caught his attention and tugged at his senses. She'd sparked a fire in him that had only grown hotter with each passing day, and the one time he'd given in to his need and made love to her, he'd only wanted her more.

Knowing that, accepting it, he shouldn't have even considered making love to her again. But he couldn't consider anything else. Not after the way she danced with him, touched him, melted against him time and again as they'd circled the dance floor in a slow rhythm that was uniquely their own. She captivated him with her smile, her touch, the passion that was in her kiss and eyes and everything she did, and there was no way he was walking away from her. Not tonight.

Giving in to the need to touch all of her, he reached for the tab of her zipper as he kissed his way down her throat. "You're so beautiful," he groaned. "Do you know what you do to me in this dress?"

"Drive you crazy, I hope," she whispered softly as the bones in her neck seemed to dissolve one by one. Her eyes closing on a sigh, she leaned against him weakly. "Mmmm," she hummed. "I love it when you do that."

She was driving him crazy, all right, and he loved it as much as she did. When she got all soft and hot, he just wanted to sweep her up in his arms and carry her off to his lair like a caveman. Giving in to the impulse, he dragged her zipper the rest of the way down, then slipped his hand beneath her knees, and lightning quick, lifted her off her feet and cradled her against his chest.

Surprised, she gasped, clinging to him as he strode toward the bed. "What are you doing? The light—"

"I want to see you," he growled, and followed her down to the bed.

Breathless, every nerve ending in her body tingling and her heart pounding wildly, she looked up at him with wide blue eyes and found herself suddenly shy and unsure. The one time they'd made love, she'd had the shadows of the night to conceal the imperfections of her body. This was the last time they would have together. She didn't want anything to ruin it. "I'm skinny."

Her sudden insecurity caught him off guard. She saw the surprise flare in his eyes, then a tenderness that was nearly her undoing. Cupping her cheek in the palm of his hand, he gently rubbed her bottom lip with his thumb. "You're perfect."

"My hair's going to be wild when it's unbraided."

Far from concerned, he only grinned crookedly at her. "I like you wild."

"I wasn't talking about me," she whispered as her lip started to throb where he rubbed her. "I was talking about my hair."

"I like you wild," he repeated, this time in a voice that sounded like sandpaper. Leaning down, he kissed the feminine braids of her red hair. "I like your hair wild. I like it when I kiss your neck and it turns you on."

Suiting his actions to his words, he pressed a lingering kiss to the side of her neck, and smiled against her sensitive skin when she moaned softly and moved under him. "And best of all," he murmured thickly, "I like it when you call my name when we're making love and you're all hot and wild and I am, too.

"Call my name, sweetheart," he urged as he kissed his way slowly back up her neck and began to ease her dress from her. "I want to hear you call my name."

Sighing at the feel of his hands on her, she opened her

mouth to do just that, but suddenly he was kissing her, making love to her with his mouth and hands and body, and she couldn't think, couldn't speak, couldn't do anything but feel. And he felt wonderful!

His hands stroked her breasts and teased her nipples and with nothing more than that, he had her shuddering. Then her clothes were gone and so were his, and he was lighting fires under her skin with the flick of his tongue. Her mind blurring, she clung to him, a sob tearing from her throat as he moved down her body and claimed it as his.

She thought she would die from the pleasure of it. He teased her and seduced her and turned her inside out in a way no man ever had, until she was wild with wanting him. But it wasn't until he moved over her, in her, his hips setting a pace that stole her breath right out of her lungs, that she finally called his name. "Lorenzo!"

With nothing more than that, she nearly destroyed him. Groaning, he kissed her fiercely. Sweet girl, she didn't have a clue how she delighted him. He should have told her, but he wanted her too badly to say the words. Caught up in the heat and fire of her, he could feel himself coming undone, and even though he wanted nothing more than to drag out the pleasure, it was too late. His control snapped, and with a hoarse cry, he buried his face against her neck and lost himself in her just as she shattered. And the last thing he heard was Eliza calling his name.

"Lorenzo…Lorenzo…Lorenzo…."

She was falling in love with him.

Staring at the snow-covered countryside as they headed for the Chambers ranch after breakfast the next morning, Eliza couldn't understand how she'd let this happen. He was a duke, for heaven's sake! There was no place in his life for a gossip columnist. She shouldn't have had to be reminded of that.

Still, she'd lost her heart to him, and it was tearing her apart. From the directions Mr. Johnson had given her, they were already halfway to the Chambers ranch. In less than a half hour, Lorenzo would come face-to-face with the prince, and she would get her exclusive…end of tale. End of the time she and Lorenzo had had together. End of the dreams she hadn't even realized she had.

And it hurt. More than she'd ever dreamed possible.

"Is something wrong?"

His husky question shattered the quiet that had kept them company all morning. Pain squeezing her heart, she wanted to tell him that she loved him—the words were right there on her tongue—but her head warned her not to be an idiot. Women made fools of themselves all the time by throwing themselves at him—she wouldn't add her name to the list. She had more pride than that.

So she locked away her hurt deep in her heart and forced a smile that didn't come easily. "No, I'm just looking for the entrance to the ranch. It should be coming up, and Mr. Johnson said you'll drive right past it without even knowing it if you're not careful."

"And it's right after a big boulder on the left?"

She nodded. "You must be excited about seeing the prince again."

He knew what she was doing, turning his attention from her to Lucas, and for a moment, he almost called her on it. She'd been quiet all morning, and although she'd tried to hide it, he'd seen the sadness in her eyes. He felt it, too. And they needed to talk about it, dammit! Ignoring the situation wasn't going to make it go away.

But she wasn't ready to discuss it, and there wasn't time, anyway. Glancing at the odometer, he realized they should have reached the entrance to the Chambers ranch. Slowing down, he searched for the boulder that marked the entrance and had just about decided he'd missed it when he saw it up ahead.

"There it is," he told Eliza, nodding toward the granite boulder that was nearly lost beneath a snow drift. "Thank God we've got four-wheel drive. We're going to need it."

The entrance hadn't been plowed recently, but he was able to avoid the deeper drifts, and moments later, they were on the Chambers ranch and winding through the trees toward the main house. From a distance, the place looked deserted, and it didn't look much different when Lorenzo pulled up in front of the house a few minutes later. The shades were drawn, no smoke spiraled from the chimney and the garage door was shut, so it was impossible to see if anyone was home.

Swearing softly under her breath, Eliza said, "I was hoping we could talk to the owner, but it looks like no one's here."

"Let's check behind the house," Lorenzo said, cutting the motor. "If Lucas is really working here, he's probably staying in some kind of bunkhouse or hired hand's cabin."

It went without saying that a hired hand wouldn't be laying in bed at nine-thirty on a beautiful winter morning—the day started early on a working ranch. If they were lucky, they would find something of his in the bunkhouse that would verify that he really was working there. Then all they would have to do was wait until someone came home.

Climbing out of the truck, they began walking around the garage to the back of the house. The snow drifts were higher there, and if they hadn't both been watching where they were walking, they might have seen the beat-up Jeep parked just inside the open doors of the barn...and the man who was trying to jimmy open the back door of the house with a tire iron. As it was, they didn't even notice either one, and the burglar was equally engrossed in what he was doing. Then Eliza stepped on the back porch.

"Oh, my God!" Startled, she stumbled to a halt and took in the scene in a single glance.

Behind her, Lorenzo did the same. "What the hell?"

As surprised as they, the burglar whirled to face them, and in the process, dropped the tire iron. He, however, was quicker to react than they were. Before they could so much as blink, he grabbed Eliza, jerked her arm up behind her back, and snatched a gun from where it was tucked in the waistband of his jeans. Eliza was still gasping when he pressed the cold barrel of the revolver to her temple.

"Back off, buddy," the man snapped at Lorenzo when he swore and took a step toward them, "or the lady buys one in the head!"

Unarmed and furious with himself for allowing Eliza to be endangered while she was in his care, Lorenzo froze. "Let her go," he growled. "Now!"

"I don't think so," he laughed nastily. "She's my ticket out of here."

To her credit, Eliza didn't get hysterical as most of the women Lorenzo knew would have. She was scared—he could see it in her eyes—but she was also livid. Refusing to cry out in pain when the bastard shoved her arm higher up her back, she warned, "You're in enough trouble already. Don't make it worse by adding kidnapping to breaking and entering. Let me go and we can just pretend this never happened."

Far from worried, her captor only mocked, "Nice try, but you're not exactly in a position to be making deals. Now tell your boyfriend to get the hell out of my way...or you can start saying your prayers."

"Tell him yourself," she retorted. "If you think I'm going to help you kidnap me, you're crazy!"

Watching her, Lorenzo didn't know if he wanted to hug her or shake her for standing up to the thug. The jackass had a gun to her head, dammit! Didn't she realize this wasn't the time to be uncooperative? If she pushed him too far, he would shoot her. Oh, she might not think so, but she couldn't see the man's eyes. There was no remorse there, no emotion whatsoever. And that scared the hell out of Lorenzo. He'd seen his kind before, and he knew better than to underestimate him.

Holding up his hand in a calming manner, he said, "Let's talk about this."

"There's nothing to talk about," the other man snarled, his patience at an end. "Move! I've got a car in the barn, and me and your lady friend are getting the hell out of here."

His heart thundering with fear for Eliza, Lorenzo had no intention of just standing there and letting the bastard drive off with her. But he also wouldn't be responsible for her death. He'd never be able to live with himself. His mind scrambling for a plan, he took a slow step to the side, giving the thug free access to the porch steps behind him.

"Lorenzo, no!" Eliza cried, stricken.

Never taking his eyes off the other man, he wanted to reassure her that he wasn't letting her go anywhere without him, but he didn't dare. "I don't have any choice," he said, pretending to capitulate. "He'll kill you if I don't."

"He'll kill me if you *do!*" she retorted, clinging to the hard male arm that threatened to crush her windpipe as her captor backed toward the steps. "Dammit, let go of me!"

"Shut up!"

Fury glinting in his soulless eyes, he dragged her with him to the edge of the porch and felt blindly behind him for the steps. Watching him like a hawk, Lorenzo knew this was the only opportunity he was likely to get. If the bastard managed to get her to the barn and in his car, she would probably never be seen or heard from again.

And Eliza knew that as well as he did. She was as pale as a ghost, her eyes silently pleading for his help. Rage burning in him that anyone would dare to try to hurt her, he sent her a silent message, warning her to be ready for anything. She was so scared, however, that Lorenzo couldn't be sure that she understood. And there was no time for second chances. Just as her captor's foot blindly found the porch step, he misjudged the width of it and momentarily lost his balance. He caught himself almost immediately, but it was too late. The gun slipped from its position against Eliza's temple, and with a growl that came from deep in his gut, Lorenzo launched himself at her attacker.

"Now, Eliza!"

At his signal, she went boneless, just like he'd hoped she would, and suddenly, her captor found himself struggling with a limp woman and an attacker who was flying right at him and looked ready to take his head off. That's when the gun went off.

Stunned, Lorenzo's heart stopped dead in his chest just as he plowed into the burglar and knocked him free of Eliza. "You bastard!" he snarled, pummeling him as they rolled across the snow. "You shot her!"

"No!" Eliza cried, scrambling up to grab the gun that had fallen at her feet. "I'm all right, Lorenzo. The bullet just went through my sleeve. Look!"

Shaking, but somehow managing to keep the gun steady on the man who had nearly killed her, she held up her arm, showing him the hole where the bullet had pierced the thick material of her sheepskin coat. "I'm all right," she assured him again. "He didn't hurt me."

He may not have, but it wasn't from lack of trying. Staring at her sleeve and seeing how close the bullet had come to her delicate skin, he realized he could have lost her. In a split second, if the trajectory of the bullet had been slightly different, he could have lost her. And that's when it hit him. He loved her.

Stunned, he wanted to reach for her, to wrap her close and never let her go. Most of all, he wanted to tell her. The words were right there on his tongue, begging to be said. But this was hardly the time or place. First, he had to take care of the man who had nearly killed her.

Subduing the thug, he jerked him to his feet and just dared him to try to get away. "If he so much as moves an eyebrow, shoot him," he told Eliza, then reached for his cell phone. Punching in 9-1-1, he growled, "I need the sheriff to come to the Chambers ranch. A burglar just tried to shoot my girlfriend."

Chapter 11

"What the hell's going on here?"

Waiting for the sheriff, and in the process of tying up the burglar with some rope he'd retrieved from the barn, Lorenzo whirled at the question to find a woman approaching, irritation glinting in her blue eyes as she inadvertently stepped in a drift and she sank up to her calf in snow. "Damn snow," she muttered to herself. "I should have headed for California after my stunt in New York. Not here."

All his senses on alert, Lorenzo assumed she was the owner of the place, but he wasn't taking any chances. Stepping closer to Eliza, who'd taken a firmer grip on the gun at the first sound of the new visitor's voice, he ignored the woman's question and said instead, "This is a matter for the sheriff, Miss. Who are you?"

"Ursula Chambers," she snapped. "The owner." Only just then noticing the gun that Eliza still held on the burglar, she gasped, "My God, what happened? Who are you people? What are you doing here?"

"They're robbers," the burglar said before Lorenzo could come up with a suitable story that wouldn't give away his and Eliza's identity and the real reason they were there. "I caught them trying to break into the place and tried to make a citizen's arrest, but they overpowered me. You've got to help me, lady."

"That's a lie!" Eliza cried, outraged. "We caught him trying to break in, then he pulled a gun on me and tried to kidnap me so he could get away."

"So what were you two doing here?" she retorted. "How do I know you weren't trying to break in, too? Who are you?"

Shooting Eliza a warning look, Lorenzo had no intention of revealing his real identity to Ursula Chambers. She seemed honest enough, but until he found Lucas and saw with his own two eyes that he was safe and sound, he wasn't telling anyone who he was or why he was in Colorado. "I'm Lawrence Peters," he lied, "and this is my fiancée, Elizabeth Rawlings. Some friends of ours from Colorado Springs stayed at a fantastic bed-and-breakfast somewhere around here last summer, and we were trying to find it. Obviously, we took a wrong turn somewhere. We'd just decided we were in the wrong place when we stumbled across this joker trying to rob you. As soon as the sheriff gets here and we give him a statement, we'll get out of your hair."

Studying him, Ursula *almost* believed him. But she'd been around the block a few times, and she didn't believe in coincidence. The ranch was ten miles from town and not an easy place to find—people didn't just wander in off the street by accident. They were here for a reason, and any first grader could have figured out why. The prince.

She couldn't say she blamed them. She was there for the same reason.

Oh, she didn't have to break in, but she, too, wanted to search the house to see if Prince Lucas had left behind anything of value, and Jessica hadn't made that easy for her. Still sick at heart over *Joe's* leaving, she'd done nothing but cry for days now. Finally, unable to bear the memories…and the loneliness…of the ranch anymore, she'd packed her things and come to stay with Ursula for a while.

And Ursula hadn't had a moment to herself since.

It wasn't that she didn't care about her sister, she told herself. She did. But, geez Louise, she had things to do— like search the ranch house, bunkhouse and barn from top to bottom to see if Joe left anything behind—and she couldn't do that with Jessica underfoot. She'd never approve. In spite of the fact that the good prince had left her high and dry with a baby in her tummy, the little idiot still had him up on a pedestal like he was some kind of Greek god or something. She refused to let Ursula contact the king and queen about the baby—she was convinced Joe would come back to her on his own…because he loved her.

Yeah, right, Ursula thought sarcastically, rolling her eyes. She'd tell that to the tooth fairy the next time she saw her. In the meantime, she didn't have the luxury of fairy tales. She was high and dry, with no career, no boyfriend, in Hickstown, U.S.A. And unlike her lucky sister, she wasn't carrying a royal baby. She had to look out for herself, and by God, that was what she was going to do. Given the chance, she planned to use the prince by whatever means necessary to make some money.

But damn, Jessica didn't make it easy for her. She'd been her shadow for days now and had refused to let her out of her sight. Then, this morning, Jessica herself had inadvertently opened a door for her to get away for a little while when she'd mentioned over breakfast that she was worried about the ranch. Seeing her chance, she'd immediately offered to drive out there and make sure everything was okay. For a moment, she'd been afraid Jessica was going to go with her, but tears had gathered in her eyes just at the mention of the ranch. She'd gladly let Ursula go by herself.

Thrilled, Ursula had thought she had it made in the shade. Jessica would expect her to be gone for a while, and so she would have all the time she needed to go through the house. She'd never dreamed that someone would try to beat her to the punch.

Her eyes narrowing on the man who called himself Lawrence Peters, she wondered where she'd seen him before. There was something vaguely familiar about him. "You said you're from Colorado Springs, Mr. Peters?"

"No, our friends live there," he said easily. "We're from a small town east of there."

She highly doubted that, but all she said was, "I see. And what do you do for a living, if you don't mind me asking?"

"No, not at all," he assured her. "To tell you the truth, I don't do a damn thing. Well, I sold insurance until last month. That's when my grandmother died and left me a fortune. Elizabeth and I both quit our jobs, and we've been trying to decide what we want to do with the money. I'd like to buy a ranch."

"And I want a bed-and-breakfast," the woman he referred to as "Elizabeth" chimed in, smiling. "I just think they're so quaint, don't you?"

"So that's why you were looking for the bed-and-breakfast," she concluded, putting two and two together and not buying it for a second. "I suppose it was on a ranch."

"We thought we'd kill two birds with one stone," the

man said. "Elizabeth would learn all the ins and outs about running a bed-and-breakfast, and I could talk to a real rancher about the pitfalls of ranching." His expression turning regretful, he shrugged. "I guess that's the breaks, huh? We'll just have to find another bed-and-breakfast somewhere else. Of course, finding a ranch is going to be a little more difficult.

"Hey," he said suddenly, "what about you, Miss Chambers? Maybe you could tell me something about running a ranch. It looks like you've got a pretty big place here. You don't run it all by yourself, do you?"

She started to tell him that Jessica actually ran the ranch, only to shut her mouth with a snap. No. Her sister—and the baby—was something she would keep to herself until she could find a way to make them pay off. "The hired hand took off a couple of days ago for a mining job in Montana. He didn't even give notice."

"No kidding? That must have been rough. How long had he worked for you?"

If Ursula needed proof that her unwanted visitors were looking for the prince, Lawrence just gave it to her. For someone who claimed to be interested in ranching in general, he seemed awfully interested in one particular ranch hand. And that irritated her to no end. So he thought he was going to pick her brain, go after the prince and collect all the glory, did he? she fumed. Over her dead body! This was her ticket to fame and glory, by God, and no one was taking it from her. She'd tell him everything he wanted to know about Prince Charming. He might fall for the wild tale the prince had told her sister about a mining job—she hoped he did. Then he and his girlfriend would take off on a wild goose chase to Montana and leave her a clear shot to the prince. *She* could find him. After all, how hard could it be? Now that Prince Lucas had, no doubt, remembered who he was, he was bound to be on his way back to Montebello. All she had to do was convince Jessica that tracking him down was the right thing to do for the baby.

But first, she reminded herself, she had to get rid of John Wayne. "I guess he was here for several months," she said with a shrug. "He came wandering in here one day looking for food, and talked me into letting him stay. I've always been a sucker for a sob story," she lied, giving an Oscar-winning performance, "and Joe just broke my heart. He'd been in a fight and got hit in the head. The poor guy couldn't remember anything. He didn't even know his real name. Joe was just something he picked out of the phone book."

"Oh, that's awful," Elizabeth murmured in sympathy. "I can't imagine not knowing my real name. He must have felt like he was walking around in a fog. Did he choose a last name?"

She nodded. "Benson. Joe Benson. He was perfect for the job—six-two and strong as a mule. He turned out to be a really hard worker. He didn't know much about cattle at the beginning, but the man knew horses. From the way he acted, he'd obviously been around them all his life."

She rattled on about the absent Joe, and as he listened to her, Lorenzo found it hard to contain his excitement. The man she spoke of had to be Lucas! He'd always been strong and athletic, and his way with horses was legendary. There couldn't be two men in Colorado that met that description, especially when Mr. Johnson had recognized Lucas's picture. Lucas and the missing Joe had to be one and the same.

Relieved—he was alive!—Lorenzo had a thousand questions. Had *Joe* said anything at all about his past? How was his health? But as much as Lorenzo wanted to grill Ursula, he couldn't. After all, his interest was supposed to be in the ranch, not a drifter who'd moved on.

Biting back his questions, all he could say was, "It's too bad he quit. It sounds like you lost a good man. Maybe he'll come back if the mining job doesn't work out."

"There's not much chance of that," she said flatly. "Ranch hands don't come back once they've moved on."

Before she could say more, the sound of a siren cut through the cold morning air. Seconds later, a black-and-white patrol car from the sheriff's department came barreling up the drive to the ranch house and the opportunity was lost.

A giant of a man, the deputy stepped out of the car and took in the scene in a single glance. His eyes narrowing on the trussed up burglar, who gave him a go-to-hell look, he then greeted Ursula with a nod, and said, "It looks like you all have had some trouble. Anybody hurt?"

"No, sir," Lorenzo said, "but it wasn't from lack of trying on this man's part." Glaring at the burglar, he added, "He held a gun to my fiancée's head and tried to kidnap her."

"Where's the gun?"

"Here," Eliza said. Stepping forward, she held it out to him in distaste.

"I'll need statements from everyone," the deputy said as he placed the gun in a plastic evidence bag, then pulled a small notebook from his coat pocket and looked expectantly at Lorenzo. "You first, sir."

Without blinking an eye, Lorenzo gave him the same story he'd given Ursula Chambers. "My fiancée and I were looking for a bed-and-breakfast..."

An hour later, the burglar was in custody and Lorenzo and Eliza were free to go. Climbing back into the truck, Eliza hardly waited until they were out of sight of the house before she turned to Lorenzo with sparkling eyes. "Well? Say something!"

Lorenzo grinned. "Something."

"Oh! You know what I mean," she laughed, hitting him lightly on the arm. "We've found him, haven't we? Joe Benson *is* Prince Lucas. Isn't he? He has to be!"

She answered her own question, but Lorenzo couldn't tease her about it. "I still need to see him with my own eyes, but, yes, I agree. I think we've found the prince."

"I knew it! The second Sally told me about him, I had a feeling we'd finally gotten lucky. Do you think he really went to Montana or he just told Ursula that?"

That question was a little more difficult to answer. "It's hard to say. If he thought she'd give him a hard time about quitting, he might have come up with another job offer to satisfy her. But it sounds like this came up pretty quickly and he didn't want to let the offer pass him by."

"So he's in Montana," Eliza concluded, sitting back in her seat with a pleased smile. "Damn, I wish we could have asked her where!"

"That might have given us away," he replied. "And finding the mine won't be a problem. We'll visit all of them if we have to."

"So we're going to Montana? Now?"

"Just as soon as I call the king and tell him about the latest developments," he assured her as he drove back into town and pulled into the motel parking lot. "He'll want to know about this."

Since they hadn't known what to expect at the Chambers ranch, they hadn't checked out, but had taken a single room for another night. As they stepped inside, Lorenzo found himself struggling with a dozen different memories...the first time they'd made love, the last...the feel of Eliza's skin under his hands, the taste of her...the moment when the gun went off at the ranch…the exact second he realized how much he loved her.

How long had he loved her? he thought, shaken. It seemed like forever…and only seconds. And he couldn't wait to tell her, to show her, to make love to her until they both were too weak to move. But first, he had to talk to the king.

Punching in the number to his aunt and uncle's private phone in the family quarters of the palace, he greeted Marcus with a quiet hello, and said, "I have news."

"He's alive?"

"I believe he is, but I haven't seen him for myself." Quickly and efficiently, he told him about Mr. Johnson's positive I.D. of Lucas's picture, then his conversation with Ursula Chambers about the missing hired hand named Joe. "We missed him by just a day or two. He quit without notice to take a job in a mine in Montana."

"A mine? Are you sure this is Lucas, Lorenzo? That doesn't sound like something he'd do at all."

"I know, but the hardware owner was positive it was him, and the description the Chambers woman gave was accurate. It's him, Marcus. He's in Montana—we just don't know where. Picking up his trail again will take some time, but I feel sure we'll be able to find him."

Well pleased, the king laughed. "He's alive, Lorenzo. That's what's important! I can't wait to tell Gwendolyn and the girls."

"It's very important that this be kept quiet until he's found, Your Highness."

"I understand," the king told him. "Don't worry. I won't put my son in jeopardy. What I tell Gwen and the girls goes no further. We have you to thank for this, Lorenzo. As always, you've done an excellent job. I want you to fly back home tonight, and you can give me all the details when you get here.''

Surprised, he said, ''But I haven't found him yet!''

''I know, but some things have come up here that only you can handle. The mood in Montebello is tense and your presence here would go a long way to soothe it. Though I never made the official announcement, most of the country guessed you were my first choice for the throne, and with Lucas still gone, and things so uncertain, it might be reassuring to the public if you returned. So I'm going to send Tyler Ramsey to take over the search for you. He's one of the mercenaries from the Noble Men who's been working for me, and I think he's the perfect man to investigate the mines in Montana. He's been following your reports and is anxious to help. So I'll see you tomorrow. All right?''

''Yes, sir. Of course,'' he replied. What else could he say? Tyler Ramsey was a good man, and the Noble Men specialized in covert operations. He was well trained to handle the job.

It wasn't, however, the search that he hated to leave behind. It was Eliza. They'd only just now found each other. How was he going to walk away?

''Well?'' she said expectantly when he hung up the phone and just sat there. ''What did he say?''

''I have to return to Montebello.''

Stunned, Eliza couldn't believe she'd heard him correctly. ''What?! When?''

''Immediately.''

''But why? We haven't found the prince yet. Surely the king doesn't expect us to give up now. We're finally on the right track!''

His face expressionless, he offered no explanation other than, ''There are some matters at home that I need to take care of. Someone else will take over the search for the prince." Reaching for the phone book, he flipped through to the yellow pages. "I need to call the airlines and make a reservation for tonight. We'll need to leave immediately if I'm going to make it back to Denver in time for my flight."

Stricken, Eliza watched him punch in the toll-free number for the airlines and couldn't believe this was happening. There had to be a mistake. She loved him! He couldn't be leaving. Not like this. Not when she'd been so sure that he loved her as much as she loved him. She'd felt his love and caring in his touch, tasted it in his kiss. She didn't care what the king said. He wouldn't just leave her!

But that was exactly what he was preparing to do, and without one word of regret. And that broke her heart. Could she have been that wrong about him and his feelings? Had she fallen in love with a man who didn't love her? Had never loved her?

Hurt lancing her heart, she opened her mouth to ask him, only to shut it with a snap. No! she told herself furiously. She did have some pride. Obviously, she didn't need to ask him anything. The fact that he was preparing to leave without expressing any regret told her everything she needed to know.

"I'll go fill the truck up with gas while you're making your reservations," she said coolly. "It's a four hour drive back to Denver, so we should be there in plenty of time for you to make an evening flight to Montebello. I'll be back in a minute." Grabbing the keys off the table, she turned and walked out with her head in the air. It wasn't until she shut the door behind her and headed for the truck that the tears began to fall.

Long after she left, Lorenzo just sat there, swearing.

The return drive to Denver was accomplished in near silence. Keeping a tight rein on her emotions, Eliza didn't try again, but she doubted that Lorenzo noticed. His face carved in granite, he hardly looked at her. And that, she decided, was for the best. Because if he'd shown the slightest interest in her feelings, if he'd spoken just once about the loving they'd shared, she was sure she would have made a complete fool of herself.

He however, didn't seem any more inclined to talk about the intimacy they'd shared than she did. When he did speak to her, he restricted the conversation to impersonal topics like the weather and traffic and highway construction.

Her heart hurting, Eliza was relieved when they finally reached Denver. The tears that had threatened all day were back, and she didn't know how much longer she was going to be able to keep them at bay. Wishing he would hurry, she just wanted the goodbyes to be over with so she could go home and cry in peace.

But it wasn't quite that easy. She couldn't just drop him at the curb outside the airport entrance and drive away. As much as she was hurting, she just couldn't be that cold. And there were details to be taken care of.

"What do you want to do about the truck?" she asked as they parked and walked into the airport. "I can sell it for you, if you like, and send the money to Montebello."

"Thanks, but that's not necessary," he said coolly. "I'm sure the king would rather have it donated to charity. I'll sign the title and have someone pick it up at your apartment tomorrow…if that's all right with you."

"That's fine," she assured him in a tone that was as polite as his. "I'm going to hate to see it go though. I'll continue the search in Montana, of course. I'm sure the king will have someone over at the palace contact me with the details of where I meet whoever is taking over for you. When the prince is found and I've finished the feature, I'll send you a copy."

So this was the way it was going to end, Lorenzo though
bitterly. He should have expected as much. All this time
she'd been with him for one reason, and one reason only–
the story. She was a reporter, for God's sake! How the he
had he allowed himself to forget that? From the very be
ginning, she'd made it clear that the only thing she wante
was an exclusive. Now that he couldn't help her with he
precious feature anymore, she was moving on to the nex
man who could help her with a headline, and kissing hi
goodbye.

Hell, he fumed silently, what the devil was he thinking
He wasn't even getting a handshake, let alone a kiss. An
that hurt—more than he'd ever dreamed possible—and th
only infuriated him. Had anything they'd done togethe
over the past few weeks meant anything to her other tha
a headline?

Don't ask, a voice in his head advised. *You don't war
to know.*

His own pride coming to his rescue, he was as cool a
she when he said, "Good. I look forward to reading it.
Overhead, a bored female voice announced the boarding c
his flight, and as far as Lorenzo was concerned, it wasn'
a moment too soon. "Well, there's my flight," he sai
"I've got to go."

His luggage had already been checked; there was nothin
to do but show the flight attendant his ticket. Afraid h
would say too much if he said a single word to Eliza, h
nodded briefly, then boarded the plane. And that, h
thought grimly, was that.

Long after he disappeared from view and the plan
pulled away from the gate, Eliza stood where she was, pa
lancing her heart. He would come back, she told hersel
swallowing a sob. Despite the king's order, he would fin

a way to return and take up the search again…so they could be together again. He wouldn't just leave her this way.

But even as she tried to convince herself that this was all some horrible mistake, his plane raced down the runway and rose gracefully into the air. Seconds later, it disappeared into the cold winter sky. It wasn't until she finally turned and headed back to the truck that she realized she was crying.

How she made it back to her apartment safely, she never knew. Tears kept welling in her eyes, blurring her vision, and more than once, she had trouble staying in her lane. At least three drivers honked at her, and one actually rolled down his window and called her a few choice names. She didn't care.

And the situation didn't get any better when she got home and began unpacking her suitcase. Somehow, his scent surrounded her, cruelly teasing her, breaking her heart. And every time she looked out her front window, she saw his truck in her parking space. She'd lost him forever, she thought, sobbing. Giving in to the pain, she collapsed on the couch and buried her face in a pillow. Hours later, long after the apartment complex had quieted down for the night, she was still crying.

In spite of the fact that he had traveled all over the world, Lorenzo was, at heart, a homebody. He supposed his need to have his own space and things around him came from the fact that he'd lost the only home he'd ever known after his parents died and he'd gone to live with the king and queen in the palace. Oh, Marcus and Gwendolyn had done everything they could to make him as comfortable at the palace as possible, and he would always love them for that, but it had never felt like home. Nothing had until he'd bought a villa on a cliff by the sea several years ago.

Small only by palace standards, it had arched window that looked out onto the endless blue of the Mediterranean an overgrown garden that called to his spirit whenever he was restless, and none of the hustle and bustle that accompanied life in the palace. It was here that he found peace just by walking through the front door.

Until he returned from America.

He went home to change before presenting himself to the king at the palace, and for the first time, he was lonely in his own home. The echo of his own footsteps mocked him as he strode through the familiar rooms. The house cleaning service he paid to keep the place neat for him had done a thorough cleaning while he was gone, but the place was as pristine as a suite at the Ritz hotel. It lacked warmth and vitality, and with a muttered curse, Lorenzo switched on the stereo, hoping to infuse some life into the house. It didn't help.

For the first time since he'd bought the place, it seemed cold and empty.

Because of Eliza.

He missed her.

His heart aching, he told himself to get a grip. They were history; whatever they'd shared was gone forever and the sooner he accepted that, the better. It never would have worked anyway. His life was here. She belonged in America.

He knew that, accepted it…and couldn't for the life of him understand why he felt like she belonged there, in his house. She'd never been there; she didn't even know that he lived apart from the palace. Yet everywhere he looked he saw her. The deep blue of the sea that glistened from every window in the house was the exact color of her eyes. He stepped out onto the patio and though he knew his imagination was playing tricks on him, he could have sworn that he could hear her voice on the breeze, calling him softly.

It was unnerving, frustrating, painful. And it only got worse when he stepped into his bedroom. He could see her there, in his bed, his arms, waking and sleeping with him, making love with him. Without even closing his eyes, he could see her carrying his baby, growing old with him, loving him.

"Don't go there," he growled, and stalked into the bathroom to strip off his clothes. A split second later, he stepped under a cold shower. It didn't help.

When he arrived at the palace, he was in a bear of a mood, but he hid it well when he stepped into the large solarium, where his aunt and uncle had retired after breakfast and were waiting for him. He smiled easily and was thankful no one could see how heavy his heart was. "Good morning, everyone."

"Lorenzo!" Greeting him with a happy smile, Gwendolyn stepped forward to hug him fiercely. "Thank God, you're back! Come...sit down and tell us about Lucas. Who is this woman he worked for? Where do you think he is now? Was he really working as a cowboy?"

"Give the boy a chance to catch his breath, Gwen," Marcus chided laughingly as he, too, came forward to greet him. Shaking his hand, he grinned. "I see you survived the company of Ms. Windmere. I was hoping you would bring her back with you."

"She had to stay with the search for her exclusive," he replied easily. "She promised to send copies of everything once she had it in print."

"Good," Gwendolyn said, pleased. "I can't wait to read

it. She was quite an enterprising young lady. Now tell us about Lucas. What did you find out? You're sure he's alive?''

Lorenzo hoped he wasn't giving them false hope, but he truly believed there was good reason to believe that Lucas and the ranch hand named Joe were one and the same man. "I didn't see him but I spoke to several people who had and yes, I think he's alive and well.''

He proceeded to tell them then about the search through what seemed like every small town in north central Colorado, ending with their search yesterday morning at the Chambers ranch. "The bullet just missed Eliza, but I have to give her credit—she kept her head.'' While he was losing his heart, he thought, and quickly stifled the thought. "We were able to subdue him and had just called the sheriff when one of the owners of the ranch arrived.''

"You were both lucky you weren't killed,'' his uncle said gruffly. "Now, about this woman who owns the ranch—''

"Ursula Chambers,'' Lorenzo said.

"Was she nice? Did she treat him well?''

"She seemed pleasant enough,'' he replied, then added with a grin, "though she was quite irritated that he had left.''

"What was Eliza's opinion of her?'' the queen asked.

Irritated that both his aunt and uncle kept bringing up her name—couldn't they just let him forget her?—he said, "She really didn't say. There were a lot of questions she wanted to ask that she couldn't—that would have given us away.''

"But she, too, thought Lucas was alive? Even though you never saw him?''

Understanding that she needed all the verification she could get, Lorenzo smiled gently. "She was sure of it

From the moment Willy Cranshaw showed her Lucas's scarf, she was positive he was alive. Nothing that's happened since has changed her mind.''

That was all Gwendolyn needed to hear. Tears glistening in her eyes, she stepped into her husband's arms. ''Oh, Marcus, we're going to find him soon, I just know it.''

Watching the two of them together and the love they made no attempt to hide, Lorenzo felt envy for the first time in his life. He and Eliza could have had that…if she'd loved him.

Lost in his thoughts, he didn't realize his uncle was watching him until he said suddenly, ''You are telling us everything, aren't you, Lorenzo? I know how protective you are of the family. You wouldn't hold something back to keep us from worrying, would you?''

The only thing he was holding back was that he'd fallen in love with a woman who wasn't looking for someone to love, but a headline. And that was no one's business but his own. ''No,'' he said huskily. ''I've told you everything of importance. Nothing else matters.''

Chapter 12

Lorenzo liked to think he was a man who could cut his losses and move on. He didn't hang on to lost dreams—what was the point? So he immersed himself in work over the next few days and almost convinced himself that he was, if not happy, then at least, content. In reality, he'd never been lonelier in his life.

Still, he thought he hid it well. He had dinner with the family several times, and if he found himself watching Julia and Rashid with their baby and imagining he and Eliza finding the same happiness, his thoughts were his own. He played with the baby and acted as if he didn't have a care in the world.

But each night when he went home, the walls of his house closed in on him. Miserably unhappy, unable to sleep, he couldn't get Eliza out of his head. Cursing the weakness he had for her, he returned to his office after dinner each night and worked until he fell asleep at his desk. Then the next day, he did the same thing all over again. He was exhausted, but too tired to dream of Eliza, and that was all that mattered.

Still, he thought he was hiding it well…until his brother walked into his office one morning and said bluntly, "What's wrong with you? You look like hell."

A weak smile curled one corner of his mouth. "It's good to see you, too, Desmond. I haven't been sleeping much since I got back," he added. "I've been working."

Excited, his brother moved to quickly shut the door to his office so that they wouldn't be overheard. "The king is very hush-hush about what you discovered. Prince Lucas *is* alive, isn't he?" he pressed. "Otherwise, the king would be announcing you as his successor."

Lorenzo hesitated, remembering his own words of caution to Marcus. But Desmond was his brother, after all, and he'd only guessed the obvious. Smiling, he said, "There's good reason to believe that he's very much alive, but I missed him by a couple of days."

"So he's in Colorado?"

Again, Lorenzo hesitated, but this time, his brother was asking more of him than he could give. The king would want only the closest family members to know about the continuing search efforts, and although Desmond was blood, there were things that Lorenzo felt instinctively that he was not entitled to know. So he played his cards close to his vest and only gave him information about where Lucas had been—not where he was going. "We traced him to the Chambers ranch in Shady Rock, Colorado, but he left before we got there."

Furious—damn him, Lorenzo *would* be king!—Desmond knew better than to let his brother see his anger. Forcing a broad smile, he raved, "Lorenzo, this is marvelous! No wonder the king is walking around like he just won the lottery. He must be thrilled that Lucas is coming home soon.''

''I wouldn't use the word *soon,*'' Lorenzo corrected him wryly, ''but yes, I think it will only be a matter of time before Lucas is back with us. It can't, of course, be too soon for the king and queen.''

Of course not, he thought snidely. The king and queen always got what *they* wanted. The lucky bastards. ''We will, no doubt, have a celebration the likes of which has never been seen in Montebello,'' he purred with well-practiced enthusiasm. ''The prince returns!''

For a moment, Lorenzo thought he caught a trace of cynicism in his voice, but he must have been mistaken. A split second later, Desmond smiled affectionately and quirked an eyebrow at him. ''I would have thought you'd be thrilled with this news,'' he said. ''In spite of my ambitions for you, you never wanted to be king. So why the long face?''

''I told you—I've been working.''

For a moment, he thought Desmond was going to question him further, but something in his expression must have warned him not to push. Stepping back, he gave in graciously. ''I'm only concerned about you. If you want to talk, give me a call.''

He had that wounded look in his eyes that had always twisted Lorenzo in knots of guilt, but Lorenzo made no attempt to call him back when Desmond turned and walked out. Considering his mood, Lorenzo really did need to be alone. Later, he would apologize.

From there, the day only went downhill.

He'd thrown himself into work and had, finally—for the moment, at least—pushed Eliza from his thoughts. Then, just when he was finally able to concentrate on anything but her, a letter arrived from her from America. With nothing more than that, she reached across the Atlantic and touched him.

For a long moment, he just sat at his desk and stared at the plain white envelope bearing her name and home address. He swore he wasn't going to touch it. The, the next thing he knew, he was tearing it open and pulling out a newspaper clipping of her column. With a will of their own, his eyes dropped to the title of the column.

THE MAN WHO WOULD BE KING!

Lorenzo had braced himself, fearful she had caved to pressure and revealed vital information about Prince Lucas in her column, now that Simon was probably clamoring for fresh headlines. Instead, much to his amazement, he found himself reading about himself. "What the hell?"

> I recently spoke to a former lover of Duke Lorenzo and for the sake of this column, we'll call this woman...Elizabeth. She'd spent quite some time in his company, and needless to say, she was just full of interesting little tidbits about the devastatingly attractive Duke. Did you know that he looks as rugged as a cowboy in boots and jeans and a cowboy hat? Or that he's as quick to protect a lady's honor as a knight of old? He might not have a lance and suit of armor, but he doesn't need one. With him, a woman can feel safe and protected, even when she's surrounded by ruffians...

She was writing about that night in the bar when that drunken cowboy tried to force himself on her, he thought, stunned. This was about their time together! His heart starting to pound, he quickly read on.

> According to Elizabeth, he's everything that a woman could want in a man—strong and caring, not

to mention resourceful. His ladylove had the most wonderful time of her life with him and wanted nothing more than to see him again. Unfortunately, his royal duties called him back to the palace, but that was just one more reason why she found dear Duke Lorenzo so fascinating. He's a man who knows the value of family. Whenever he chooses a duchess, she will be the luckiest woman on earth.

At those words, Lorenzo's heart stopped dead in his chest. What did she mean? What was she trying to tell him? Did she love him? Hurriedly scanning the column again, he told himself he was a fool to read anything into her words. But his heart refused to accept that he'd misunderstood. In her writing, he could hear her voice, see the sparkle in her eyes, the flash of her smile, feel the softness of her kiss. Memories swirled, warming the ice that had encased his heart over the last few days, and the loneliness of his own existence slapped him right in the face. Dear God, he missed her!

And if he'd read her words correctly, she missed him, too.

His lady love had the most wonderful time of her life with him and wanted nothing more than to see him again... Whenever he chooses a duchess, she will be the luckiest woman on earth.

Did she want to be his duchess? Is that what she was saying?

"Lorenzo, we need to talk about this report from London—"

Stepping into his office, the king stopped short, a frown

knitting his brow as his gaze dropped to the newspaper clipping spread out on his desk, then lifted to the confusion and longing Lorenzo couldn't quite hide in his eyes. "What's wrong?"

"Nothing!" Cursing himself for not shutting his office door before opening Eliza's package—with his palace office located so close to the king's his uncle frequently wandered in whenever he needed to discuss something with him—he gathered up the newspaper clipping and stuffed it back into the envelope. "I was just reading Eliza's column."

Surprised, the king frowned. "There wasn't anything there that puts Lucas in jeopardy, is there?"

"No, of course not. Eliza wouldn't do that," Lorenzo said, giving voice to the certainty that had grown in him as he had gotten to know Eliza—a certainty he had been able to deny until he read her column today.

Pleased that he recognized that, Marcus said, "No, she wouldn't. I like that girl—but I digress. If the column's not bothering you, it must be something else."

When Lorenzo gave him a look that would have intimidated anyone else, he only grinned. "I'm the king—I get to be as nosey as I like and no one gets to tell me to buzz off."

He had a point, one that Lorenzo couldn't help but appreciate. His lips twitching, he growled, "I really hate it when you pull rank."

"Too bad," he tossed back. "Now tell me what's really troubling you. Or maybe I should say who. You have the look of a man who's been thinking about a woman. Is there any chance this woman might be an American reporter?"

"Who said there was a woman?"

Marcus smiled ruefully. "I was young once. I know the signs. Did you fall in love with her?"

"No!"

"Really? I find it odd, then, that you're letting someone you don't care anything about make you this miserable. And don't try to convince me that I'm imagining things," he added quickly. "You've been putting on a good front for Gwen and the rest of the family since you returned from America, but I could always tell when something was eating at you. You get this look in your eyes that gives you away every time. You've got it now."

Cornered, Lorenzo swore softly. Why hadn't anyone told him about "this look" before now? A man couldn't very well deny something when his face gave him away. "She's a reporter, Marcus. A gossip columnist. How can I be in love with someone who makes a living reporting to the world what we eat for breakfast?"

Marcus, to his credit, didn't laugh, but he couldn't quite stop his lips from twitching. "I read a few of Eliza's columns while you were gone. She never once mentioned anyone's breakfast."

Far from amused, Lorenzo just looked at him. "You know what I mean."

Sobering, he nodded. "Yes, I do. So let's talk about this. We both know there are writers out there who are vicious and can't wait to stir up a scandal. Eliza's not one of them. Personally, I think she's quite amazing. She didn't have to bring Lucas's scarf to us, Lorenzo. She didn't have to tell us anything at all. She could have published her story and we would have learned our son was alive when someone stuck a microphone in our face and asked us what we thought of the news."

"She was after bigger fish. She wants a Pulitzer and will do anything to get one."

"Really? I didn't find her that way, at all. In fact, she

was quite accommodating when I asked her to step back and let Tyler Ramsey finish the search for Lucas alone.''

"What?! When did this happen?''

"I placed a call to her home the night you left," he replied, "and explained that I was afraid that too many people had learned of the search. I have enemies who would take advantage of the situation, and I didn't want to place her in danger. I assured her she would still get her exclusive—she's more than earned it—but for now, it's essential that Tyler work alone.''

"And she agreed to that?''

"I told you she was an amazing woman," his uncle said with a smile. "Above all else, she wants a happy ending for her story. That means Lucas's safe return. She didn't want to do anything that would jeopardize that.''

Lorenzo didn't know why he was so surprised. In his heart, he had known for quite some time that she was as noble and good as the heroines in the fairy tales she'd loved as a child. "She does love happy endings," he admitted ruefully.

"And you love her.''

No longer able to deny it, Lorenzo sighed miserably. "She's all I can think about.''

"Then why aren't you with her?" A sudden thought hit him, and he frowned. "She's in love with you, too, isn't she?''

"We didn't exactly discuss it," Lorenzo hedged. "She didn't seem the least bit concerned that I was leaving, so I didn't say anything." When Marcus rolled his eyes, he said, "I've got my share of pride, just like the next man.''

He expected Marcus to agree that he couldn't have done anything any differently. Instead, his uncle swore softly. "I can't believe this! Do you like being alone?" he demanded. "Is that what you're telling me? Because in case you hadn't noticed, your pride's just about all you've got right now. Is that what you want?''

''No, of course not.''

''You've been alone for a long time,'' Marcus said gruffly. ''It doesn't have to be that way anymore. Take a chance and go after her. If you put your heart on the line and tell her you love her, I promise you you won't regret it.''

Deep inside, Lorenzo felt his heart expand, and he realized his uncle was right. He *had* been alone a long time—ever since his parents died when he was a boy—and he wanted someone he could claim as his own. But not just anyone. He wanted Eliza. It seemed like he had from the moment he'd first met her and her blue eyes had flashed fire at him. And that wasn't ever going to change. She'd gotten under his skin, into his heart, and he couldn't imagine going through the rest of his life without her. There was no reason he had to.

Rising to his feet abruptly, he told Marcus, ''I won't be able to go to Geneva for you tomorrow. I know I promised I would, but I can't. I'm going to Denver, instead.''

Pleased, Marcus grinned. ''Take one of the jets. I'll have it fueled and ready for you by the time you reach the airport.''

He didn't have to tell Lorenzo twice. He started for the door, only to stop suddenly and turn back into the office. Reaching his uncle in three strides, he surprised him with a bear hug. ''Thanks,'' he said huskily.

His eyes glistening with emotion, the king patted him on the shoulder. ''Bring her home, son. We'll have a party to welcome her into the family.''

''I'll hold you to that,'' he said with a smile, and strode out.

* * *

Some days, it didn't pay to get out of bed.

Rereading the piece she'd just written for tomorrow's column, Eliza wrinkled her nose. It wasn't that bad, she supposed. Deborah couldn't have written anything half that good if she'd had a year to work on it. And her readers would enjoy it. Still, Eliza knew it didn't have her usual punch. And regardless of how hard she tried, she just couldn't get it back.

Nothing meant anything to her. Life had no sparkle— *she* had no sparkle! Over the past few days, she'd lost five pounds she couldn't afford to lose, and all of it in tears. How could one woman have so many tears in her? If anyone so much as looked at her wrong, she cried.

And it had to stop! This wasn't who she was. She'd been hurt before and she'd always been able to shake it off without missing a beat. She had her career to turn to, and her friends. That had always been enough for her in the past. Why wasn't it now?

Because she'd never known anyone quite like Lorenzo.

Pain squeezed her heart at the mere thought of him, and with a muttered oath, she hit the print button on her computer. No! she told herself furiously as she waited for the printer to do its job. She wouldn't do this. She wouldn't let him make her miserable again. She spent her days daydreaming about him, her nights reaching for him in her sleep, and she couldn't take it anymore. Every time she wrote about a royal—any royal!—she found her thoughts drifting to him. It was nuts, crazy, unacceptable! If she didn't get a grip on her emotions, and damn soon, she was going to ask Simon to transfer her to sports. Maybe then she'd find someone else to dream about!

"Hey, there's our wonder girl," Simon teased when she walked into his office with her latest column. "Guess who

I had lunch with today? The big man himself! And he couldn't stop singing your praises. The readers love your column about Duke Lorenzo and Elizabeth. Sales are up, and Mr. Jones is convinced it's because of you. He can't wait to see the feature you do on the prince when he's found. Just wait, Red. When all this is said and done, you're going to get a big bonus...maybe even that Pulitzer you've been chasing.''

That was high praise, indeed, from Simon, and the old Eliza would have been crowing like a proud peacock at the first sign of a compliment. But a Pulitzer was no longer the be-all and end-all of her existence. Oh, she still wanted one, of course. But she didn't need one to make her happy. She couldn't say the same thing about Lorenzo, which was why she'd written the column telling him how she felt. He had to know. But even though she'd sent him a copy of the column, she hadn't heard from him. And that hurt. She'd hoped—

"Eliza? Have you heard a word I've said?"

Startled out of her silent, painful musings, she jumped...and glanced up to find him watching her with knowing eyes that saw far too much. "Of course," she replied, only to curse the revealing color that stained her cheeks. "Mr. Jones is pleased with my work."

"So am I," he said gruffly. "So why don't you tell me why the hell you have such a long face? You've been moping around here for days. You didn't even notice when Debbie got snooty with you yesterday."

"Deborah's attitude is not my concern."

"See? That's what I mean! Has an alien invaded your body? This isn't you! You don't let that little twit get by with sneezing in public without putting her in her place. What's wrong? C'mon, you can tell Uncle Simon. You know I won't tell anyone."

For the first time in days, she laughed. "Nice try, La-Gree. What is this? The new, improved, gentler you? I don't think so."

Far from offended, he only grinned crookedly. "Okay, so I went a little far. I'm worried about you, dammit! I've never seen you like this, and I don't like it. You fell in love with him, didn't you?"

The question came out of left field and caught her completely off guard. Stiffening, she said, "I beg your pardon?"

"Damn, I knew this was going to happen! That Lorenzo fellow's not your ordinary namby-pamby duke—if he had been, you never would have looked twice at him."

"Wait a minute. I never said—"

"He's a military hero, and royalty, to boot," he continued as if she hadn't spoken. "Guts, brains and a title would be a hard combination for you to resist. And I can't blame you for that. You spent a lot of time alone with him, and he was probably charming as hell."

"Actually, there were times when he could be the most irritating man I'd ever met," she retorted.

"Then there you go," he said, pleased. "He got your blood boiling. Smart man. There's no faster way to get a woman's attention than to get her all hot and bothered. No wonder you fell for him. You always did love a good confrontation."

He summed her up in just a few short sentences—and hit the nail on the head. He'd never even met Lorenzo or seen them together, she thought, stunned. How had he known? Studying him through narrowed eyes, she said, "What did you do? Have us followed? How'd you know that?"

His brown eyes twinkling, he shrugged. "I'm psychic." His smile faded. "The point is, I don't need to be psychic to figure this one out, Red. I wish I could take you to lunch and order champagne and celebrate your being in love. There's no better feeling in the world. But royals don't make commitments to commoners. You know that as well as I do.''

If anyone else but Simon had told her that, she might have resented it, but she knew he was only trying to help her in his gruff, tell-it-like-it-is way. And she appreciated it. But it still hurt. Stupid tears once again stinging her eyes, she smiled sadly. "I screwed up. I couldn't help it. It just happened.''

"It happens to all of us at one time or another," he retorted with a grimace. "That's life, Red. Cry your tears, then let go of it and find someone else. Trust me. That's the fastest way to get over a broken heart.''

He would have said more, but the phone on his desk rang then, and he snatched it up. "Yes?"

"Mr. Maxwell? This is George, at the front desk. There's a Duke Lorenzo Sebastiani down here to see Eliza Windmere. I buzzed her desk, but she didn't answer.''

Surprised, Simon nearly dropped the phone. "What?!"

"Ms. Windmere has a visitor," he repeated. "Should I send him up or take a message?''

Glancing at Eliza, who didn't have a clue what the call was about, he said, "No, don't take a message. Ask him to wait. I want to speak to him. I'll be right there.''

"Problems?" Eliza asked with a frown when he hung up and quickly came to his feet. "What's wrong?"

"Nothing," he assured her quickly. "I just have to take care of something downstairs. It'll only take a minute. So stay right here, okay? I'll be back in just a second.''

Not giving her time to question him further, he hurried out of his office and quickly strode to the wall of elevators down the hall. A split second later, he was on his way to the lobby, worry knitting his brow in a scowl. He didn't know what the duke wanted, but if he thought he was going to come here and make Eliza more miserable than she already was, he would soon learn he was sadly mistaken.

Now that he had his courage up, Lorenzo didn't like cooling his heels in the lobby, but he didn't have much choice. The security guard wouldn't even tell him if she was there, and now someone by the name of Maxwell was coming down to speak with him. Great. All he wanted to do was see Eliza and tell her he loved her. Why did everyone have to make it so complicated?

Frowning impatiently, he turned away from the reception desk just in time to see the elevator doors open and a short, rounded man step out into the lobby. His shirt was wrinkled, his tie loosened, and the only hair on his head was his busy gray eyebrows, which were currently knit in a straight line across his sharp brown eyes. Immediately spying Lorenzo near the reception desk, he headed straight for him.

"Your Grace? I'm Simon Maxwell," he said, holding out his hand to him. "I understand you're here to talk to Eliza."

So this was the infamous Simon, he thought. From what Eliza had told him, he was a gruff, shrewd man who didn't care about anything but the newspaper. So why had he come downstairs instead of Eliza? Had she refused to see him?

His heart constricting at the thought, he returned his handshake with a frown. "If Eliza's not here, I can come back later."

"Actually, she's upstairs in my office," the older man retorted. "I didn't tell her you were here. I wanted to talk to you first and get a few things straight."

Well, that was certainly blunt enough. If anyone else had

talked to him in that tone, Lorenzo would have put them in their place. But despite Eliza's claims to the contrary, Simon obviously had more than printer's ink in his veins. His dark eyes were grim with determination and held a concern that couldn't be denied.

And Lorenzo couldn't hold that against him. How could he? She had friends who cared about her as much as he did. Only a self-centered man would resent that. "All right," he said quietly. "What did you want to discuss?"

"Your intentions," he growled. "What are they?"

In spite of the seriousness of the question, Lorenzo couldn't help but smile. "You don't beat around the bush, do you?"

"Life's too short," he said simply. "You're here for a reason, and I want to know what it is. Granted, I don't really have the right—I'm not her father or family—but she's a damn good kid and I don't want to see her get hurt. So like it or not, I'm asking. What are your intentions?"

Lorenzo didn't so much as blink. "I love her. I came back to ask her to marry me."

He'd expected a nod of approval from the older man. What he got was a broad smile and a slap on the back. "It's about damn time! What took you so long?"

"I didn't think she loved me," he replied honestly. "I didn't want to make a fool of myself."

Simon couldn't believe he was serious, but there was no doubting the less than confident look in his eyes. Stunned, he nearly dropped his teeth. He was a duke, for God's sake! With movie star looks. He wasn't the kind of man women usually turned down. Now if he'd looked like him, Simon thought ruefully, that would have been another matter. It took a rare woman like his Ginger to see beneath his rough exterior to the catch that he was.

Curious, he said, "I know you haven't talked to Red—

I would have been able to tell.'' She'd been moping around the office like a sick duck for days, though that was something Simon didn't intend to tell him. That was privileged information. "So what changed your mind? You got her column, didn't you? About you and Elizabeth?''

He didn't deny it. "Yes, but I still don't know if she loves me. After reading her column, though, I'm no longer afraid of making a fool of myself. I love her. I have to tell her.''

Just that easily, he bared his soul, and any last lingering doubts that Simon had about him vanished. Eliza needed a man with guts. She'd found one. "She's in my office," he said huskily. "Take the elevator to the third floor and turn right. It's the second door on the left.''

Later, Lorenzo never remembered taking the elevator to the third floor. Suddenly, he found himself standing outside the open door of Simon's office, and there was Eliza right in front of him. Seated at a chair on the visitor side of her boss's desk, she was reading what looked to be a tabloid that she must have taken from the stack on one corner of the desk.

Not surprised that she was keeping abreast of what other publications were doing, he drank in the sight of her and couldn't stop smiling. It hadn't even been a week since they'd parted at the airport, but it seemed like a lifetime since he'd seen her. He wanted to reach for her, to pull her into his arms and hold her like he would never let her go, but he couldn't. Not yet. First, they had to talk.

Stepping into the office, he quietly shut the door behind him. "Hello, Eliza.''

At the first sound of his voice, Eliza froze, sure her ears were playing tricks on her. But her imagination wasn't that good, and with a soft gasp, she jumped to her feet and

whirled to face him. When he smiled crookedly at her, her
heart threatened to pound right out of her breast. "Lorenzo!
What are you doing here? I thought—"

"That I was still in Montebello? I flew in this morning.
How are you?"

Stunned, she hardly heard him. He was back and all she
wanted to do was step into his arms. She'd missed him so
much! She just wanted to touch him, to lose herself in the
taste of him, and forget the last six days had ever existed.

But even as she started to take a step toward him, she
stopped. Just because he was back didn't mean that he'd
come back for her. He'd left her once already, and devastated her in the process. She wouldn't let him do that again.
She wouldn't even begin to let herself hope until she knew
why he was there.

"Has the king reassigned you to the search?" she asked
quietly. "Is that why you're here?"

His smile faded slightly, but his eyes never left hers.
"Actually, I forgot to wrap up a few things before I left."

He couldn't have hurt her more if he'd slapped her. How
could he be so cruel? If he hadn't come back for her, why
had he even bothered to contact her? Hadn't he read her
column? Couldn't he see what he was doing to her? Didn't
he realize this was killing her?

Or did he think she would want to take up the search
with him where they'd left off?

Struck by the thought, she froze. Could she do that? If
he asked her, could she forget she loved him and pick up
the prince's trail again?

The answer came without hesitation. Yes. She had no
pride. She loved him. She'd go to the moon and back with
him and pretend it was for a story if she could spend time
with him.

"If you need any help, all you have to do is ask," she

said quietly. "I'm sure Simon would give me some time. He'd be thrilled if we could pick up where we left off."

Last week, that would have been enough to send Lorenzo out the door and back home. But not now. He wasn't giving up that easily—especially when they were talking about two different things. "Actually," he said huskily, "we won't be picking up the search again. My business here has nothing to do with the prince."

"It doesn't? But you said—"

"That I forgot to wrap up a few things before I left," he finished for her. "I was talking about you."

He watched her eyes go wide, then well with tears, and he couldn't wait any longer to touch her. Eliminating the space between them with a single step, he reached for her. "I love you," he rasped. "I couldn't tell you last week. I've never loved anyone the way I love you, and I was afraid of getting hurt. But living without you hurt like hell and I can't do it anymore. That's why I really came back. I love you, and I had to tell you. I hoped, after reading your column, that you felt the same way."

"Oh, Lorenzo, I do!" Joy flooding her heart, she stepped into his arms and lifted her mouth for his kiss. "I love you, too. I was heartbroken when you left. I thought you didn't love me—"

"I thought the same thing. You should have seen me. I couldn't sleep, and I was jealous of everyone who had someone in their life—"

"Me, too," she said, chuckling. "Simon threatened to fire me if I didn't stop feeling sorry for myself. He wouldn't have, of course—I could tell he was just worried about me—but I couldn't help it. I've never been so miserable in all my life."

"I should have told you," he said, kissing her softly,

over and over again. "But you acted like the only thing you were interested in was your next headline—"

"Because you couldn't wait to get home—"

"And I didn't think I could bear the rejection. It wasn't until I got home that I realized what I really couldn't bear was being without you."

"I couldn't bear it, either," she said softly. "Please don't ever leave me again."

"I won't," he promised huskily. "I can't. I love you too much. Will you marry me, sweetheart? And run away with me to Montebello? You could still work for Simon—you wouldn't have to give up your column—you'd just be a foreign correspondent. What do you say? Do you think you'd like that?"

For a woman who made a living with words, it only took one to answer all his questions and change both their lives forever. Her heart in her eyes, she kissed him sweetly and grinned. "Yes."

* * * * *

Chapter 1

Anna Sebastiani stood at the window, arms folded across her chest, and stared outside but paid little attention to the lovely view. She'd seen the well-tended gardens and the sparkling Mediterranean beyond practically every day of her life, and though she loved it all dearly, it held no interest for her this morning. The landscape she wanted to see at that very moment was vastly different—miles of barren plains, rugged mountains so rocky that that was the name they bore, forests and glaciers and lakes.

She wanted to be in America, in the state called Montana. That was where her older sister, Dr. Christina Sebastiani-Dalton, the esteemed researcher, lived with her husband. It was where Christina had escaped the confines of life in the capital city of San Sebastian and found true happiness.

And it was where their brother, Prince Lucas of Montebello, was reported to have gone.

Since Lucas's disappearance following a plane crash one

year past, life for the royal Sebastiani family of Montebello had been chaotic. First Lucas had been believed dead, though the family had continued to hope that he'd survived. Now evidence had surfaced that he *was* alive, though possibly not well. Rumors had placed him in Colorado, and the last people to have contact with him there had steered the search to Montana.

She wanted to be part of that search.

Lucas was the eldest of her siblings and her only brother, and she loved him dearly. Of his three sisters, he'd favored her, and not simply because she was the youngest. They'd shared a genuine closeness that his relationship with the others had lacked, and staying home in Montebello while her father's men conducted the search for him was making her crazy. She was utterly convinced she could help in the search.

And her father would be equally convinced she couldn't.

That was why she'd asked permission to visit Christina in America. Her father would think it perfectly natural for Anna to miss her elder sister and to crave the comfort a sister could give in a time of trouble. He would probably be delighted to send her off into Christina's competent care, leaving him with one less worry at home.

Of course, it was too much to hope that she could escape without a bodyguard, but she'd had no little experience in her twenty-five years in sneaking away for a few hours of freedom. All she need do this time—in the event her father granted permission, which he surely would; how could he tell the apple of his eye no!—was sneak away for a few weeks. Just long enough to visit the sites where Lucas had allegedly gone looking for employment.

Quiet footsteps approached on the marble floor, causing Anna to turn. It was her father's secretary, Albert, a small, bespectacled man who'd held the position for more years than Anna had lived. "Your father will see you now, Princess."

"Thank you." Fortifying herself with a deep breath, Anna crossed the solarium, heading down the long elegant hallway, past the entry foyer to the tall, elaborately carved doors that led into her father's office. On the inside, she might be worrying about Lucas and her plan, but on the outside, she knew no hint of it showed. Her mouth curved of its own accord into an affectionate smile the instant she saw her father, sitting behind a desk strewn with papers, maps and other necessities for the daily running of Montebello. To the rest of the world, he was King Marcus, much-loved monarch of Montebello, but to her, he was simply…"Papa."

He returned her smile and opened his arms. She embraced him, then leaned against the desk, her fingers loosely trapped by his.

"And to what do I owe the honor of this visit?" he asked.

"You know what, Papa. You promised me an answer today."

"An answer? To what?"

She attempted to fix a stern gaze on him, but it was difficult when the corners of her mouth kept twitching. "To my request to visit Christina in America."

"Ah, yes, that I did. Such impatience, Anna. The day isn't even half gone yet."

She didn't hesitate to let her features slide fluidly into a pout. "Do you know how long it's been since I've seen Christina?"

"Yes, *bambina*, little girl. It was the same time I last saw her. But will it make so much difference if you see her tomorrow as opposed to next week?"

Next week? Anna's heart sank. By next week Lucas

could be on his way to any of the other forty-eight states he hadn't yet been spotted in. He could be getting himself more and more lost. Naturally she didn't point that out. Instead, she sweetly asked, "You tell me, Papa. You'll be the one on the receiving end of my pouting if you make me wait until next week."

He laughed. "You are spoiled rotten, *mia figlia.*"

She gave him an appropriate spoiled-daughter smile. "As you should know, since you're the one who spoiled me."

"Very well. I'll send you off to visit your sister and get that scary face out of my sight for a few weeks." He gently pinched her cheek, bringing a smile from her. "Naturally you'll travel with an escort."

"Naturally. I thought Roberto would enjoy visiting the 'Wild West.'" Roberto had served the family for years, and his penchant for all things cowboy was well known. John Wayne movies, Louis L'Amour books, videocassettes of *Bonanza, Maverick, Rawhide* and *Paladin.* "Have gun, will travel." He had a gun, he liked to tease—what bodyguard didn't—and serving the royal family certainly allowed him to travel.

"I'm sure he would enjoy it. However, I've chosen someone else."

He gestured to someone behind her, and instantly Anna became aware that they weren't alone in the room. Ordinarily, she was more attuned to others' presence than that. She could attribute her lack of awareness only to the fact that these were far from ordinary circumstances.

Slowly she turned to see the man, his back to her, standing near the bookcases that lined one wall. Evidently it had been *his* meeting with her father that had kept her waiting. He turned as slowly as she had, and her heart took an unexpected leap in her chest.

Tyler Ramsey! She had just pouted, sweet-talked and manipulated her father with Tyler Ramsey there to witness every word. Heat surged into her cheeks as she fought the urge to take cover behind her father's chair. The man was a frequent visitor at the palace, due to the work he and his brother did for the king as well as the friendship between his father and hers, but he'd hardly noticed she was alive.

But *she* had noticed *him*. He stood six feet tall, more than half a foot above her, and he was—to put it in simple American terms—to die for. Though he hadn't followed his father and brother into the military, his auburn hair was military-short. A few of her friends thought the style too severe, but she thought it accentuated the clean lines and sharp angles of his face. With his green eyes and decidedly muscular body, he belonged on a recruiting poster.

He'd certainly recruited more than a few Montebellans, one princess included, to the spectator sport of Ogling Tyler Ramsey.

"I believe the two of you have met," her father said as Tyler came toward them.

"Yes, of course." Anna straightened. Rather than offer her hand, she tucked both hands behind her back, and since she didn't offer, neither did Tyler. His own hands were clasped before him—large hands, long fingers, more comfortable with a gun, according to gossip, than with a woman. Not that there was any doubt of his interest in women. He simply hadn't yet met one who could compete with his fierce dedication to duty.

And that dedication might prove a problem. Escaping Roberto would be child's play. Escaping one as driven by duty as Tyler might prove impossible.

Calling on every bit of regal bearing she'd learned over the years, she inclined her head slightly. "Mr. Ramsey."

He mimicked the action. "Princess Anna."

In the preceding centuries, Montebello had fallen under the control of many peoples—the British, Greeks, Italians, Arabs and others—so its population was a potpourri of them all. She loved the diversity of the people, their customs and their languages...ah, but there was something special about English as spoken by Tyler Ramsey.

Or perhaps there was simply something special about him, period.

"Tyler was already scheduled to travel to America on business for me," her father said. "If you'd waited one more day to make your request, he would have already been gone, and I would have been forced to turn you down, no matter how prettily you pouted."

"No, Papa," she disagreed. "You merely would have been forced to send someone else in his stead." Like Roberto, Salim, Nikos—any of the guards in the king's employ, any one of whom she could charm as easily as she did her father.

"Perhaps. But since Tyler *is* going, it makes perfect sense for him to deliver you into your sister's care. You get to visit your sister, and I get to know you're safe. We'll both be happy."

"Yes, Papa," she said dutifully. "We'll leave this afternoon—"

"You'll leave tomorrow."

"But I've made reservations!"

King Marcus laughed. "Were you so sure of me, *bambina?* And did you reserve two seats?"

"One for my escort and one for me."

He gave a patient, indulgent shake of his head. "You'll leave in the morning, and you'll take the Gulfstream jet. No arguments. Run along now, Anna. Tyler and I have things to discuss."

"Yes, Papa." Though her ego chafed at her being dismissed like a small child, Anna embraced her father once more, then gave her newly appointed bodyguard another cool nod as she walked past. ''Mr. Ramsey.''

He nodded, but didn't say a word.

Too bad. She would have liked to hear him speak her name once more. But it was a long flight to America. She would have plenty of chances to listen to the sound of his voice.

* * * * *

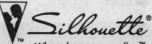

Silhouette —
where love comes alive—online...

eHARLEQUIN.com

your romantic
books

♥ Shop online! Visit Shop eHarlequin and discover a wide selection of new releases and classic favorites at great discounted prices.

Read our daily and weekly Internet exclusive serials, and participate in our interactive novel in the reading room.

♥ Ever dreamed of being a writer? Enter your chapter for a chance to become a featured author in our Writing Round Robin novel.

your romantic
magazine

♥ Check out our feature articles on dating, flirting and other important romance topics and get your daily love dose with tips on how to keep the romance alive every day.

♥ Learn what the stars have in store for you with our daily Passionscopes and weekly Erotiscopes.

♥ Get the latest scoop on your favorite royals in Royal Romance.

your
community

♥ Have a Heart-to-Heart with other members about the latest books and meet your favorite authors.

♥ Discuss your romantic dilemma in the Tales from the Heart message board.

All this and more available at
www.eHarlequin.com

AT TWILIGHT...

they awaken with a growing
hunger and need.
Yet the yearning isn't always for blood,
but rather a true joining....

**Born in Twilight
"Beyond Twilight"**

Don't miss these wonderful, stirring stories
from *USA Today* bestselling author

MAGGIE SHAYNE's
WINGS IN THE NIGHT

series, coming to your local stores
February 2002.

Available at your favorite retail outlet.

Silhouette®
Where love comes alive™

Silhouette®

INTIMATE MOMENTS™

LONE STAR
LCC
COUNTRY CLUB
EST. 1923

Where Texas society reigns supreme—and appearances are everything!

When a bomb rips through the historic Lone Star Country Club, a mystery begins in Mission Creek....

Available February 2002
ONCE A FATHER (IM #1132)
by Marie Ferrarella
A lonely firefighter and a warmhearted doctor fall in love while trying to help a five-year-old boy orphaned by the bombing.

Available March 2002
IN THE LINE OF FIRE (IM #1138)
by Beverly Bird
Can a lady cop on the bombing task force and a sexy ex-con stop fighting long enough to realize they're crazy about each other?

Available April 2002
MOMENT OF TRUTH (IM #1143)
by Maggie Price
A bomb tech returns home to Mission Creek and discovers that an old flame has been keeping a secret from him....

And be sure not to miss the Silhouette anthology

Lone Star Country Club: The Debutantes

Available in May 2002

Available at your favorite retail outlet.

Silhouette®
Where love comes alive™